C000224756

Paul Bowles was born in New Y[...]
1931, and in 1938 married Jane [...]
Jane Bowles moved to Tangier, a[...]
published his first novel *The Shelte*[...]
acclaim. He is the author of th[...]
confirmed his reputation as a wr[...]
well as several collections of short stories, an autobiography
and travel writing. In 1990 Abacus publish his travel book
Their Heads are Green, his remarkable novel *Let it Come Down*,
and two collections of stories, *Pages from Cold Point* and *A
Thousand Days for Mokhtar*.

Call at Corazón

and Other Stories

PAUL BOWLES

AN ABACUS BOOK

First published in Great Britain by Peter Owen Publishers 1988

Published by Sphere Books Ltd in Abacus 1989

Copyright © Paul Bowles 1939, 1946, 1947, 1949, 1950, 1957, 1958, 1982, 1983, 1984, 1985

Printed and bound in Great Britain by
The Guernsey Press Co. Ltd, Guernsey, Channel Islands.

ISBN 0349 10099 3

Sphere Books Ltd
A Division of
Macdonald and Co. (Publishers) Ltd,
66/73 Shoe Lane, London EC4P 4AB

A member of Maxwell Pergamon Publishing Corporation plc

Preface

The stories in this volume were written during a period
which covers approximately fifty years. Many are the result
of nostalgia for places left behind; the composition of these
began with an evocation of the *ambiance* of the locale, a
general atmosphere out of which the protagonists were
born. It seems a practical procedure to let the place determine
the characters who will inhabit it.

Often the settings used are precise descriptions of actual
places. 'At Paso Rojo' takes place at a ranch in Guanacaste,
Costa Rica, 'Under the Sky' in a sinister town called Tonalá,
in Chiapas, Mexico, 'The Successor' in a café (now destroyed
to make room for a hotel) which once stretched along the
edge of a cliff above the city of Fez. 'The Hours after
Noon' is set in a pension which used to exist on the Old
Mountain outside Tangier, and 'The Frozen Fields' uses a
farm in New England where I used to go in my early
childhood. Excepting in the last-mentioned story, characters,
being determined by the backdrop, are necessarily almost
entirely improvised, as is the action in which they become
involved. For me the pleasure of writing stories, as opposed
to novels, lies in the liberty of allowing protagonists to
invent their own personalities as they emerge from the
landscape.

More rarely both protagonists and events are taken directly
from life, as in two of the Monologues ('Tangier 1975' and
'Massachusetts 1932') where only certain decorative details
are fictional; the rest actually happened. But I prefer to let
nostalgia indicate the place, and to leave imagination free
to wander in the unconscious, where it can select whatever
elements seem propitious to the elaboration of a tale.

Contents

Call at Corazón

'But why would you want a little horror like that to go along with us? It doesn't make sense. You know what they're like.'

'I know what they're like,' said her husband. 'It's comforting to watch them. Whatever happens, if I had that to look at, I'd be reminded of how stupid I was ever to get upset.'

He leaned farther over the railing and looked intently down at the dock. There were baskets for sale, crude painted toys of hard natural rubber, reptile-hide wallets and belts, and a few whole snakeskins unrolled. And placed apart from these wares, out of the hot sunlight, in the shadow of a crate, sat a tiny, furry monkey. The hands were folded, and the forehead was wrinkled in sad apprehensiveness.

'Isn't he wonderful?'

'I think you're impossible – and a little insulting,' she replied.

He turned to look at her. 'Are you serious?' He saw that she was.

She went on, studying her sandalled feet and the narrow deck-boards beneath them: 'You know I don't really mind all this nonsense, or your craziness. Just let me finish.' He nodded his head in agreement, looking back at the hot dock and the wretched tin-roofed village beyond. 'It goes without saying I don't mind all that, or we wouldn't be here together. You might be here alone . . .'

'You don't take a honeymoon alone,' he interrupted.

'*You* might.' She laughed shortly.

He reached along the rail for her hand, but she pulled it

away, saying, 'I'm still talking to you. I expect you to be crazy, and I expect to give in to you all along. I'm crazy too, I know. But I wish there were some way I could just once feel that my giving in meant anything to you. I wish you knew how to be gracious about it.'

'You think you humour me so much? I haven't noticed it.' His voice was sullen.

'I don't *humour* you at all. I'm just trying to live with you on an extended trip in a lot of cramped little cabins on an endless series of stinking boats.'

'What to you mean?' he cried excitedly. 'You've always said you loved the boats. Have you changed your mind, or just lost it completely?'

She turned and walked toward the prow. 'Don't talk to me,' she said. 'Go and buy your monkey.'

An expression of solicitousness on his face, he was following her. 'You know I won't buy it if it's going to make you miserable.'

'I'll be more miserable if you don't, so please go and buy it.' She stopped and turned. 'I'd love you to have it. I really would. I think it's sweet.'

'I don't get you at all.'

She smiled. 'I know. Does it bother you very much?'

After he had bought the monkey and tied it to the metal post of the bunk in the cabin, he took a walk to explore the port. It was a town made of corrugated tin and barbed wire. The sun's heat was painful, even with the sky's low-lying cover of fog. It was the middle of the day and few people were in the streets. He came to the edge of the town almost immediately. Here between him and the forest lay a narrow, slow-moving stream, its water the colour of black coffee. A few women were washing clothes; small children splashed. Gigantic grey crabs scuttled between the holes they had made in the mud along the bank. He sat down on some elaborately twisted roots at the foot of a tree and took out the notebook he always carried with him. The day before, in a bar at Pedernales, he had written: 'Recipe for dissolving the impression of hideousness made by a thing: Fix the attention upon the given object or situation so that the various elements, all familiar, will regroup themselves.

Frightfulness is never more than an unfamiliar pattern.'

He lit a cigarette and watched the women's hopeless attempts to launder the ragged garments. Then he threw the burning stub at the nearest crab, and carefully wrote: 'More than anything else, woman requires strict ritualistic observance of the traditions of sexual behaviour. That is her definition of love.' He thought of the derision that would be called forth should he make such a statement to the girl back on the ship. After looking at his watch, he wrote hurriedly: 'Modern, that is, intellectual education, having been devised by males for males, inhibits and confuses her. She avenges . . .'

Two naked children, coming up from their play in the river, ran screaming past him, scattering drops of water over the paper. He called out to them, but they continued their chase without noticing him. He put his pencil and notebook into his pocket, smiling, and watched them patter after one another through the dust.

When he arrived back at the ship, the thunder was rolling down from the mountains around the harbour. The storm reached the height of its hysteria just as they got under way.

She was sitting on her bunk, looking through the open porthole. The shrill crashes of thunder echoed from one side of the bay to the other as they steamed toward the open sea. He lay doubled up on his bunk opposite, reading.

'Don't lean your head against that metal wall,' he advised. 'It's a perfect conductor.'

She jumped down to the floor and went to the washstand. 'Where are those two quarts of White Horse we got yesterday?'

He gestured. 'In the rack on your side. Are you going to drink?'

'I'm going to *have* a drink, yes.'

'In this heat? Why don't you wait until it clears, and have it on deck?'

'I want it now. When it clears I won't need it.'

She poured the whisky and added water from the carafe in the wall bracket over the washbowl.

'You realize what you're doing, of course.'

She glared at him. 'What am I doing?'

He shrugged his shoulders. 'Nothing, except just giving in to a passing emotional state. You could read, or lie down and doze.'

Holding her glass in one hand, she pulled open the door into the passageway with the other, and went out. The noise of the slamming door startled the monkey, perched on a suitcase. It hesitated a second and hurried under its master's bunk. He made a few kissing sounds to entice it out, and returned to his book. Soon he began to imagine her alone and unhappy on the deck, and the thought cut into the pleasure of his reading. He forced himself to lie still a few minutes, the open book face down across his chest. The boat was moving at full speed now, and the sound of the motors was louder than the storm in the sky.

Soon he rose and went on deck. The land behind was already hidden by the falling rain, and the air smelt of deep water. She was standing alone by the rail, looking down at the waves, with the empty glass in her hand. Pity seized him as he watched, but he could not walk across to her and put into consoling words the emotion he felt.

Back in the cabin he found the monkey on his bunk, slowly tearing the pages from the book he had been reading.

The next day was spent in leisurely preparation for disembarking and changing of boats: in Villalta they were to take a smaller vessel to the opposite side of the delta.

When she came in to pack after dinner, she stood a moment studying the cabin. 'He's messed it up, all right,' said her husband, 'but I found your necklace behind my big valise, and we'd read all the magazines anyway.'

'I suppose this represents man's innate urge to destroy,' she said, kicking a ball of crumpled paper across the floor. 'And the next time he tries to bite you, it'll be man's basic insecurity.'

'You don't know what a bore you are when you try to be caustic. If you want me to get rid of him, I will. It's easy enough.'

She bent to touch the animal, but it backed uneasily under the bunk. She stood up. 'I don't mind him. What I mind is you. *He* can't help being a little horror, but he keeps reminding me that you could if you wanted.'

Her husband's face assumed the impassivity that was characteristic of him when he was determined not to lose his temper. She knew he would wait to be angry until she was unprepared for his attack. He said nothing, tapping an insistent rhythm on the lid of a suitcase with his fingernails.

'Naturally I don't really mean you're a horror,' she continued.

'Why not mean it?' he said, smiling pleasantly. 'What's wrong with criticism? Probably I am, to you. I like monkeys because I see them as little model men. You think men are something else, something spiritual or God knows what. Whatever it is, I notice you're the one who's always being disillusioned and going around wondering how mankind can be so bestial. I think mankind is fine.'

'Please don't go on,' she said. 'I know your theories. You'll never convince yourself of them.'

When they had finished packing, they went to bed. As he snapped off the light behind his pillow, he said, 'Tell me honestly. Do you want me to give him to the steward?'

She kicked off her sheet in the dark. Through the porthole, near the horizon, she could see stars, and the calm sea slipped by just below her. Without thinking she said, 'Why don't you drop him overboard?'

In the silence that followed she realized she had spoken carelessly, but the tepid breeze moving with languor over her body was making it increasingly difficult for her to think or speak. As she fell asleep it seemed to her she heard her husband saying slowly, 'I believe you would. I believe you would.'

The next morning she slept late, and when she went up for breakfast her husband had already finished his and was leaning back, smoking.

'How are you?' he asked brightly. 'The cabin steward's delighted with the monkey.'

She felt a flush of pleasure. 'Oh,' she said, sitting down, 'did you give it to him? You didn't have to do that.' She glanced at the menu; it was the same as every other day. 'But I suppose really it's better. A monkey doesn't go with a honeymoon.'

'I think you're right,' he agreed.

Villalta was stifling and dusty. On the other boat they had grown accustomed to having very few passengers around, and it was an unpleasant surprise to find the new one swarming with people. Their new boat was a two-decked ferry painted white, with an enormous paddle wheel at the stern. On the lower deck, which rested not more than two feet above the surface of the river, passengers and freight stood ready to travel, packed together indiscriminately. The upper deck had a salon and a dozen or so narrow staterooms. In the salon the first-class passengers undid their bundles of pillows and opened their paper bags of food. The orange light of the setting sun flooded the room.

They looked into several of the staterooms.

'They all seem to be empty,' she said.

'I can see why. Still, the privacy would be a help.'

'This one's double. And it has a screen in the window. This is the best one.'

'I'll look for a steward or somebody. Go on in and take over.' He pushed the bags out of the passageway where the *cargador* had left them, and went off in search of an employee. In every corner of the boat the people seemed to be multiplying. There were twice as many as there had been a few moments before. The salon was completely full, its floor space occupied by groups of travellers with small children and elderly women, who were already stretched out on blankets and newspapers.

'It looks like Salvation Army headquarters the night after a major disaster,' he said as he came back into the stateroom. 'I can't find anybody. Anyway, we'd better stay in here. The other cubicles are beginning to fill up.'

'I'm not so sure I wouldn't rather be on deck,' she announced. 'There are hundreds of cockroaches.'

'And probably worse,' he added, looking at the bunks.

'The thing to do is take those filthy sheets off and just lie on the mattresses.' She peered out into the corridor. Sweat was trickling down her neck. 'Do you think it's safe?'

'What do you mean?'

'All those people. This old tub.'

He shrugged his shoulders.

'It's just one night. Tomorrow we'll be at Cienaga. And

it's almost night now.'

She shut the door and leaned against it, smiling faintly.

'I think it's going to be fun,' she said.

'The boat's moving!' he cried. 'Let's go on deck. If we can get out there.'

Slowly the old boat pushed across the bay toward the dark east shore. People were singing and playing guitars. On the bottom deck a cow lowed continuously. And louder than all the sounds was the rush of water made by the huge paddles.

They sat on the deck in the middle of a vociferous crowd, leaning against the bars of the railing, and watched the moon rise above the mangrove swamps ahead. As they approached the opposite side of the bay, it looked as if the boat might plough straight into the shore, but a narrow waterway presently appeared, and the boat slipped cautiously in. The people immediately moved back from the railing, crowding against the opposite wall. Branches from the trees on the bank began to rub against the boat, scraping along the side walls of the cabins, and then whipping violently across the deck.

They pushed their way through the throng and walked across the salon to the deck on the other side of the boat; the same thing was happening there.

'It's crazy,' she declared. 'It's like a nightmare. Whoever heard of going through a channel no wider than the boat! It makes me nervous. I'm going in to read.'

Her husband let go of her arm. 'You can never enter into the spirit of a thing, can you?'

'You tell me what the spirit is, and I'll see about entering into it,' she said, turning away.

He followed her, 'Don't you want to go down on to the lower deck? They seem to be going strong down there. Listen.' He held up his hand. Repeated screams of laughter came up from below.

'I certainly don't!' she called, without looking around.

He went below. Groups of men were seated on bulging burlap sacks and wooden crates, matching coins. The women stood behind them, puffing on black cigarettes and shrieking with excitement. He watched them closely, reflecting that with fewer teeth missing they would be a handsome people. 'Mineral deficiency in the soil,' he commented to himself.

Standing on the other side of a circle of gamblers, facing him, was a muscular young native whose visored cap and faint air of aloofness suggested official position of some sort aboard the boat. With difficulty the traveller made his way over to him, and spoke to him in Spanish.

'Are you an employee here?'

'Yes, sir.'

'I am in cabin number eight. Can I pay the supplementary fare to you?'

'Yes, sir.'

'Good.'

He reached into his pocket for his wallet, at the same time remembering with annoyance that he had left it upstairs locked in a suitcase. The man looked expectant. His hand was out.

'My money is in my stateroom.' Then he added, 'My wife has it. But if you come up in half an hour I can pay you the fare.'

'Yes, sir.' The man lowered his hand and merely looked at him. Even though he gave an impression of purely animal force, his broad, somewhat simian face was handsome, the husband reflected. It was surprising when, a moment later, that face betrayed a boyish shyness as the man said, 'I am going to spray the cabin for your señora.'

'Thank you. Are there many mosquitoes?'

The man grunted and shook the fingers of one hand as if he had just burned them.

'Soon you will see how many.' He moved away.

At that moment the boat jolted violently, and there was great merriment among the passengers. He pushed his way to the prow and saw that the pilot had run into the bank. The tangle of branches and roots was a few feet from his face, its complex forms vaguely lighted by the boat's lanterns. The boat backed laboriously and the channel's agitated water rose to deck level and lapped the outer edge. Slowly they nosed along the bank until the prow once more pointed to midstream, and they continued. Then almost immediately the passage curved so sharply that the same thing happened again, throwing him sideways against a sack of something unpleasantly soft and wet. A bell clanged below deck in the interior of the boat; the passengers' laughter was louder.

Eventually they pushed ahead, but now the movement became painfully slow as the sharpness of the curves in the passage increased. Under the water the stumps groaned as the boat forced its sides against them. Branches cracked and broke, falling on to the forward and upper decks. The lantern at the prow was swept into the water.

'This isn't the regular channel,' muttered a gambler, glancing up.

Several travellers exclaimed 'What?' almost in unison.

'There's a pile of passages through here. We're picking up cargo at Corazón.'

The players retreated to a square inner arena which others were forming by shifting some of the crates. The husband followed them. Here they were comparatively safe from the intruding boughs. The deck was better lighted here, and this gave them the idea of making an entry in his notebook. Bending over a carton marked *Vermifugo Santa Rosalia*, he wrote: 'November 18th. We are moving through the bloodstream of a giant. A very dark night.' Here a fresh collision with the land knocked him over, knocked over everyone who was not propped between solid objects.

A few babies were crying, but most of them still slept. He slid down to the deck. Finding his position fairly comfortable, he fell into a dozing state which was broken irregularly by the shouting of the people and the jolting of the boat.

When he awoke later, the boat was quite stationary, the games had ceased, and the people were asleep, a few of the men continuing their conversation in small groups. He lay still, listening. The talk was all about places; they were comparing the unpleasant things to be found in various parts of the republic: insects, weather, reptiles, diseases, lack of food, high prices.

He looked at his watch. It was half-past one. With

difficulty he got to his feet, and found his way to the stairs. Above, in the salon, the kerosene lamps illumined a vast disorder of prostrate figures. He went into the corridor and knocked on the door marked with an eight. Without waiting for her to answer, he opened the door. It was dark inside. He heard a muffled cough nearby, and decided that she was awake.

'How are the mosquitoes? Did my monkey man come and fix you up?' he asked.

She did not answer, so he lit a match. She was not in the bunk on the left. The match burned his thumb. With the second one, he looked at the right-hand bunk. A tin insecticide sprayer lay there on the mattress; its leak had made a large circle of oil on the bare ticking. The cough was repeated. It was someone in the next cabin.

'Now what?' he said aloud, uncomfortable at finding himself upset to this degree. A suspicion seized him. Without lighting the hanging lamp, he rushed to open her valises, and in the dark felt hurriedly through the flimsy pieces of clothing and the toilet articles. The whisky bottles were not there.

This was not the first time she had gone on a solitary drinking bout, and it would be easy to find her among the passengers. However, being angry, he decided not to look for her. He took off his shirt and trousers and lay down on the left-hand bunk. His hand touched a bottle standing on the floor by the head of the bunk. He raised himself enough to smell it; it was beer and the bottle was half full. It was hot in the cabin, and he drank the remaining warm, bitter liquid with relish and rolled the bottle across the room.

The boat was not moving, but voices shouted out here and there. An occasional bump could be felt as a sack of something heavy was heaved aboard. He looked through the little square window with the screen in it. In the foreground, dimly illumined by the boat's lanterns, a few dark men, naked save for their ragged underdrawers, stood on a landing made in the mud and stared toward the boat. Through the endless intricacies of roots and trunks behind them he saw a bonfire blazing, but it was far back in the swamp. The air smelt of stagnant water and smoke.

Deciding to take advantage of the relative silence, he lay down and tried to sleep; he was not surprised, however, by the difficulty he found in relaxing. It was always hard to sleep when she was not there in the room. The comfort of her presence was lacking, and there was also the fear of being awakened by her return. When he allowed himself to, he would quickly begin to formulate ideas and translate them into sentences whose recording seemed the more urgent because he was lying comfortably in the dark. Sometimes he thought about her, but only as an unclear figure whose character lent flavour to a succession of backdrops. More often he reviewed the day just completed, seeking to convince himself that it had carried him a bit further away from his childhood. Often for months at a time the strangeness of his dreams persuaded him that at last he had turned the corner, that the dark place had finally been left behind, that he was out of hearing. Then, one evening as he fell asleep, before he had time to refuse, he would be staring closely at a long-forgotten object – a plate, a chair, a pincushion – and the accustomed feeling of infinite futility and sadness would recur.

The motor started up, and the great noise of the water in the paddle wheel recommenced. They pushed off from Corazón. He was pleased. Now I shan't hear her when she comes in and bangs around, he thought, and fell into a light sleep.

He was scratching his arms and legs. The long-continued, vague malaise eventually became full consciousness, and he sat up angrily. Above the sounds made by the boat he could hear another sound, one which came through the window: an incredibly high and tiny tone, tiny but constant in pitch and intensity. He jumped down from the berth and went to the window. The channel was wider here, and the overhanging vegetation no longer touched the sides of the boat. In the air, nearby, far away, everywhere, was the thin wail of mosquito wings. He was aghast, and completely delighted by the novelty of the phenomenon. For a moment he watched the tangled black wilderness slip past. Then with the itching he remembered the mosquitoes inside the cabin. The screen did not reach quite to the top of the window; there was ample space for them to crawl in. Even there in the dark as he moved his fingers along the frame to find the handle he could feel them; there were that many.

Now that he was fully awake, he lighted a match and went to her bunk. Of course she was not there. He lifted the Flit gun and shook it. It was empty, and as the match went out, he saw that the spot on the mattress had spread even farther.

'Son of a bitch!' he whispered, and going back to the window he tugged the screen vigorously upward to close the crack. As he let go of it, it fell out into the water, and almost immediately he was concious of the soft caress of tiny wings all about his head. In his undershirt and trousers he rushed out into the corridor. Nothing had changed in the salon. Almost everyone was asleep. There were screen doors giving on to the deck. He inspected them: they appeared to be more firmly installed. A few mosquitoes brushed against his face, but it was not the horde. He edged in between two women who were sleeping sitting with their backs against the wall, and stayed there in acute discomfort until again he dozed. It was not long before he opened his eyes to find the dim light of dawn in the air. His neck ached. He arose and went out on to the deck, to which most of the people from the salon had already crowded.

The boat was moving through a wide estuary dotted with clumps of plants and trees that rose out of the shallow water. Along the edges of the small islands stood herons, so white in the early grey light that their brightness seemed to come from inside them.

It was half-past five. At this moment the boat was due in Cienaga, where it was met on its weekly trip by the train that went into the interior. Already a thin spit of land ahead was being identified by eager watchers. Day was coming up swiftly; sky and water were the same colour. The deck reeked of the greasy smell of mangoes as people began to breakfast.

And now at last he began to feel pangs of anxiety as to where she might be. He determined to make an immediate and thorough search of the boat. She would be instantly recognizable in any group. First, he looked methodically through the salon, then he exhausted the possibilities on the upper decks. The he went downstairs, where the gambling had already begun again. Toward the stern, roped to two flimsy iron posts, stood the cow, no longer bellowing. Nearby was an improvised lean-to, probably the crew's quarters. As he passed the small door, he peered through the low transom above it, and saw her lying beside a man on the floor. Automatically he walked on; then he turned and went back. The two were asleep, and half-clothed. In the warm air that came through the screened transom there was the smell of whisky that had been drunk and whisky that had been spilled.

He went upstairs, his heart beating violently. In the cabin, he closed her two valises, packed his own, set them all together by the door and laid the raincoats on top of them. He put on his shirt, combed his hair carefully, and went on deck. Cienaga was there ahead, in the mountains' morning shadow: the dock, a line of huts against the jungle behind, and the railway station to the right beyond the village.

As they docked, he signalled the two urchins who were waving for his attention, screaming, '*Equipajes!*' They fought a bit with one another until he made them see his two fingers held aloft. Then to make them certain, he pointed at each of them in turn, and they grinned. Still grinning, they stood beside him with the bags and coats, and he was among the first of the upper-deck passengers to get on land. They went down the street to the station with the parrots screaming at them from each thatched gable along the way.

On the crowded, waiting train, with the luggage finally in the rack, his heart beat harder than ever, and he kept his eyes painfully on the long dusty street that led back to the dock. At the far end as the whistle blew, he thought he saw a figure in white running among the dogs and children toward the station, but the train started up as he watched, and the street was lost to view. He took out his notebook, and sat with it on his lap, smiling at the shining green landscape that moved with increasing speed past the window.

At Paso Rojo

When old Señora Sanchez died, her two daughters Lucha and Chalía decided to visit their brother at his ranch. Out of devotion they had agreed never to marry while their mother lived, and now that she was gone and they were both slightly over forty there seemed just as little likelihood of a wedding in the family as there ever had. They would probably not admit this even to themselves, however. It was with complete understanding of his two sisters that Don Federico suggested they leave the city and go down to Paso Rojo for a few weeks.

Lucha arrived in black crêpe. To her, death was one of the things that happen in life with a certain regularity, and it therefore demanded outward observance. Otherwise her life was in no way changed, save that at the ranch she would have to get used to a whole new staff of servants.

'Indians, poor things, animals with speech,' she said to Don Federico the first night as they sat having coffee. A bare-footed girl had just carried the dessert dishes out.

Don Federico smiled. 'They are good people,' he said deliberately. Living at the ranch so long had lowered his standards, it was said, for even though he had always spent a month or so of each year in the capital, he had grown increasingly indifferent to the social life there.

'The ranch is eating his soul little by little,' Lucha used to say to Señora Sanchez.

Only once the old lady had replied. 'If his soul is to be eaten, then let the ranch do it.'

She looked around the primitive dining-room with its dry decorations of palm leaves and branches. He loves it

22

here because everything is his, she thought, and some of the things could never have been his if he had not purposely changed to fit them. That was not a completely acceptable thought. She knew the ranch had made him happy and tolerant and wise; to her it seemed sad that he could not have been those things without losing his civilized lustre. And that he certainly had lost. He had the skin of a peasant – brown and lined everywhere. He had the slowness of speech of men who have lived for long periods of time in the open. And the inflexions of his voice suggested the patience that can come from talking to animals rather than to human beings. Lucha was a sensible woman; still, she could not help feeling a certain amount of regret that her little brother, who at an earlier point in his life had been the best dancer among the members of the country club, should have become the thin, sad-faced, quiet man who sat opposite her.

'You've changed a great deal,' she suddenly said, shaking her head from side to side slowly.

'Yes. You change here. But it's a good place.'

'Good, yes. But so sad,' she said.

He laughed. 'Not sad at all. You get used to the quiet. And then you find it's not quiet at all. But you never change much, do you? Chalía's the one who's different. Have you noticed?'

'Oh, Chalía's always been crazy. She doesn't change either.'

'Yes. She is very much changed.' He looked past the smoking oil lamp, out into the dark. 'Where is she? Why doesn't she take coffee?'

'She has insomnia. She never takes it.'

'Maybe our nights will put her to sleep,' said Don Federico.

Chalía sat on the upper veranda in the soft night breeze. The ranch stood in a great clearing that held the jungle at bay all about, but the monkeys were calling from one side to the other, as if neither clearing nor ranch house existed. She had decided to put off going to bed – that way there was less darkness to be borne in case she stayed awake. The lines of a poem she had read on the train two days before were still in her mind: '*Aveces la noche*'. . . . Sometimes the night takes you with it, wraps you up and rolls you along, leaving you washed in sleep at the morning's edge.' Those lines were comforting. But there was the terrible line yet to come: 'And sometimes the night goes on without you.' She tried to jump from the image of the fresh sunlit morning to a completely alien idea: the waiter at the beach club in Puntarenas, but she knew the other thought was waiting there for her in the dark.

She had worn riding breeches and a khaki shirt open at the neck, on the trip from the capital, and she had announced to Lucha her intention of going about in those clothes the whole time she was at Paso Rojo. She and Lucha had quarrelled at the station.

'Everyone knows Mamá had died,' said Lucha, 'and the ones who aren't scandalized are making fun of you.'

With intense scorn in her voice Chalía had replied, 'You have asked them, I suppose.'

On the train as it wound through the mountains toward *tierra caliente* she had suddenly said, apropos of nothing: 'Black doesn't become me.' Really upsetting to Lucha was the fact that in Puntarenas she had gone off and bought some crimson nail-polish which she had painstakingly applied herself in the hotel room.

'You can't, Chalía!' cried her sister, wide-eyed. 'You've never done it before. Why do you do it now?'

Chalía had laughed immoderately. 'Just a whim!' she had said, spreading her decorated hands in front of her.

Loud footsteps came up the stairs and along the veranda, shaking it slightly. Her sister called: 'Chalía!'

She hesitated an instant, then said, 'Yes.'

'You're sitting in the dark! Wait. I'll bring out a lamp from your room. What an idea!'

'We'll be covered with insects,' objected Chalía, who, although her mood was not a pleasant one, did not want it disturbed.

'Federico says no!' shouted Lucha from inside. 'He says

there are no insects! None that bite, anyway!'

Presently she appeared with a small lamp which she set on a table against the wall. She sat down in a nearby hammock and swung herself softly back and forth, humming. Chalía frowned at her, but she seemed not to notice.

'What heat!' exclaimed Lucha finally.

'Don't exert yourself so much,' suggested Chalía.

They were quiet. Soon the breeze became a strong wind, coming from the direction of the distant mountains; but it too was hot, like the breath of a great animal. The lamp flickered, threatened to go out. Lucha got up and turned it down. As Chalía moved her head to watch her, her attention was caught by something else, and she quickly shifted her gaze to the wall. Something enormous, black and swift had been there an instant ago; now there was nothing. She watched the spot intently. The wall was faced with small stones which had been plastered over and whitewashed indifferently, so that the surface was very rough and full of large holes. She rose suddenly and, approaching the wall, peered at it closely. All the holes, large and small, were lined with whitish funnels. She could see the long, agile legs of the spiders that lived inside, sticking out beyond some of the funnels.

'Lucha, this wall is full of monsters!' she cried. A beetle flew near to the lamp, changed its mind and alighted on the wall. The nearest spider darted forth, seized it and disappeared into the wall with it.

'Don't look at them,' advised Lucha, but she glanced about the floor near her feet apprehensively.

Chalía pulled her bed into the middle of the room and moved a small table over to it. She blew out the lamp and lay back on the hard mattress. The sound of the nocturnal insects was unbearably loud – an endless, savage scream above the noise of the wind. All the vegetation out there was dry. It made a million scraping sounds in the air as the wind swept through it. From time to time the monkeys called to each other from different sides. A night bird scolded occasionally, but its voice was swallowed up in the insistent insect song and the rush of wind across the hot countryside. And it was absolutely dark.

Perhaps an hour later she lit the lamp by her bed, rose, and in her nightgown went to sit on the veranda. She put the lamp where it had been before, by the wall, and turned her chair to face it. She sat watching the wall until very late.

At dawn the air was cool, full of the sound of continuous lowing of cattle, nearby and far. Breakfast was served as soon as the sky was completely light. In the kitchen there was a hubbub of women's voices. The dining-room smelled of kerosene and oranges. A great platter heaped with thick slices of pale pineapple was in the centre of the table. Don Federico sat at the end, his back to the wall. Behind him was a small niche, bright with candles, and the Virgin stood there in a blue and silver gown.

'Did you sleep well?' said Don Federico to Lucha.

'Ah, wonderfully well!'

'And you?' to Chalía.

'I never sleep well,' she said.

A hen ran distractedly into the room from the veranda and was chased out by the serving-girl. Outside the door a group of Indian children stood guard around a square of clothes-line along which was draped a red assortment of meat: strips of flesh and loops of internal organs. When a vulture swooped low, the children jumped up and down, screaming in chorus, and drove it into the air again. Chalía frowned at their noise. Don Federico smiled.

'This is all in your honour,' he said. 'We killed a cow yesterday. Tomorrow all that will be gone.'

'Not the vultures!' exclaimed Lucha.

'Certainly not. All the cowboys and servants take some home to their families. And they manage to get rid of quite a bit of it themselves.'

'You're too generous,' and Chalía. 'It's bad for them. It makes them dissatisfied and unhappy. But I suppose if you didn't give it to them, they'd steal it anyway.'

Don Federico pushed back his chair.

'No one here has ever stolen anything from me.' He rose and went out.

After breakfast while it was still early, before the sun got too high in the sky, he regularly made a two-hour tour of the ranch. Since he preferred to pay unexpected visits to the vaqueros in charge of the various districts, he did not always cover the same regions. He was explaining this to Lucha as he untethered his horse outside the high barbed-wire fence that enclosed the house. 'Not because I hope to find something wrong. But this is the best way always to find everything right.'

Like Chalía, Lucha was sceptical of the Indian's ability to do anything properly. 'A very good idea,' she said. 'I'm sure you are much too lenient with those boys. They need a strong hand and no pity.'

Above the high trees that grew behind the house the red and blue macaws screamed, endlessly repeating their elliptical path in the sky. Lucha looked looked up their direction and saw Chalía on the upper porch, tucking a khaki shirt into her breeches.

'Rico, wait! I want to go with you,' she called, and rushed into her room.

Lucha turned back to her brother. 'You won't take her? She couldn't! With Mamá ...'

Don Federico cut her short, so as not to hear what would have been painful to him. 'You both need fresh air and exercise. Come, both of you.'

Lucha was silent a moment, looking aghast into his face. Finally she said, 'I couldn't,' and moved away to open the gate. Several cowboys were riding their horses slowly up from the paddock toward the front of the house. Chalía appeared on the lower porch and hurried to the gate, where Lucha stood looking at her.

'So you're going horseback riding,' said Lucha. Her voice had no expression.

'Yes. Are you coming? I suppose not. We should be back soon; no, Rico?'

Don Federico disregarded her, saying to Lucha: 'It would be good if you came.'

When she did not reply, but went through the gate and

shut it, he had one of the cowboys dismount and help Chalía on to his horse. She sat astride the animal beaming down at the youth.

'Now you can't come. You have no horse!' she cried, pulling the reins taut violently so that the horse stood absolutely still.

'Yes, señora. I shall go with the señores.' His speech was archaic and respectful, the speech of the rustic Indian. Their soft, polite words always annoyed her, because she believed, quite erroneously, that she could detect mockery underneath. 'Like parrots who've been taught two lines of Góngora!' she would laugh, when the subject was being discussed. Now she was further nettled by hearing herself addressed as señora. The idiot! she thought. He should know that I'm not married. But when she looked down at the cowboy again she noticed his white teeth and his very young face. She smiled, saying, 'How hot it is already', and undid the top button of her shirt.

The boy ran to the paddock and returned immediately, riding a larger and more nervous horse. This was a joke to the other cowboys, who started ahead, laughing. Don Federico and Chalía rode side by side, and the boy went along behind them, by turns whistling a tune and uttering soothing words to his skittish horse.

The party went across the mile or so of open space that lay between the house and the jungle. Then the high grass swept the riders' legs as the horses went downward to the river, which was dry save for a narrow stream of water in the middle. They followed the bed downstream, the vegetation increasing in height along the banks as they progressed. Chalía had enamelled her fingernails afresh before starting out and was in a good humour. She was discussing the administration of the ranch with Don Federico. The expenses and earning capacity interested her particularly, although she had no clear idea of the price of anything. She had worn an enormous soft straw sombrero whose brim drooped to her shoulders as she rode. Every few minutes she turned around and waved to the cowboy who still remained behind, shouting to him: 'Muchacho! You're not lost yet?'

Presently the river was divided into two separate beds by a large island which loomed ahead of them, its upper reaches a solid wall of branches and vines. At the foot of the giant trees among some grey boulders was a score or so of cows, looking very small indeed as they lay hunched up in the mud or ambled about seeking the thickest shade. Don Federico galloped ahead suddenly and conferred loudly with the other vaqueros. Almost simultaneously Chalía drew in her reins and brought her horse to a halt. The boy was quickly abreast of her. As he came up she called to him: 'It's hot, isn't it?'

The men rode on ahead. He circled around her. 'Yes, señora. But that is because we are in the sun. There' – he indicated the island – 'it is shady. Now they are almost there.'

She said nothing, but took off her hat and fanned herself with the brim. As she moved her hand back and forth she watched her red nails. 'What an ugly colour,' she murmured.

'What, señora?'

'Nothing.' She paused. 'Ah, what heat!'

'Come, señora. Shall we go on?'

Angrily she crumpled the crown of the sombrero in her fist. 'I am not señora,' she said distinctly, looking at the men ahead as they rode up to the cows and roused them from their lethargy. The boy smiled. She went on. 'I am señorita. That is not the same thing. Or perhaps you think it is?'

The boy was puzzled; he was conscious of her sudden emotion, but he had no idea of its cause. 'Yes, señorita,' he said politely, without conviction. And he added, with more assurance, 'I am Roberto Paz, at your orders.'

The sun shone down upon them from above and was reflected by the mica in the stones at their feet. Chalía undid another button of her shirt.

'It's hot. Will they came back soon?'

'No, señorita. They return by the road. Shall we go?' He turned his horse toward the island ahead.

'I don't want to be where the cows are,' and Chalía with

petulance. 'They have *garrapatas*. The *garrapatas* get under your skin.'

Roberto laughed indulgently. 'The *garrapatas* will not molest you if you stay on your horse, señorita.'

'But I want to get down and rest. I'm so tired!' The discomfort of the heat became pure fatigue as she said the words; this made it possible for the annoyance she felt with him to transform itself into a general state of self-pity and depression that came upon her like a sudden pain. Hanging her head she sobbed: *'Ay, madre mía!* My poor mamá!' She stayed that way a moment, and her horse began to walk slowly toward the trees at the side of the river-bed.

Roberto glanced perplexedly in the direction the others had taken. They had all passed out of sight beyond the head of the island; the cows were lying down again. 'The señorita should not cry.'

She did not reply. Since the reins continued slack, her horse proceeded at a faster pace toward the forest. When it had reached the shade at the edge of the stream, the boy rode quickly to her side. 'Señorita!' he cried.

She sighed and looked up at him, her hat still in her hand. 'I'm very tired,' she repeated. 'I want to get down and rest.'

There was a path leading into the forest. Roberto went ahead to lead the way, hacking at stray vines and bushes with his machete. Chalía followed, sitting listlessly in the saddle, calmed by the sudden entrance into the green world of silence and comparative coolness.

They rode slowly upward through the forest for a quarter of an hour or so without saying anything to each other. When they came to a gate Roberto opened it without dismounting and waited for Chalía to pass through. As she went by him she smiled and said: 'How nice it is here.'

He replied, rather curtly, she thought: 'Yes, señorita.'

Ahead, the vegetation thinned, and beyond lay a vast, open, slightly undulating expanse of land, decorated here and there, as if by intent, with giant white-trunked ceiba trees. The hot wind blew across this upland terrain, and the cry of cicadas was in the air. Chalía halted her horse and jumped down. The tiny thistlelike plants that covered the ground crackled under her boots. She seated herself carefully in the shade at the very edge of the open land.

Roberto tied the two horses to a tree and stood looking at her with the alert, hostile eyes of the Indian who faces what he does not understand.

'Sit down. Here,' she said.

Stonily he obeyed, sitting with his legs straight on the earth in front of him, his back very erect. She rested her hand on his shoulder. '*Qué calor,*' she murmured.

She did not expect him to answer, but he did, and his voice sounded remote. 'It is not my fault, señorita.'

She slipped her arm around his neck and felt the muscles grow tense. She rubbed her face over his chest; he did not move or say anything. With her eyes shut and her head pressing hard against him, she felt as if she were hanging to consciousness only by the ceaseless shrill scream of the cicadas. She remained thus, leaning ever more heavily upon him as he braced himself with his hands against the earth behind him. His face had become an impenetrable mask; he seemed not to be thinking of anything, not even to be present.

Breathing heavily, she raised her head to look at him, but found she did not have the courage to reach his eyes with her gaze. Instead she watched his throat and finally whispered, 'It doesn't matter what you think of me. It's enough for me to hold you like this.'

He turned his head stiffly away from her face, looking across the landscape to the mountains. Gruffly he said, 'My brother could come by this place. We must go back to the river.'

She tried to bury her face in his chest, to lose herself once more in the delicious sensation. Without warning, he moved quickly and stood up, so that she tumbled forward with her face against the ground.

The surprise of her little fall changed her mood instantly. She sprang up, dashed blindly for the nearer of the two horses, was astride it in an instant, and before he could cry, 'It's the bad horse!' had pounded the animal's flanks with her heels. It raised its head wildly; with a violent bound it began to gallop over the countryside. At the first movement she realized dimly that there had been a change, that it was not the same horse, but in her excitement she let her observation stop there. She was delighted to be moving swiftly across the plain against the hot wind. Roberto was left behind.

'*Idiota!*' she screamed into the air. '*Idiota! Idiota!*' with all her might. Ahead of her a tremendous vulture, panic-stricken at the approaching hoof sounds, flapped clumsily away into the sky.

The saddle, having been strapped on for less vigorous action, began to slip. She gripped the pommel with one hand, and seizing her shirt with the other gave it a convulsive tug that ripped it completely open. A powerful feeling of exultation came to her as she glanced down and saw her own skin white in the sunlight.

In the distance to one side, she dimly saw some palm trees reaching above a small patch of lower vegetation. She shut her eyes: the palms looked like shiny green spiders. She was out of breath from the jolting. The sun was too hot. The saddle kept slipping farther; she could not right it. The horse showed no sign of being aware of her existence. She pulled on the reins as hard as she could without falling over backward, but it had no effect on the horse, which continued to run at top speed, following no path and missing some of the trees by what seemed no more than inches.

'Where shall I be in an hour?' she asked herself. 'Dead, perhaps?' The idea of death did not frighten her the way it did some people. She was afraid of the night because she could not sleep; she was not afraid of life and death because she did not feel implicated to any extent in either one. Only other people lived and died, had their lives and deaths. She, being inside herself, existed merely as herself and not as a part of anything else. People, animals, flowers and stones were objects, and they all belonged to the world outside. It was their juxtapositions that made hostile or friendly patterns. Sometimes she looked at her own hands and feet for several minutes, trying to fight off an indefinite sensation thay gave her of belonging also to the world outside. But this never troubled her deeply. The impressions were received and accepted without question; at most she could combat them when they were too strong for her comfort.

Here in the hot morning sun, being pulled forward through the air, she began to feel that almost all of her had slipped out of the inside world, that only a tiny part of her was still she. The part that was left was full of astonishment and disbelief; the only discomfort now lay in having to accept the fact of the great white tree trunks that continued to rush by her.

She tried several times to make herself be elsewhere: in her rose garden at home, in the hotel dining-room at Puntarenas, even as a last resort, which might prove feasible since it too had been unpleasant, in her bed back at the ranch, with the dark around her.

With a great bound, the horse cleared a ditch. The saddle slipped completely around and hung underneath. Having no pommel to cling to, she kept on as best she could, clutching the horse's flanks with her legs and always pulling on the reins. Suddenly the animal slowed down and stepped briskly into a thicket. There was a path of sorts; she suspected it was the same one they had used coming from the river. She sat listlessly, waiting to see where the horse would go.

Finally it came out into the river-bed as she had expected, and trotted back to the ranch. The sun was directly overhead when they reached the paddock. The horse stood outside, waiting to be let in, but it seemed that no one was around. Making a great effort, she slid down to the ground and found she had difficulty in standing because her legs were trembling so. She was furious and ashamed. As she hobbled toward the house she was strongly hoping Lucha would not see her. A few Indian girls appeared to be the only people about. She dragged herself upstairs and shut herself in her room. The bed had been pushed back against the wall, but she did not have the force to pull it out into the centre where she wanted it.

When Don Federico and the others returned, Lucha, who had been reading downstairs, went to the gate. 'Where's Chalía? she cried.

'She was tired. One of the boys brought her back a while

ago,' he said. 'It's just as well. We went half-way to Cañas.'

Chalía had her lunch in bed and slept soundly until late in the afternoon. When she emerged from her room on to the veranda, a woman was dusting the rocking-chairs and arranging them in a row against the wall.

'Where's my sister?' demanded Chalía.

'Gone to the village in the truck with the señor,' the women replied, going to the head of the stairs and beginning to dust them one by one, as she went down backward.

Chalía seated herself in a chair and put her feet up on the porch railing, reflecting as she did so that if Lucha had been there she would have disapproved of the posture. There was a bend in the river – the only part of it that came within sight of the house – just below her, and a portion of the bank was visible to her through the foliage from where she sat. A large breadfruit tree spread its branches out almost to the opposite side of the stream. There was a pool at the turn, just where the tree's trunk grew out of the muddy bank. An Indian sauntered out of the undergrowth and calmly removed his trousers, then his shirt. He stood there a moment, stark nakèd, looking at the water, before he walked into it and began to splash and swim. When he had finished bathing he stood again on the bank, smoothing his blue-black hair. Chalía was puzzled, knowing that few Indians would be so immòdest as to bathe naked in full view of the upstairs veranda. With a sudden strange sensation as she watched him, she realized it was Roberto and that he was wholly conscious of her presence at that moment.

He knows Rico is gone and that no one can see him from downstairs, she thought, resolving to tell her brother when he came home. The idea of vengeance upon the boy filled her with a delicious excitement. She watched his deliberate movements as he dressed. He sat down on a rock with only his shirt on and combed his hair. The late afternoon sun shone through the leaves and gave his brown skin an orange cast. When finally he had gone away without once glancing up at the house, she rose and went into her room. Manoeuvring the bed into the middle of the floor once more, she began to walk around it; her mood was growing more and more turbulent as she circled about the room.

She heard the truck door slam, and a moment later, voices downstairs. With her finger to her temple, where she always put it when her heart was beating very fast, she slipped out on to the veranda and downstairs. Don Federico was in the commissary, which he opened for a half-hour each morning and evening. Chalía stepped inside the door, her mouth already open, feeling the words about to burst from her lungs. Two children were pushing their copper coins along the counter, pointing at the candy they wanted. By the lamp a women was looking at a bolt of goods. Don Federico was on a ladder, getting down another bolt. Chalía's mouth closed slowly. She looked down at her brother's desk by the door beside her, where he kept his ledgers and bills. In an open cigar box almost touching her hand was a pile of dirty banknotes. She was back in the room before she knew it. She shut the door and saw that she had four ten-colon notes in her hand. She stuffed them into her breeches pocket.

At dinner they made fun of her for having slept all the afternoon, telling her that now she would lie awake again all night.

She was busy eating. 'If I do, so much the worse,' she said, without looking up.

'I've arranged a little concert after dinner,' said Don Federico. Lucha was ecstatic. He went on: 'The cowboys have some friends here, over from Bagaces, and Raul has finished building his marimba.'

The men and boys began to assemble soon after dinner. There was laughter, and guitars were strummed in the dark on the terrace. The two sisters went to sit at the end near the dining-room, Don Federico was in the middle with the vaqueros, and the servants were ranged at the kitchen end. After several solo songs by various men with guitars, Raul and a friend began to play the marimba. Roberto was seated on the floor among the cowboys who were not performing.

'Suppose we all dance,' said Don Federico, jumping up and seizing Lucha. They moved about together at one end of the terrace for a moment, but no one else stirred.

'*A bailar!*' Don Federico shouted, laughing.

Several of the girls started to dance timidly in couples, with loud giggling. None of the men would budge. The marimba players went on pounding out the same piece over and over again. Don Federico danced with Chalía, who was stiff from her morning ride; soon she excused herself and left. Instead of going upstairs to bed she crossed on to the front veranda and sat looking across the vast moonlit clearing. The night was thick with eternity. She could feel it there, just beyond the gate. Only the monotonous, tinkling music kept the house within the confines of time, saved it from being engulfed. As she listed to the merry-making progress, she had the impression that the men were taking more part in it. Rico has probably opened them a bottle of rum, she thought with fury.

At last it sounded as though everyone were dancing. Her curiosity having risen to a high pitch, she was about to rise and return to the terrace, when a figure appeared at the other end of the veranda. She needed no one to tell her it was Roberto. He was walking soundlessly toward her; he seemed to hesitate as he came up to her, then he squatted down by her chair and looked up at her. She had been right: he smelled of rum.

'Good evening, señorita.'

She felt impelled to remain silent. Nevertheless, she said, 'Good evening.' She put her hand into her pocket, saying to herself that she must do this correctly and quickly.

As he crouched there with his face shining in the moonlight, she bent forward and passed her hand over his smooth hair. Keeping her fingers on the back of his neck, she leaned still farther forward and kissed his lips. The rum was very strong. He did not move. She began to whisper in his ear, very low: 'Roberto, I love you. I have a present for you. Forty colones. Here.'

He turned his head swiftly and said out loud, 'Where?'

She put the bills into his hand, still holding his head, and whispered again: 'Sh! Not a word to anyone. I must go now. I'll give you more tomorrow night.' She let go of him.

He rose and went out the gate. She went straight upstairs to bed, and as she went to sleep the music was still going on.

Much later she awoke and lit her lamp. It was half-past four. Day would soon break. Feeling full of an unaccustomed energy, Chalía dressed, extinguished the lamp and went outdoors, shutting the gate quietly behind her. In the paddock the horses stirred. She walked by it and started along the road to the village. It was a very silent hour: the night insects had ceased their noises and the birds had not yet begun their early-morning twitter. The moon was low in the sky, so that it remained behind the trees most of the time. Ahead of her Venus flared like a minor moon. She walked quickly, with only a twinge of pain now and then in her hip.

Something dark lying in the road ahead of her made her stop walking. It did not move. She watched it closely, stepping cautiously toward it, ready to run the other way. As her eyes grew accustomed to its form, she saw that it was a man lying absolutely still. And as she drew near, she knew it was Roberto. She touched his arm with her foot. He did not respond. She leaned over and put her hand on his chest. He was breathing deeply, and the smell of liquor was almost overpowering. She straightened and kicked him lightly in the head. There was a tiny groan from far within. This also, she said to herself, would have to be done quickly. She felt wonderfully light and powerful as she slowly manoeuvred his body with her feet to the right-hand side of the road. There was a small cliff there, about twenty feet high. When she got him to the edge, she waited a while, looking at his features in the moonlight. His mouth was open a little, and the white teeth peeked out from behind the lips. She smoothed his forehead a few times and with a gentle push rolled him over the edge. He fell very heavily, making a strange animal sound as he hit.

She walked back to the ranch at top speed. It was getting light when she arrived. She went into the kitchen and ordered her breakfast saying, 'I'm up early.' The entire day she spent around the house, reading and talking to Lucha. She thought Don Federico looked preoccupied when he set out on his morning tour of inspection, after closing the commissary. She thought he still did when he returned; she told him so at lunch.

'It's nothing,' he said. 'I can't seem to balance my books.'

'And you've always been such a good mathematician,' said Chalía.

During the afternoon some cowboys brought Roberto in. She heard the commotion in the kitchen and the servants' cries of '*Ay, Dios!*' She went out to watch. He was conscious, lying on the floor with all the other Indians staring at him.

'What's the matter?' she said.

One of the cowboys laughed. 'Nothing of importance. He had too much . . .', the cowboy made a gesture of drinking from a bottle, 'and fell off the road. Nothing but bruises, I think.'

After dinner Don Federico asked Chalía and Lucha into his little private office. He looked drawn, and he spoke more slowly than usual. As Chalía entered she saw Roberto was standing inside the door. He did not look at her. Lucha and Chalía sat down; Don Federico and Roberto remained standing.

'This is the first time anyone has done this to me,' said Don Federico, looking down at the rug, his hands locked behind him. 'Roberto has stolen from me. The money is missing. Some of it is in his pocket still, more than his monthly wages. I know he has stolen it because he had no money yesterday and because,' he turned to Chalía, 'because he can account for having it only by lying. He says you gave it to him. Did you give Roberto any money yesterday?'

Chalía looked puzzled. 'No,' she said. 'I thought of giving him a colon when he brought me back from the ride yesterday morning. But then I thought it would be better to wait until we were leaving to go back to the city. Was it much? He's just a boy.'

Don Federico said: 'It was forty colones. But that's the same as forty centavos. Stealing . . .'

Chalía interrupted him. 'Rico!' she exclaimed. 'Forty colones! That's a great deal! Has he spent much of it? You could take it out of his wages little by little.' She knew her brother would say what he did say, a moment later.

'Never! He'll leave tonight. And his brother with him.'

In the dim light Chalía could see the large purple bruise on Roberto's forehead. He kept his head lowered and did not look up, even when she and Lucha rose and left the room at a sign from their brother. They went upstairs together and sat down on the veranda.

'What barbarous people they are!' said Lucha indignantly. 'Poor Rico may learn some day how to treat them. But I'm afraid one of them will kill him first.'

Chalía rocked back and forth, fanning herself lazily. 'With a few more lessons like this he may change,' she said. 'What heat!'

They heard Don Federico's voice below by the gate. Firmly it said, '*Adiós.*' There were muffled replies and the gate was closed. Don Federico joined his sisters on the veranda. He sat down sadly.

'I didn't like to send them away on foot at night,' he said, shaking his head. 'But that Roberto is a bad one. It was better to have him go once and for all, quickly. Juan is good, but I had to get rid of him too, of course.'

'*Claro, claro,*' said Lucha absently. Suddenly she turned to her brother full of concern. 'I hope you remembered to take away the money you said he still had in his pocket.'

'Yes, yes,' he assured her, but from the tone of his voice she knew he had let the boy keep it.

Don Federico and Lucha said good-night and went to bed. Chalía sat up a while, looking vaguely at the wall with the spiders in it. Then she yawned and took the lamp into her room. Again the bed had been pushed back against the wall by the maid. Chalía shrugged her shoulders, got into the bed where it was, blew out the lamp, listened for a few minutes to the night sounds, and went peacefully to sleep, thinking of how surprisingly little time it had taken her to get used to life at Paso Rojo, and even, she had to admit now, to begin to enjoy it.

Doña Faustina

No one could understand why Doña Faustina had bought the inn. It stood on one of the hairpin curves in the old highway leading up from the river valley to the town, but the route had been made useless by the building of the new paved road. Now it was impossible to reach the inn except by climbing up a stony path over the embankment and walking several hundred feet down the old road which, no longer kept in repair, already was being washed away by the rains and strangled by the shiny vegetation of that lowland region.

On Sundays the people used to walk out from the town, the women carrying parasols and the men guitars (for this was before the days of the radio, when almost everyone knew how to make a little music); they would get as far as the great breadfruit tree and look up the road at the faded façade of the building, more than half hidden by young bamboo and banana plants, stare a few seconds, and turn around to go back. 'Why does she leave the sign up?' they would say. 'Does she think anyone would ever spend the night there now?' And they were quite right: no one went near the inn any more. Only the people of the town knew that it existed, and they had no need of it.

There remained the mystery of why she had bought it. As usual when there is something townspeople cannot understand, they invented a whole series of unpleasant explanations for Doña Faustina's behaviour. The earliest and most common one, which was that she had decided to transform the place into a house of ill-repute, soon fell to pieces, for there was absolutely nothing to substantiate such

41

a theory. No one had been seen to go near the inn for weeks, except Doña Faustina's younger sister Carlota who arrived from Jalapa, and the old servants José and Elena, who went to market each morning and minded their business strictly enough to satisfy even the most vicious gossips. As for Carlota, she appeared occasionally at mass, dressed in black. It was said that she had taken their father's death very much to heart, and would probably not remove the mourning, ever.

The other suppositions evolved by the people of the town in their effort to bring light to the mystery proved as unlikely as the first. It was rumoured that Doña Faustina was giving asylum to Chato Morales, a bandit whom the police of the region had been trying for months to capture, but he was caught soon afterwards in a distant part of the province. Then it was said that the inn was a depository for a drug ring; this also proved to be false. The leaders of the ring, having been arrested, divulged their secrets, and the cache proved to be in a room above the Farmácia Ideal. There were darker hints to the effect that Carlota might be luring lone voyagers to the inn, where they met the fate that traditionally befalls such solitary visitors to lonely inns. But people did not take such suggestions seriously. The opinion grew that Doña Faustina had merely gone a little mad, and that her madness, having taken an anti-social turn, had induced her to retire to the outskirts of town where she could live without ever seeing anyone. To be sure, this theory was contested by certain younger members of the community who claimed that she was no more crazy than they, that on the contrary she was extremely crafty. They said that having a great deal of money she had bought the inn because of the ample lands which surrounded it, and that there in the privacy of the plant-smothered gardens and orchards she had devised all kinds of clever ways of hiding her riches. The older citizens of the town took no stock in this, however, since they clearly remembered both her husband and her father, neither of whom had evinced any unusual prowess in collecting money. And she had bought the inn for practically nothing. 'Where would she have got the pesos?' they said sceptically. 'Out of the trees, perhaps?'

2

Once when a child disappeared from the town (small children were often stolen in those days and taken off to distant places where they were made to work), the parents insisted that the police search the inn. Doña Faustina, who was a large women in the prime of life, met the little policeman at the door and refused to let him in. Indeed, she was so brusque with him and glared at him with such malignity that he felt obliged to go back to the *comisaría* and get reinforcements. When he and the three extra men returned to the inn, they made a complete but unrewarding search of the place, followed at every step by Doña Faustina, who did not cease to shower them with insults until they had left the premises. But they returned to town with a story. The rooms were a shambles, they said, the furniture was broken, there was rubbish and garbage everywhere in the corridors, the railing of the second-storey balcony had given way and been replaced by a single strand of barbed wire, and the place looked generally as though innumerable picnic parties had been held there over a period of years. This report helped to fortify people in their belief that Doña Faustina had more or less lost her mind, and for a time the town ceased thinking about her.

Some time afterwards it was noted that she and her sister had taken to making trips to neighbouring towns; they had been seen in such widely separated places as Tlacotalpam and Zempoala. But even these peregrinations failed to elicit true interest. Heads were shaken, sympathetically or otherwise, and it was remarked that Doña Faustina was growing less and less sane, but that was all.

When the mistresses of the house were absent they did not return for three or four days, and José and Elena remained alone to guard the property, not even venturing forth to the town for marketing until the two reappeared. On their return the sisters would take an old covered carriage that went each day to the station to await the train. They would pile their numerous bundles and baskets in and drive as far as the curve, where they would get down, the driver helping them up the embankment with their effects and then leaving them to get to the house in whatever way they could. Carlota would go and bring up José to help carry the things, but Doña Faustina always insisted on carrying the heaviest baskets herself. A few trips would be made back and forth through the undergrowth, and then the abandoned road would be quiet again until the old servants went to market the next morning.

In another fortnight or so they would set out once more, always to a new place; necessarily this led them farther and farther afield. Someone even claimed to have seen them once in Vera Cruz, although, given the number of false stories which were circulated about the two women, there was no particular reason to believe this.

Before the house had been made into an inn it had been a prosperous *finca,* with terraced lands planted with fruit trees, leading downward rather steeply for a mile or so to a high bluff above the river. For fifty years or more the land had been totally neglected, so that now it was hard to find the avocado and mango trees in the tangle of new, eager parasites which had sprung up on every side and often reached above even the tallest of the older trees. Lianas looped down from the branches, climbing plants stretched up to clutch at them, and a person could not stray more than fifty feet down one of the orchard paths from the house without coming face to face with an impenetrable curtain of leaves. And now no one really knew how far it was from the house to the river, because the borders of the property gave on even thicker jungle.

3

Not even José would have known the tank existed, if he had not strayed a bit farther down than usual one afternoon, to see if he could find some mameyes. In the deep silence of the undergrowth there, far beneath the regions where the sun could reach, he had heard a heavy splash not far distant, as though a boulder had been flung into deep water. He had listened intently, but there had been no other sound. The next afternoon during siesta time he went back to the same spot carrying a machete, and laboriously hacked his way through the stubborn vegetation. It was nearly twilight when he caught sight of the water ahead. Finally he stood near the edge of the tank. The stagnant water gave off a heavy odour, and insects hovered in swarms in the still air above it. And as he watched, it seemed to him that there was a faint movement down in the brown depths; for some reason the water was not completely motionless. For a while he stood there staring downward, lost in contemplation; then, as the light was fading, he turned and started back, resolving, without knowing why he did so, to say nothing about the tank to Elena when he returned to the house.

Several times in the course of the following months José returned there, always with the hope of discovering what had made the splash. Even a man diving into the tank could scarcely have caused such a noise. There was a stone-paved ramp at the far end (the tank doubtless had been built to bathe cattle) and on two occasions he found the ramp partially wet, which merely added to his perplexity. The second time he noticed this, he began to cut his way through the vines along the edge, in order to examine the ramp closely. And half-way along he found the path. Someone had cleared a narrow but practicable passage to the tank from some point back near the house. Abandoning his project, he followed the path and came out in a corner of what had once been a rose garden, on a lower terrace between the door to the laundry and the ruined stables. As he stood blinking in the sunlight, Doña Faustina appeared coming down the short flight of steps outside the laundry door. By its handle she carried a basket with a newspaper tucked over the top. Automatically old José walked towards her to take the basket from her. Evidently she had not been expecting to see him, for when she looked up and realized he was near her, her face took on an extraordinary expression. But all she said was: 'What are you doing down here? Go to the kitchen.' The she stepped to a stone bench under an arbour near her and sat down, putting the basket on the bench beside her.

As he went on up towards the house José thought he had never seen his *patrona* look quite so fierce. She was always

severe, and often forbidding, but not to the point of being
able to frighten him as she had today. It was as if a demon
had peered out at him for a moment from beneath her heavy
lids.

It must be true, he thought. Doña Faustina is going mad.
What will become of Elena and me?

This time when he got to the kitchen he took Elena into
a corner and whispered to her, telling her his fears, and of
how strange the señora had looked in the garden. Elena
crossed herself. 'Oh, God,' she murmured. But he did not
mention the tank to her, either now or later. He did not
even want to think about it, because he suspected that in
some way it was connected with Doña Faustina's madness,
and being the only one who knew about it gave him a
certain feeling of security which he would have lost had he
shared the knowledge with Elena.

4

One cold evening of *llovizna*, as the mealy fog slowly turned
to water and drenched the countryside, there was a knock
at the entrance door. Doña Faustina, who spent much of
her time pottering about in the basement where the baths
and laundry were, heard it from there, and straightway
mounted the stairs, her face dark with fury. Carlota stood
in the *comedor*, undecided as to whether she should answer.
The knocking was repeated as Doña Faustina reached her.

'Again the police?' said Carlota a bit fearfully.

'*Ya veremos,*' muttered Doña Faustina. And she went out
and stood behind the door, calling out in a loud voice:
'Who?'

There was no answer.

'Don't open it,' whispered Carlota, who stood behind
her.

Doña Faustina made an impatient gesture to silence her
sister. They waited several minutes, but the knock did not
come again. There was only the irregular dripping of the
water from the balcony above on to the ground.

'Stay here,' said Doña Faustina, and she went through

the *comedor*, down the stairs and into the laundry again. Here she gathered up all the refuse that strewed the floor and the wash-tubs, and packing it into two large baskets, continued out of the side door which gave on the grape arbour. From here, descending the steps slowly, she disappeared into the darkness of the rose garden.

Within a half-hour she was back in the entrance hall where Carlota still stood listening by the door.

'Nothing,' said Carlota in answer to Doña Faustina's questioning gesture. Doña Faustina beckoned to her. They went into the *comedor* and whispered together. One candle flame cowered behind a pitcher on the newspaper-covered sideboard.

'It's not the police,' said Doña Faustina. 'Your room has a key. Go immediately. Lock the door and go to bed.'

'But you . . . ?'

'I'm not afraid.'

Left alone in the *comedor*, Doña Faustina poured herself a glass of water and drank it. Then she took the candle and went up the long staircase to her room. She closed the door and set the candle down. By her sagging bed, around which Elena had draped the patched mosquito-net, stood a man. Swiftly he stepped over to her, and putting one arm around her neck tightly, stuffed a crumpled cloth into her mouth. She swung her arms about wildly, and managed to hit him once in the face, but almost immediately he had tied her wrists together. There was no further struggle. He propelled her roughly to the bed, yanked aside the netting and pushed her down. She looked at him: he was a tall young man, a *mestizo* probably, and badly dressed. As he moved about the room looking into the crates and boxes that lay in wild disorder about the floor, he snorted with distaste. Finally he overturned a chair in anger and with a scornful gesture swept all the empty bottles and piles of newspapers off the bureau on to the floor. He approached the bed again and looked at Doña Faustina in the wavering light. Then, to her surprise (although it cannot be said to her annoyance) he lay down and had his way with her quietly, impersonally. A few minutes later he sat up and pulled the cloth out of her mouth. She lay perfectly still and looked up at him.

Finally she said: 'What do you want here? I have no money.'

'Who knows if you have or not?'

'I tell you there is none.'

'We'll see.'

He got up. Again he spent a quarter of an hour or so searching the room, scuffing piles of refuse under the tables, kicking the furniture over to examine the under part, emptying drawers of their dust and litter. He lit a small cigar and returned to the bed. His oblique eyes looked almost closed in the light of the candle.

'Where is it?' he said.

'There is none. But I have something more precious.'

'What?' He looked at her with scornful disbelief. What could be more precious than money?

'Untie my hands.'

He gave her the use of one hand, holding the other arm firmly while she fumbled in her clothing. In a moment she drew forth a small parcel done up in newspaper, and handed it to him. He placed it on the bed and bound her hands together. Then in a gingerly fashion he lifted the parcel and smelled of it. It was soft, and slightly wet.

'What is it?'

'Open it, *hombre*. Eat it. You know what it is.'

Suspiciously he removed the outer layer of paper and held the contents close to the candle.

'What is this?' he cried.

'*Ya sabes, hombre,*' she said calmly. '*Cómelo.*'

'What is it?' he said again, trying to sound stern; but there was fear in his voice.

'Eat it, son. You don't have the chance every day.'

'Where did you get it?'

'Ah!' Doña Faustina looked mysterious and wise, and gave no further answer.

'What do I want of it?' said the young man presently, looking down at the little object in his hand.

'Eat it! Eat it and have the power of two,' she said cajolingly.

'*Brujerías!*' he exclaimed, still without putting the thing down.

A moment later he added, speaking slowly: 'I don't like

witchcraft. I don't like it.'

'Bah!' Doña Faustina snorted. 'Don't be stupid, son. Don't ask questions. Eat it, and go on your way with the force of two. Who will ever know? Tell me that! Who?'

This argument appeared to weigh with the young man. Suddenly he lifted the thing to his mouth and bit into it as if it had been a plum. While he ate he looked once at Doña Faustina darkly. When he had finished, he walked around the room tentatively for a moment, his head slightly on one side. Doña Faustina watched him closely.

'How do you feel?' she inquired.

'*Bien*,' he said.

'Two,' she reminded him. 'Now you have the power of two.'

As if inspired by the fortifying suggestion, he walked to the bed, threw himself down on it and lay with her again briefly. This time she kissed his forehead. When it was over he rose, and without undoing the rope that bound her hands, without saying a word, he went out of the door and down the stairs. A minute or so later she heard the front door close. At the same time the candle, which had burned down to its base, began to flicker wildly, and soon the room was in darkness.

5

All night Doña Faustiña lay perfectly still on her bed, sleeping now and then, and during the periods of wakefulness listening to the slow dripping of the mist outside her windows. In the morning Carlota, still fearful, opened her door a crack, and apparently finding everything in the corridors in a normal state went to Doña Faustina's room.

'*Ay, Dios!*' she cried when she saw Doña Faustina lying with her clothing partially ripped away and her hands lashed together. 'Oh God! Oh God!'

But Doña Faustina was calm. As Carlota undid the rope, she said: 'He did no harm. But I had to give him the heart.'

Carlota looked at her sister with horror.

'You're mad!' she cried. 'The police will be here any

minute.'

'No, no,' Doña Faustina reassured her, and she was right: no police arrived to search the house again. Nothing happened. At the end of two weeks thay made another trip, and a little while later still another. Two days after they had returned from this one, Doña Faustina called Carlota into her room and said to her: 'There will be a child.'

Carlota sat down slowly on the bed.

'How terrible!'

Doña Faustina smiled. 'No, no. It's perfect. Think. It will have the power of thirty-seven.'

But Carlota did not seem convinced. 'We don't know about those things,' she said. 'It may be a vengeance.'

'No, no, no,' said Doña Faustina, shaking her head. 'But now we must be more careful than ever.'

'No more trips?' said Carlota hopefully.

'I shall think about it.'

A few days later they were both in the rose garden sitting on a bench.

'I have thought,' said Doña Faustina. 'And there will be no more trips.'

'Good,' replied Carlota.

Towards the end of the year Doña Faustina was confined to bed, awaiting the birth of the child. She lay back comfortably in the crooked old bed, and had Elena come and sweep out the room for the first time in many months. Even when the floor was clean, the room still reeked of the garbage that had lain there for so long. Carlota had bought a tiny crib in the town; the purchase had reawakened interest in their activities on the part of the townspeople.

When the time arrived, Elena and Carlota were both in the room to assist at the birth. Doña Faustina did not scream once. The baby was washed and laid beside her in the bed.

'A boy,' said Elena, smiling down at her.

'Of course,' said Doña Faustina, beginning to nurse him.

Elena went down to the kitchen to tell José the good news. He shook his head gloomily.

'Something bad in all this,' he muttered.

'In all what?' said Elena sharply.

'Who is the father?' said José, looking up.

'That is Doña Faustina's secret,' Elena replied smugly, rather as if it had been her own.

'Yes. I think so too,' said José meaningfully. 'I think there is no father, if you want to know. I think she got the child from the Devil.'

Elena was scandalized. 'Shameless!' she cried. 'How can you say such a thing?'

'I have reasons,' said José darkly. And he would say no more.

Things went smoothly at the inn. Several months passed. The baby had been named Jesus Maria and was in perfect health – '*un torito*,' said Elena, 'a real little bull.'

'Of course,' Doña Faustina had replied on that occasion. 'He has the power of thirty-seven . . .' Exactly then Carlota had been taken with a violent fit of coughing which managed to cover the rest of the sentence. But Elena had noticed nothing.

The rainy season had finished again, and the bright days of sunlight and green leaves had come. José went in search of fruit once more, wandering down through the garden, crouching over most of the time to creep beneath the hanging walls of vines and tendrils. Again one day he cut his way to the tank, and stood on the edge of it looking towards the ramp. And this time he saw the monster just as it slid forward and disappeared beneath the surface of the water. His mouth dropped open. Only one word came out: '*Caimán!*'

He stood still for several minutes looking down at the dark water. Then he edged along the side of the tank to the place where the path had been the year before. It had completely disappeared. No one had been to the tank in many months; there was no indication that such a corridor had ever existed there in the mass of vegetation. He returned the way he had come.

It was a scandal, thought José, that such a beast should be living on Doña Faustina's property, and he determined to speak to her about it immediately. He found her in the kitchen talking with Elena. From his face she saw that something was wrong, and fearful perhaps that he was going to say what he did say a moment later, she tried to get him out of the room.

'Come upstairs. I want you to do something for me,' she said, walking over to him and pulling him by the arm.

But José's excitement was too great. He did not even notice that she was touching him. 'Señora!' he cried. 'There is a crocodile in the garden!'

Doña Faustina looked at him with black hatred. 'What are you saying?' she said softly and with a certain concern in her voice, as if the old man needed to be treated with gentleness.

'An enormous *caimán*! I saw it!'

Elena looked at him apprehensively. 'He's ill,' she whispered to Doña Faustina. José heard her. 'Ill!' he laughed scornfully. 'Come with me and wait a little. I'll show you who's ill! Just come!'

'You say in the garden?' repeated Doña Faustina incredulously. 'But where?'

'In the great tank, señora.'

'Tank? What tank?'

'The señora doesn't know about the tank? There's a tank down below in the orchard. *Sí, sí, sí*,' he insisted, seeing Elena's face. 'I've been there many times. It's not far. Come.'

Inasmuch as Elena seemed to be on the point of removing her apron and, accepting his invitation, Doña Faustina changed her tactics. 'Stop this nonsense!' she shouted. 'If you're ill, José, go to bed. Or are you drunk?' She stepped close to him and sniffed suspiciously. 'No? *Bueno*. Elena, give him some hot coffee and let me know in an hour how he is.'

But in her room Doña Faustina began to worry.

6

They got out just in time. Carlota was not sure they ought to leave. 'Where shall we go?' she said plaintively.

'Don't think about that,' said Doña Faustina.

'Think about the police. We must go. I know. What good does it do me to have the power of thirty-seven if I pay no attention to what they tell me? They say we must leave. Today.'

As they sat in the train, ready to pull out of the station, surrounded by baskets, Doña Faustina held Jesus Maria up to the window and made his tiny arm wave goodbye to the town. 'The capital is a better place for him in any case,' she whispered.

They went to a small *fonda* in the capital, where the second day Doña Faustina conceived the idea of applying at the nearest *comisaría* for employment as police matron. Her physical build, plus the fact that, as she told the lieutenant, she was afraid of no human being, impressed those who interviewed her, and after various examinations, she was accepted into the force.

'You'll see,' she said to Carlota when she returned that evening in high spirits. 'From now on we have nothing to worry about. Nothing can harm us. We have new names. We are new people. Nothing matters but Jesus Maria.'

At that very moment the inn was swarming with police. The news of the *caimán*, which José in his obstinacy insisted was really there, first to Elena and then to others in the market, had reached them and awakened their curiosity once again. When it was found that there was not one, but a pair of the beasts, in the hidden tank, the police began to look more closely. No one really believed even now that it was Doña Faustina and her sister who were responsible for the disappearance of the dozens of infants who had vanished during the past two or three years, but it was felt that it would do no harm to investigate.

In a dark corner of the laundry, under one of the wash-tubs, they found a bundle of bloodstained rags which on closer inspection proved beyond a doubt to be the garments of an infant. Then they discovered other such rags stuffed in the windows to fill the spaces left by broken panes. 'They must be Jesus Maria's,' said the loyal Elena. 'The señora will be back in a day or so, and she will tell you.' The police leered.

The *jefe* came and looked around the laundry. 'She was

not stupid,' he said admiringly. 'She did the work here, and *they*', he pointed out towards the orchard, 'took care of the rest.'

Little by little all the stories from round about concurred to make one unified mass of evidence; there was no longer much doubt as to Doña Faustina's guilt, but finding her was another matter. For a while the papers were full of the affair. Indignant articles were spread across the pages, and always there was the demand that the readers be on the look-out for the two monstrous women. But it turned out that no picture was available of either of them.

Doña Faustina saw the newspapers, read the articles, and shrugged her shoulders. 'All that happened long ago,' she said. 'It has no importance now. And even if it had, they could not catch me. I have too much power for them.' Soon the papers spoke of other things.

Fifteen years passed quietly. Jesus Maria, who was unusually bright and strong for his age, was offered a position as servant in the home of the Chief of Police. He had seen the boy about with his mother for several years, and liked him. This was a great triumph for Doña Faustina.

'I know you will be a great man,' she told Jesus Maria, 'and will never bring dishonour upon us.'

But eventually he did, and Doña Faustina was inconsolable.

After three years he grew bored with his menial work, and went into the army, carrying with him a recommendation from his employer to a close friend, a certain colonel who saw to it that Jesus Maria was pleasantly treated in the barracks. Everything went well for him; he was constantly promoted, so that by the time he was twenty-five he had become a colonel himself. It may be observed that to be a colonel in the Mexican army is not so great an attainment, nor is it necessarily a sign of exceptional merit. However, there is little doubt that Jesus Maria's military career would have continued its upward course, had he not happened to be in Zacatecas at the time of the raids on the villages thereabout by Fermín Figueroa and his band. As one more privilege in the endless chain of favours granted him by his superiors he was put in charge of the punitive expedition that was sent out in pursuit of Figueroa. Jesus Maria could not have been completely without ability, none the less, since on the third day out he succeeded in taking the leader prisoner along with thirty-six of his men.

No one ever really knew what happened in the small mountain village where the capture took place, save that Figueroa and the bandits had all been tied up in a sheep corral, ready to be shot, and when a few hours later a corporal had arrived with six soldiers to carry out the execution, the corral was empty. And it was even said, after Jesus Maria had been stripped of his rank, that a sheep-herder had seen him enter the corral in the bright afternoon sunlight when everyone else was asleep, loosen the ropes that bound Figueroa, and then hand him his knife, whereupon he turned his back and walked away. Few believed the sheep-herder's story: colonels do not do such things. Still, it was agreed that he had been inexcusably careless, and that it was entirely his fault that the thirty-seven bandits had escaped and thus lived to continue their depredations.

The evening Jesus Maria arrived back at his barracks in the capital, he stood alone in the latrine looking at himself in the fly-specked mirror. Slowly he began to smile, watching the movements of his facial muscles. 'No,' he said, and tried again. He opened his eyes wider and smiled with all his might. The man's face had looked something like that; he would never be able to get it exactly, but he would to on trying because it made him happy to recall that moment – the only time he had ever known how it feels to have power.

Under the Sky

Inland from the sea on the dry coastal plain lay the town, open, spread out under the huge high sky. People who lived outside in the country, and even some of the more educated town-dwellers, called the town 'the Inferno' because nowhere in the region was the heat so intense. No other place around was quite so shadowless and so dusty; it seemed that the clouds above shrank upwards to their farthest possible positions. Many miles above, and to all sides, they hung there in their massive patterns, remote and motionless. In the spring, during the nights, the lightning constantly jumped from one cloud to another, revealing unexpected distances between them. Then, if anyone ever looked at the sky, he was surprised to see how each flash revealed a seemingly more distant portion of the heavens to which still more clouds had receded. But people in the town seldom turned their heads upward. They knew at what time of the year the rains would come, and it was unnecessary to scan those vast regions in order to say what day that would be. When the wind had blown hard for two weeks so that the dust filled the wide empty streets, and the lightning grew brighter each night until finally there was a little thunder, they could be sure the water would soon fall.

Once a year when the lightning was in the sky Jacinto left his village in the mountains and walked down to the town, carrying with him all the things his family had made since his last trip. There were two days of walking in the sierra where it was cool; the third day the road was through the hot lands, and this was the day he preferred, because the road was flat and he could walk faster and leave the

56

others behind. He was taller and prouder than they, and he refused to bend over in order to be able to trot uphill and downhill as they did. In the mountains he laboured to keep up with them, but on the plain he strode powerfully ahead and sometimes arrived at the market before sunset.

Now he stood in the public square with a small paper parcel in his hand. He had arrived the day before. Instead of sitting in the side-street near the fountain and discussing the sales with the others from his village, he walked into the municipal garden and sat down on a concrete bench marked '1936'. He looked up and down the walk. No one paid him any attention. He was barefoot, so the shoeshine boys passed him by.

Tearing open the paper packet he emptied the dried leaves into his left hand. With his right he picked out all the little round, black berries and tossed them away. Then he crushed the leaves and slowly rolled them into five thin cigarettes. This took all his attention for a half-hour.

A voice beside him said: 'That's pretty.'

He looked up. It was a town-dweller; he had never seen him before, so he did not answer.

'All for you?' said the other in the silken town voice that Jacinto had learned to distrust.

'I bought it. I made them,' said Jacinto.

'But I like *grifas* too,' smiled the stranger. He was poorly dressed and had black teeth.

Jacinto covered the cigarettes completely with one big hand which he placed on the seat of the bench. The stranger pointed to a soldier sleeping on another bench near the iron bandstand.

'He wants one and I want one. You should be more careful. It's three months now for possessing marijuana. Don't you know?'

'No,' said Jacinto. 'I don't know.' Then he slowly handed over two of the cigarettes. The man took them.

'So long,' he said.

Jacinto stood up full of fury, and with the other three cigarettes still in his hand, he walked out into the plaza and down the long street that led to the station. It was nearly time for the daily train from the north. Sometimes crazy people got off, who would give a man enough money for two good meals, just for carrying a bundle into the town for them. There was a cemetery behind the roundhouse where some of the railroad employees went to smoke the weed. He remembered it from the preceding year; he had met an inspector there who had taken him to see a girl. She had proved to be ugly – one side of her face was mottled with blue and purple.

At the station the train had already arrived. The people trying to get on were fighting with those who were trying to get off. He wondered why with all those open windows everyone insisted on going through the two little doors at the ends of the cars. It would have been very simple the other way, but these people were too stupid to think of it. His defeat at the hands of the townsman still bothered him; he wanted to have a gun so he could pull it out and shout: 'I am the father of all of you!' But is was not likely that he ever would have a gun.

Without approaching the platform where so many people were moving about, he stood and impassively watched the confusion. From the crowd three strange-looking people suddenly emerged. They all had very white skin and yellow hair. He knew, of course, that they were from a far-away place because everyone knows that when people look as strange as that they are from the capital or even farther. There were two women and one man, and as they approached him, he noticed that they were speaking a language which only they could understand. Each one carried a leather bag covered with small squares of coloured paper stuck on at different angles. He stepped back, keeping his eyes on the face of the younger woman. He could not be sure whether he found her beautiful or revolting. Still he continued to look at her as she passed, holding on to the man's arm. The other woman noticed him, and smiled faintly as she went by.

He turned angrily and walked toward the tracks. He was angry at her stupidity – for thinking he could have enough money to pay her as much as she would surely want. He walked on until he came to the cemetery. It was empty save for the grey lizards that scurried from the path at his feet.

In the farthest corner there was a small square building with a white stone woman on top. He sat in the shade of the little building and took out his cigarettes.

The train whistled; it was starting on its trip to the sea where the people eat nothing but fish and travel on top of the water. He drew in the first few breaths very slowly and deliberately, holding the smoke in his lungs until he felt it burning the edges of his soul. After a few minutes the feeling began to take shape. From the back of his head it moved down to his shoulders. It was as if he were wearing a tight metal garment. At that instant he looked at ·the sky and saw far above him the tiny black dots that were vultures, moving ever so slowly in circles as they surveyed the plain in the afternoon sunlight. Beyond them stood the clouds, deep and monumental. 'Ay!' he sighed, shutting his eyes, and it occurred to him that this was what the dead people, who were lying on all sides of him, looked at day after day. This was all they could see – the clouds, and the vultures, which they did not need to fear, hidden safely as they were, deep in holy ground.

He continued to smoke, going deeper and deeper into delight. Finally he lay back and murmured: 'Now I am dead too.' When he opened his eyes it was still the same day, and the sun was very low in the sky. Some men were talking nearby. He listened; they were trainmen come to smoke, discussing wages and prices of meals. He did not believe any of the figures they so casually mentioned. They were lying to impress one another, and they did not even believe each other. He smoked half of the second cigarette, rose, stretched, and jumped over the cemetery wall, going back to the station by a roundabout path in order not to have to speak to the trainmen. Those people, when they smoked, always wanted more and more company; they would never let a fellow smoker go quietly on his way.

He went to the cantina by the station, and standing in the street, watched the railway employees playing billiards inside. As night approached, the lightning became increasingly visible. He walked up the long street toward the centre of town. Men were playing marimbas in the doorways and in front of the houses – three or four together, and sometimes only one, indolently. The marimbas and the marijuana were the only good things in the town, reflected Jacinto. The women were ugly and dirty, and the men were all thieves and drunkards. He remembered the three people at the station. They would be in the hotel opposite the plaza. He walked a little faster, and his eyes, bloodshot from lack of sleep and too much of the drug, opened a bit wider.

After he had eaten heartily in the market sitting by the edge of the fountain, he felt very well. By the side wall of the cathedral were all the families from the mountains, some already asleep, the others preparing for the night. Almost all the stalls in the market were dark; a few figures still stood in front of the cold fruit-juice stand. Jacinto felt in his pocket for the stub and the whole cigarette, and keeping his fingers around them, walked across to the park. The celestial fireworks were very bright, but there was no thunder. Throughout the town sounded the clink and purr of the marimbas, some near and some far away. A soft breeze stirred the branches of the few lemon trees in the park. He walked along thoughtfully until he came to a bench directly opposite the entrance of the hotel, and there he sat down and brazenly began to smoke his stub. After a few minutes it was easier to believe that one of the two yellow-haired women would come out. He flicked away the butt, leaned back and stared straight at the hotel. The manager had put a square loudspeaker over the entrance door, and out of it came a great crackling and hissing that covered the sound of the marimbas. Occasionally a few loud notes of band music rose above the chaos, and from time to time there seemed to be a man's voice speaking behind the noise. Jacinto was annoyed: the women would want to stay inside where they could hear the sound better.

A long time went by. The radio was silenced. The few voices in the park disappeared down the streets. By the cathedral everyone was asleep. Even the marimbas seemed to have stopped, but when the breeze occasionally grew more active, it brought with it, swelling and dying, long marimba trills from a distant part of the town.

It grew very late. There was no sound but the lemon leaves rubbing together and the jet of water splashing into the basin in the centre of the market. Jacinto was used to waiting. And half-way through the night a woman stepped out of the hotel, stood for a moment looking at the sky, and walked across the street to the park. From his bench in the dark he watched her as she approached. In the lightning he saw that it was not the younger one. He was disappointed. She looked upward again before moving into the shade of the lemon trees, and in a moment she sat down on the next bench and lighted a cigarette. He waited a few minutes. Then he said: 'Señorita.'

The yellow-haired woman cried: 'Oh!' She had not seen him. She jumped up and stood still, peering toward his bench.

He moved to the end of the seat and calmly repeated the word. 'Señorita.'

She walked uncertainly toward him, still peering. He knew this was a ruse. She could see him quite clearly each second or so, whenever the sky lighted up. When she was near enough to the bench, he motioned for her to sit down beside him. As he had suspected, she spoke his tongue.

'What is it?' she asked. The talk in the strange language at the station had only been for show, after all.

'Sit down, señorita.'

'Why?'

'Because I tell you to.'

She laughed and threw away her cigarette.

'That's not a reason,' she said, sitting down at the other end of the bench. 'What are you doing here so late?' She spoke carefully and correctly, like a priest. He answered this by saying: 'And you, what are you looking for?'

'Nothing.'

'Yes. You are looking for something,' he said solemnly.

'I was not sleeping. It is very hot.'

'No. It is not hot,' said Jacinto. He was feeling increasingly sure of himself, and he drew out the last cigarette and began to smoke it. 'What are you doing here in this town?' he asked her after a moment.

'Passing on my way south to the border,' she said, and she told him how she was travelling with two friends, a husband and wife, and how she often took a walk when they had gone to bed.

Jacinto listened as he drew in the smoke and breathed it out. Suddenly he jumped up. Touching her arm, he said: 'Come to the market.'

She arose, asking: 'Why?' and walked with him across the park. When they were in the street, he took her wrist fiercely and pressing it, said between his teeth: 'Look at the sky.'

She looked up wonderingly, a little fearfully. He went on in a low, intense voice: 'As God is my witness, I am going into the hotel to kill the man who came here with you.'

Her eyes grew large. She tried to wrest her arm away, but he would not let it go, and he thrust his face into hers. 'I have a pistol in my pocket and I am going to kill that man.'

'But why?' she whispered weakly, looking up and down the empty street.

'I want his wife.'

The woman said: 'It is not possible. She would scream.'

'I know the proprietor,' said Jacinto, rolling his eyes and grinning. The woman seemed to believe him. Now he felt that a great thing was about to happen.

'And you,' he said, twisting her arm brutally, 'you do not scream.'

'No.'

Again he pointed to the sky.

'God is my witness. You can save the life of your friend. Come with me.'

She was trembling violently, but as they stumbled through the street and he let go of her an instant, she began to run. With one bound he had overtaken her, and he made her stop and look at the sky again as he went through his threats once more. She saw his wide, red-veined eyes in a bright flash of lightning, and his utterly empty face. Mechanically she allowed him to push her along through the streets. He did not let go of her again.

'You are saving your friend's life,' he said. 'God will reward you.'

She was sobbing as she went along. No one passed them

as they moved unsteadily on toward the station. When they
were nearly there they made a great detour past the edge
of town, and finally came to the cemetery.

'This is a holy place,' he murmured, swiftly crossing
himself. 'Here you are going to save your friend's life.'

He took off his shirt, laid it on the stony ground, and
pushed her down. There was nothing but the insistent,
silent flashing in the sky. She kept her eyes shut, but she
shuddered at each flash, even with her lids closed. The wind
blew harder, and the smell of the dust was in her nostrils.

He took her back as far as the park and there he let go
of her. Then he said: 'Good night, señorita,' and walked
away very quickly. He was happy because she had not asked
for any money.

The next year when he came down to the town he waited
at the station four afternoons to see the train come in. The
last afternoon he went to the cemetery and sat near the
small square building that had the stone woman on top of
it. On the ground the dust blew past. The enormous clouds
hung in the sky and the vultures were there high above
him. As he smoked he recalled the yellow-haired woman.
After a time he began to weep, and rolled over on to the
earth, clutching the pebbles as he sobbed. An old woman
of the town, who came every day to her son's grave, passed
near to him. Seeing him, she shook her head and murmured
to herself: 'He has lost his mother.'

The Echo

Aileen pulled out her mirror; the vibration of the plane shook it so rapidly that she was unable to see whether her nose needed powder or not. There were only two other passengers and they were asleep. It was noon; the tropical sun shone violently down upon the wide silver wings and cast sharp reflections on the ceiling. Far below, the uniform green carpet of the jungle moved slowly by. She was sleepy, but she was also excited to be going to a new home. From her handbag she pulled a folded letter which she read again intently, as if to decipher a meaning that did not lie in the sequence of the words. It was in her mother's script:

Aileen, Sweet –

I must begin (and finish) this before supper. Prue has gone out for her shower, and that means that by the time she has Luz (the cook) heat the water and can find José (the gardener) to carry it up on the roof to the tank, it will be about an hour. Add to that the time it takes her to do her actual bathing and to dress, and you can see I'll have just about time for a nice chat.

Perhaps I should begin by saying that Prue and I are sublimely happy here. It is absolute heaven after Washington, as you can pretty well imagine. Prue, of course, never could stand the States, and I felt, after the trouble with your father, that I couldn't face anyone for a while. You know how much importance I have always attached to relaxation. And this is the ideal spot for that.

Of course I did feel a little guilty about running off down here without seeing you. But I think the trip to

Northampton would have sealed my doom. I honestly don't believe I could have stood it. And Prue was nervous about the State Department's passing some new law that would prevent citizens from leaving the US because of the disturbed conditions, and so on. I also felt that the sooner we got down here to Jamonocal the more of a home we could make out of the old place, for you to spend your vacation in. And it *is* going to be beautiful. I won't drag out my reasons for not letting you know beforehand or it will sound apologetic, and I know I never have to apologize to you for anything. So I'll leave that and get on. I'm sure anyway that the eight months passed very quickly up there for you.

We have had swarms of men working on the house ever since last October. Mr Forbes happened to be in Barranquilla for a new American project in the interior, and I wanted to be sure of having him supervise the construction of the cantilever in the foundation. That man is really a prince. They don't come much finer. He was up again and again, and gave orders down to the last detail. I felt guilty about making him work so hard, but I honestly think he enjoyed himself with us girls. In any case it seemed silly, when one of the best architects in the US was right here in Colombia and happened to be an old friend, not to use him when I needed him. Anyway, the old house is now the old wing and the new part, which is so exciting I can't wait for you to see it, is built right out over the gorge. I think there's not likely to be another house like it in the world, if I do say it myself. The terrace makes me think of an old cartoon in the *New Yorker* showing two men looking over the edge of the Grand Canyon, and one is saying to the other: 'Did you ever want to spit a mile, Bill? Now's your chance.'

We are all installed. The weather has been wonderful, and if Luz could only learn a little more about what white people like to eat and how they like it served, the set-up would really be perfect. I know you will enjoy being here with Prue. She and you have many things in common, even if you do claim to 'remember not liking her much'. That was in Washington and you were, to put it mildly, at a difficult age. Now, as an adult (because you really are one by now), you'll be more understanding, I'm sure. She loves books, especially on philosophy and psychology and other things your poor mother just doesn't try to follow her in. She has rigged up a kiln and studio in the old guest house which you probably don't remember. She works at her ceramics out there all day, and I have all I can do keeping the house tidy and seeing that the marketing is done. We have a system by which Luz takes the list to her brother every afternoon, and he brings the things from town the following day. It just about keeps him fully busy getting up and down the mountain on his horse. The horse is a lazy old nag that has done nothing but plod back and forth between house and valley all its life, so it doesn't know the meaning of the word speed. But after all, why hurry, down here?

I think you will find everything to your liking, and I'm sure you won't require more than five minutes to see that Prue is a dear, and not at all 'peculiar', as you wrote in your letter. Wire me as soon as you receive this, and let me know just what week you'll be finishing classes. Prue and I will meet you in Barranquilla. I have a list of things I want you to get me in New York. Will wire it to you as soon as I hear. Prue's bath finished. Must close.

                    Love,
                    Mother

Aileen put the letter away, smiling a little, and watched the wings diving in and out of the small thick clouds that lay in the plane's way. There was a slight shock each time they hit one, and the world outside became a blinding whiteness. She fancied jumping out and walking on such solid softness, like a character in an animated cartoon.

Her mother's letter had put her in mind of a much earlier period in her life: the winter she had been taken to visit Jamonocal. All she could recall in the way of incidents was that she had been placed on a mule by one of the natives, and had felt a painful horror that the animal would walk in

the wrong direction, away from the house toward the edge
of the gorge. She had no memory of the gorge. Probably
she had never seen it, although it was only a few paces
from the house, through a short but thick stretch of
canebrake. However, she had a clear memory of its presence,
of the sensation of enormous void beyond and below that
side of the house. And she recalled the distant, hollow sound
of water falling from a great height, a constant, soft backdrop
of sound that slipped into every moment of the day –
between the conversations at mealtimes, in the intervals of
play in the garden, and at night between dreams. She
wondered if really it were possible to remember all that
from the time when she had been only five.

In Panama there was a plane change to be made. It was
a clear green twilight, and she took a short walk beyond
the airport. Parakeets were fighting in the upper branches
of the trees; suddenly they became quiet. She turned back
and went inside, where she sat reading until it was time to
go aboard.

There was no one there to meet her when she arrived
at Barranquilla in the early hours of the morning. She
decided to go into town and take a room in the hotel. With
her two valises she stepped outside and looked about for a
cab. They had all gone to the town with passengers, but a
man sitting on a packing case informed her that they would
soon be coming back. Then suddenly he said, 'You want
two ladies?'

'What? No. What do you mean?'

'You want two ladies look for you this night?'

'Where are they?' said Aileen, understanding.

'They want a drink,' he answered with an intimate grin.

'Where? Barranquilla?'

'No. Here.' He pointed down the dark road.

'Where? Can I walk?'

'Sure, I go you.'

'No! No thanks. You stay here. Thank you. I can go all
right. Where is it? How far?'

'OK.'

'What is it? A bar? What's the name?'

'They got music. La Gloria. You go. You hear music.

You look for two ladies. They drinking.'

She went inside again and checked the bags with an airline employee who insisted on accompanying her. They strode in silence along the back road. The walls of vegetation on each side sheltered insects that made an occasional violent, dry noise like a wooden ratchet being whirled. Soon there was the sound of drums and trumpets playing Cuban dance music.

'La Gloria,' said her escort triumphantly.

La Gloria was a brilliantly lighted mud hut with a thatch-covered veranda giving on to the road. The juke-box was outside, where a few drunken Negroes sprawled.

'Are they here?' she said out loud, but to herself.

'La Gloria,' he answered, pointing.

As they came opposite the front of the building, she caught a glimpse of a woman in blue jeans, and although instantaneously she knew it was Prue, her mind for some reason failed to accept the fact, and she continued to ask herself, 'Are they here or not?'

She turned to go toward the veranda. The record had finished playing, The ditch lay in the dark between the road and the porch. She fell forward into it and heard herself cry out. The man behind her said, '*Cuidado!*' She lay there panting with fury and pain, and said, 'Oh! My ankle!' There was an exclamation inside the bar. Her mother's voice cried, 'That's Aileen!' Then the juke-box began to scratch and roar again. The Negroes remained stationary. Someone helped her up. She was inside the bar in the raw electric glare.

'I'm all right,' she said, when she had been eased into a chair.

'But darling, where've you been? We've been waiting for you since eight, and we'd just about given up. Poor Prue's ill.'

'Nonsense, I'll recover,' said Prue, still seated at the bar. 'Been having a touch of the trots, that's all.'

'But darling, are you all right? This is absurd, landing here this way.'

She looked down at Aileen's ankle.

'Is it all right?'

Prue came over from the bar to shake her hand.

'A dramatic entrance, gal,' she said.

Aileen sat there and smiled. She had a curious mental habit. As a child she had convinced herself that her head was transparent, that the thoughts there could be perceived immediately by others. Accordingly, when she found herself in uncomfortable situations, rather than risk the danger of being suspected of harbouring uncomplimentary or rebellious thoughts, she had developed a system of refraining from thinking at all. For a while during her childhood this fear of having no mental privacy had been extended to anyone; even persons existing at a distance could have access to her mind. Now she felt open only to those present. And so it was that, finding herself face to face with Prue, she was conscious of no particular emotion save the familiar vague sense of boredom. There was not a thought in her head, and her face made the fact apparent.

Mornings were hard to believe. The primeval freshness, spilled down out of the forest about the house, was held close to the earth by the mist. Outside and in, it was damp and smelled like a florist's shop, but the dampness was dispelled each day when the stinging sun burned through the thin cape of moisture that clung to the mountain's back. Living there was like living sideways, with the land stretching up on one side and down on the other at the same angle. Only the gorge gave a feeling of perpendicularity; the vertical walls of rock on the opposite side of the great amphitheatre were a reminder that the centre of gravity lay below and not obliquely to one side. Constant vapour rose from the invisible pool at the bottom, and the distant, indeterminate calling of water was like the sound of sleep itself.

For a few days Aileen lay in bed listening to the water and the birds, and to the nearby, unfamiliar, domestic sounds. Her mother and Prue both had breakfast in bed, generally appeared just before the midday meal for a few minutes of conversation until Concha brought the invalid's lunch tray. In the afternoons she thumbed through old magazines and read murder mysteries. Usually it began to rain about three; the sound at first would be like an augmentation of the waterfall in the distance, and then as its violence increased it came unmistakably nearer – a great roar all around the house that covered every other sound. The black clouds would close in tightly around the mountain, so that it seemed that night would soon arrive. She would ring a small bell for Concha to come and light the oil lamp on the table by the bed. Lying there looking at the wet banana leaves outside the window, with the rain's din everywhere, she felt completely comfortable for the precarious moment. There was no necessity to question the feeling, no need to think – only the subsiding of the rain, the triumphant emergence of the sun into the steaming twilight and an early dinner to look forward to. Each evening after dinner her mother came for a lengthy chat, usually about the servants. The first three nights Prue had come too, carrying a highball, but after that her mother came alone.

Aileen had asked to be put into the old part of the house, rather than into a more comfortable room in the new wing. Her window looked on to the garden, which was a small square of lawn with young banana plants on either side. At the far end was a fountain; behind it was the disordered terrain of the mountainside with its recently cut underbush and charred stumps, and still farther beyond was the high forest whose frontier had been sliced in a straight line across the slopes many years ago to make the plantation. Here in her room she felt at least that the earth was somewhere beneath her.

When her ankle ceased to pain her, she began going downstairs for lunch, which was served out on the terrace at a table with a beach umbrella stuck in its centre. Prue was regularly late in coming from her studio, and she arrived in her blue jeans, which were caked with clay, with smears of dirt across her face. Because Aileen could not bring herself to think what she really felt, which was that Prue was ungracious, ugly and something of an interloper, she remained emotionally unconscious of Prue's presence, which is to say that she was polite but bored, scarcely present in the mealtime conversations. Then, too, Aileen was definitely uncomfortable on the terrace. The emptiness was too near and the balustrade seemed altogether too low for safety. She liked the meals to be as brief as possible, with no unnecessary time spent sipping coffee afterward, but it never would have occurred to her to divulge her reasons. With Prue around she felt constrained to behave with the utmost decorum. Fortunately her ankle provided her with a convenient excuse to get back upstairs to her room.

She soon discovered a tiny patio next to the kitchen where heavy vines with sweet-smelling flowers grew up an arbour that had been placed at one side. The air was full of the humming of hundreds of bees that clung heavily to the petals and moved slowly about in the air. After lunch she would pull a deck-chair into the arbour's shade and read until the rain began. It was a stifling, airless spot, but the sound of the bees covered that of the waterfall. One afternoon Prue followed her there and stood with her hands in her hip pockets looking at her.

'How can you take this heat?' she asked Aileen.

'Oh, I love it.'

'You do?' She paused. 'Tell me, do you really like it here, or do you think it's a bloody bore?'

'Why, I think it's absolutely wonderful.'

'Mm. It is.'

'Don't you like it?'

Prue yawned. 'Oh, I'm all for it. But I keep busy. Wherever I can work, I get on, you know.'

'Yes, I suppose so,' said Aileen. Then she added, 'Are you planning on staying long?'

'What the hell do you mean?' said Prue, leaning backward against the house, her hands still behind her. 'I live here.'

Aileen laughed shortly. To anyone but Prue it would have sounded like a merry, tinkling laugh, but Prue narrowed her eyes and thrust her jaw forward a bit.

'What's so funny?' she demanded.

'I think you're funny. You're so tied up in knots. You get upset so easily. Perhaps you work too hard out there in your little house.'

Prue was looking at her with astonishment.

'God Almighty,' she said finally, 'your IQ's showing, gal.'

'Thank you,' said Aileen with great seriousness. 'Anyway, I think it's fine that you're happy here, and I hope you go on being happy.'

'That's what I came to say to you.'

'Then everything's fine.'

'I can't make you out,' said Prue, frowning.

'I don't know what you're talking about,' replied Aileen, fingering the pages of her book impatiently. 'It's the most pointless conversation I've ever had.'

'That I *don't* think,' Prue said, going into the kitchen.

The same evening, when her mother came for her usual after-dinner chat, she looked a little unhappy.

'You don't seem to be getting on very well with Prue,' she said reproachfully, as she sat down at the foot of the bed.

'Why, we get on perfectly well. Oh. You're talking about this afternoon, probably.'

'Yes, I am, probably. Really, Aileen. You simply can't be rude to a woman her age. She's my guest, and you're my guest, and you've got to be civil to each other. But she's always civil and I have a feeling you're not.'

Aileen caught her breath and said, 'I'm your guest . . .'

'I invited you here for your vacation and I want things pleasant, and I don't see the slightest reason why they shouldn't be.'

Suddenly Aileen cried, 'She's a maniac!'

Her mother rose and quickly left the room.

In the quiet days that followed, the incident was not mentioned by any of them. Aileen continued to haunt the little patio after lunch.

There came a morning sweeter than the rest, when the untouched early mist hung inside her bedroom, and the confusion of shrill bird cries came down with perfect clarity from the uncut forest. She dressed quickly and went out. There was a white radiance in the air that she had never seen before. She walked along the path that led by the native huts. There was life stirring within; babies were crying and captive parrots and songbirds laughed and sang. The path swung into a stretch of low trees that had been planted to shield the coffee bushes. It was still almost nocturnal in here; the air was streaked with chill, and the vegetable odours were like invisible festoons drooping from the branches as she walked through. A huge bright spider walked slowly across the path at her feet. She stood still and watched it until it had disappeared in the leaves at one side. She put her hand over her heart to feel how insistently it was beating. And she listened to its sound in her head for a moment, not wanting to break into its rhythm by starting to walk again. Then she began to walk ahead fast, following the path upward toward the lightest part of the sky. When it came out suddenly on to an eminence directly above the plantation, she could barely discern the cluster of roofs through the mist. But here the sound of the waterfall was stronger; she supposed she was near the gorge, although there was no sign of it. The path turned here and went along rough open ground upward. She climbed at a steady gait, breathing slowly and deeply, for perhaps half an hour, and was surprised to find that the jungle had been cut away on all sides in this portion of the mountainside. For a time she thought the sky was growing brighter, and that the sun was about to break through, but as the path levelled out and she was able to see for some distance ahead, she saw that the mist was even thicker up here than down below.

At certain points there was a steep declivity on each side of the path. It was impossible to see how deeply the land fell away. There were a few nearby plants and rocks, the highest fronds of a tree-fern a little beyond, and white emptiness after that. It was like going along the top of a wall high in the air. Then the path would make a wide turn and go sharply upward and she would see a solitary tree above her at one side.

Suddenly she came up against a row of huts. They were less well made than those down at the plantation, and smaller. The mist was full of woodsmoke; there was the smell of pigs. She stood still. A man was singing. Two small naked children came out of the door of one hut, looked at her a moment in terror, and ran quickly back inside. She walked ahead. The singing came from behind the last hut. When she came opposite the hut, she saw that it was enclosed by a tangled but effective fence of barbed wire which left a runway about six feet wide all the way around. A young man appeared from the farther side of the closed-in space. His shirt and pants were tattered; the brown skin showed in many places. He was singing as he walked toward her, and he continued to sing, looking straight into her face with bright, questioning eyes. She smiled and said, '*Buenos días.*' He made a beckoning gesture, rather too dramatically. She stopped walking and stood still, looking hesitantly back at the other huts. The young man beckoned again and then stepped inside the hut. A moment later he came out, and still staring fascinatedly at her, made more summoning motions. Aileen stood perfectly quiet, not taking her eyes from his face. He walked slowly over to the fence and grasped the wire with both hands, his eyes growing wider as he pressed the barbs into his palms. Then he leaned across, thrusting his head toward her, his eyes fixing hers with incredible intensity. For several seconds they watched each other; then she stepped a little nearer, peering into his face and frowning. At that point with a cry he emptied his mouth of the water he had been holding in it, aiming with force at Aileen's face. Some of it struck her cheek, and the rest the front of her dress. His fingers unclenched themselves from around the wire, and straightening himself, he backed slowly into the hut, watching her face closely all the while.

She stood still an instant, her hand to her cheek. Then she bent down, and picking up a large stone from the path she flung it with all her strength through the door. A terrible cry came from within; it was like nothing she had ever heard. Or yes, she thought as she began to run back past the other huts, it had the indignation and outraged innocence of a small baby, but it was also a grown man's cry. No one appeared as she passed the huts. Soon she was back in the silence of the empty mountainside, but she kept running, and she was astonished to find that she was sobbing as well. She sat down on a rock and calmed herself by watching some ants demolish a bush as they cut away squares of leaf and carried them away in their mouths. The sky was growing brighter now; the sun would soon be through. She went on. By the time she got back to the high spot above the plantation the mist had turned into long clouds that were rolling away down the mountainside into the ravines. She was horrified to see how near she stood to the ugly black edge of the gorge. And the house looked insane down there, leaning out over as if it were trying to see the bottom. Far below the house the vapour rose up from the pool. She followed the sheer sides of the opposite cliff upward with her eye, all the way to the top, a little above the spot where she stood. It made her feel ill, and she stumbled back down to the house with her hand to her forehead, paying no attention to the natives who greeted her from their doorways.

As she ran past the garden a voice called to her. She turned and saw Prue washing her hands in the fountain's basin. She stood still.

You're up early. You must feel better,' said Prue, drying her hands on her hair. 'Your mother's been having a fit. Go in and see her.'

Aileen stared at Prue a moment before she said, 'I was going in. You don't have to tell me.'

'Oh, I thought I did.'

'You don't have to tell me anything. I think I can manage all right without your help.'

'Help isn't exactly what I'd like to give you,' said Prue, putting her hands into her pockets. 'A swift kick in the teeth would be more like it. How do you think I like to see your mother worrying about you? First you're sick in bed, then you just disappear into the goddamn jungle. D'you think I like to have to keep talking about you, reassuring her every ten minutes? What the hell d'you think life is, one long coming-out party?'

Aileen stared harder, now with unmasked hatred. 'I think', she said slowly, 'that life is pretty awful. Here especially. And I think you should look once in the mirror and then jump off the terrace. And I think Mother should have her mind examined.'

'I see,' said Prue, with dire inflexion. She lit a cigarette and strode off to her studio. Aileen went into the house and up to her room.

Less than an hour later, her mother knocked at her door.
As she came into the room, Aileen could see she had been
crying only a moment before.

'Aileen darling, I've got something to say to you,' she
began apologetically, 'and it breaks my heart to say it. But
I've got to.'

She stopped, as though waiting for encouragement.

'Mother, what is it?'

'I think you probably know.'

'About Prue, I suppose. No?'

'It certainly is. I don't know how I can ever make it right
with her. She told me what you said to her, and I must say
I found it hard to believe. How could you?'

'You mean just now in the garden?'

'I don't know where you said it, but I do know this can't
go on. So I'm just forced to say this. . . . You'll have to
go. I can't be stirred up this way, and I can tell just how
it'll be if you stay on.'

'I'm not surprised at all,' said Aileen, making a show of
calm. 'When do you want me to leave?'

'This is terribly painful . . .'

'Oh, stop! It's all right. I've had a vacation and I can get
a lot of work done before the term starts. Today?
Tomorrow?'

'I think the first of the week. I'll go to Barranquilla with
you.'

'Would you think I was silly if I had all my meals up
here?'

'I think it's a perfect idea, darling, and we can have nice
visits together, you and I, between meals.'

Now, when the tension should have been over, somehow
it was not. During the four nights before she was to leave,
Aileen had endless excruciating dreams. She would wake
up in the darkness too agonized even to move her hand. It
was not fear; she could not recall the dreams. It was rather
as if some newly discovered, innermost part of her being
were in acute pain. Breathing quickly, she would lie
transfixed for long periods listening to the eternal sound of
the waterfall, punctuated at great intervals by some slight,
nearby nocturnal noise in the trees. Finally, when she had

summoned sufficient energy to move, she would change her position in the bed, sigh profoundly, and relax enough to fall back into the ominous world of sleep.

When the final day came, there was a light tapping on her door just after dawn. She got up and unbolted it. Her mother was there, smiling thinly.

'May I come in?'

'Oh. Good morning. Of course. It's early, isn't it?'

Her mother walked across to the window and stood looking down at the misty garden.

'I'm not so well today,' she said. 'I'm afraid I can't take you to Barranquilla. I'm not up to getting on to a horse today. It's just too much, that three-hour trip to Jamonocal, and then the train and the boat all night. You'll just have to forgive me. I couldn't stand all three. But it won't matter, will it?' she went on, looking up at last. 'We'll say goodbye here.'

'But Mother, how can I go alone?'

'Oh, José'll go all the way to Barranquilla with you and be back by Wednesday night. You don't think I'd let you go off by yourself?'

She began to laugh intensely, then stopped suddenly and looked pensive.

'I rather hate to be here two nights without him, but I don't see any other way to get you down there by tomorrow. You can go shipside to Panama. There's usually a seat somewhere. Now, breakfast, breakfast. . . .'

Patting Aileen's cheek, she hurried out and downstairs to the kitchen.

The birds' morning song was coming down from the forest; the mist lay ragged in the tops of the great trees up there. Aileen shifted her gaze to the garden at her feet. Suddenly she felt she could not leave; in a sense it was as if she were leaving love behind. She sat down on the bed. 'But what is it?' she asked herself desperately. 'Not Mother. Not the house. Not the jungle.' Automatically she dressed and packed the remaining toilet articles in her overnight case. But the feeling was there, imperious and enveloping in its completeness.

She went downstairs. There was the sound of voices and the clatter of china in the kitchen. Concha and Luz were preparing her breakfast tray. She went out and watched them until everything was ready.

'*Ya se va la señorita?*' said Concha sadly.

She did not answer, but took the tray from her and carried it through the house, out on to the terrace, where she set it on the table. Everything on the terrace was wet with dew and moisture from the gorge. She turned the chair-cushion over and sat down to eat. The sound of the waterfall took her appetite away, but she thought, This is the last time. She felt choked with emotions, but they were too disparate and confused for her to be able to identify any one of them as outstanding. As she sat there eating intently, she was suddenly aware that someone was watching her. She started up and saw Prue standing in the doorway. She was wearing pyjamas and a bathrobe, and in her hand she held a glass of water. She looked very sleepy.

'How are you?' she said, sipping her water.

Aileen stood up.

'We're all up bright and early this morning,' Prue went on cheerily.

'I'm . . . leaving. I've got to go. Excuse me, it's late,' mumbled Aileen, glancing about furtively.

'Oh, take your time, gal. You haven't said goodbye to your mother yet. And José is still saddling the nags. You've got a lot of grips with you.'

'Excuse me,' said Aileen, trying to slip past through the doorway.

'Well, shake,' Prue said, reaching for Aileen's hand.

'Get away!' cried Aileen, struggling to keep clear of her. 'Don't touch me!' But Prue had succeeded in grasping one frantic arm. She held it fast.

'A dramatic entrance is enough. We don't have to have the same sort of exit. Say goodbye to me like a human being.' She twisted the arm a bit, in spite of herself. Aileen leaned against the door and turned very white.

'Feel faint?' said Prue. She let go of her arm, and holding up her glass of water, flicked some of it into Aileen's face with her fingers.

The reaction was instantaneous. Aileen jumped at her with vicious suddenness, kicking, ripping and pounding all at once. The glass fell to the stone floor; Prue was caught off her guard. Mechanically, with rapid, birdlike fury, the girl hammered at the woman's face and head, as she slowly impelled her away from the doorway and across the terrace.

From Prue's lips came several times the word 'God'. At first she did very little to defend herself; she seemed half asleep as she moved toward the outer edge beneath the onslaught. Then suddenly she threw herself to the floor. Aileen continued to kick her where she lay doubled over, trying to protect her face.

'Nobody! Nobody! Nobody! Nobody can do that to me!' she cried rhythmically as she kicked.

Her voice rose in pitch and volume; she stopped for an instant, and then, raising her head, she uttered the greatest scream of her life. It came back immediately from the black wall of rock across the gorge, straight through the noise of water. The sound of her own voice ended the episode for her, and she began to walk back across the terrace.

Concha and Luz stood frightened in the doorway; it was as if they had come to watch a terrible storm pass over the countryside. They stepped aside as Aileen walked through.

Outside the stable, José was whistling as he finished saddling the horses. The valises were already strapped on the burro.

Still in the midst of her deep dream, Aileen turned her head toward the house as they rode past. For a brief second, between the leaves, she saw two figures of her mother and Prue standing side by side on the terrace, the wall of the gorge looming behind. Then the horses turned and began to descend the trail.

An Inopportune Visit

After several hundred years of travelling in space Santa Rosenda conceived a desire to return to earth. Recently she had been homesick for her native land, and she had an unreasoning belief that feeling the Spanish earth beneath her feet once more would make her happy. She did not announce her arrival. If she were recognized, the attention she would attract would make the peace she sought an impossibility.

Yet for Santa Rosenda to feel entirely in touch with the earth, it was necessary for her to materialize; only then could she be persuaded of the reality of what was around her. This of course made her visible – a drawback, partially because of her anachronistic clothing, and even more because the slight aura around her head bore the unmistakable form of a halo.

Her arrival was sudden: she simply appeared one afternoon from behind a clump of bushes in the public garden of a provincial Spanish city. A woman who taught chemistry at the nearby college was sitting on a bench. When she saw Santa Rosenda she sprang up in a panic and ran off. This did not augur well for a restful time on earth, and Santa Rosenda realized then that she must avoid cities.

Accordingly she made a landing in a field outside a small village on the island of Menorca. She had chosen to come down in the field because the contours of the landscape pleased her, and she believed it to be deserted. But a village girl was crouched there gathering greens, and the sudden arrival of Santa Rosenda made her spring up in amazement. At this, Santa Rosenda quickly dematerialized, but it was too late. The girl rushed back to the village crying that she had witnessed a miracle. Her story was given complete credence. Several hundred people hurried to the field hoping for a glimpse of the saintly presence. Hovering above, Santa Rosenda observed them with distaste, and determined to transfer herself to the mainland. The problem was to find a pleasant spot where she could stay without fear of being seen.

Considering the various difficulties with which she had to contend, it is surprising that she did not renounce her project and return to space. She had no means of communicating with people, even if she had desired to do so, since she was without a voice. She could neither read nor write, for in her time literacy had not been considered necessary, even for saints.

These were not ideal conditions under which to return to her homeland, but she had no choice in the matter. If she wanted to be on earth she must accept them. Such minor disadvantages, however, were more than outweighed by her having no need either to eat or to sleep, and above all by her ability to dematerialize at any moment if necessary, much as she disliked the sensation. In any case, she had not returned in order to converse with people; on the contrary, she hoped to avoid all contact with them.

Thus when she found an inviting cave in the side of a hill, she established herself not far from its entrance where she could gaze out at the sunlit landscape, and then close her eyes and meditate upon the differences which had come about since she had last left the earth. She knew that stasis did not exist on the planet, that everything was in a state of constant flux, thus she was not astonished by the extraordinary changes which she could sense had come about during her absence. Her clothing preoccupied her principally, for she realized that more than anything else it was the garments she wore which called attention to the disparity between her appearance and that of other women. She would not find the peace she sought until somehow she had managed to make herself indistinguishable from them. With this in mind, she wrapped her head in a rag she had found there in the cave. At least, she thought, the halo would not show.

One afternoon when she opened her eyes for a moment, she discovered two small boys playing not far from the entrance to the cave. They had seen her, she realized, but they appeared to take no particular notice of her. Reassured, she shut her eyes again. The next time she opened them, the boys were gone. They came nearly every day, always remaining at some distance from the cave.

What she did not know was that the boys had told their parents about the strange woman who was always seated there in the same spot, day after day. Since there was a military barracks with an airstrip on the other side of the hill, the public had been requested to report any suspicious-looking individuals in the vicinity.

The boys' father spoke to a civil guard about the continued presence of a woman in the cave, with the result that Santa Rosenda was visited by a group of soldiers, who obliged her to accompany them to a jeep waiting in the road on the other side of the woods. They plied her with questions which she heard and partially understood, but could not answer. Impelled largely by curiosity, she decided to acquiesce and go along with them; perhaps she could discover what they wanted of her. Besides, it seemed to her that there would be something highly indelicate about effecting a transformation and disappearing in front of them. She preferred to do that in private.

She was taken first to a police station, where she understood nothing of what was going on around her. From there they took her to a hospital, explaining to the nurse at the entrance that their charge was a deaf-mute. Another nurse led her to a small room and left her there by herself, locking the door. The doctor who was to examine her had caught a glimpse of her as she was brought into the building, and because of the outlandish clothing and the rag wrapped around her head, immediately suspected her of being a man in disguise. Hearing from the nurse that she could not speak merely strengthened his suspicion.

'*Vamos a ver*,' he said to himself as he opened the door of the room where she had been left. A moment earlier, Santa Rosenda, incensed at being shut into so tiny a room and wearied by the entire senseless procedure, had dematerialized. The room was empty. The doctor, in a fury, called the nurse and told her that her carelessness had allowed what was probably a dangerous criminal to escape. The nurse replied that the door had been locked, and that in any case, her opinion was that the woman was mentally deficient, nothing more. Nevertheless, the police were alerted and a search was inaugurated, beginning inside the hospital.

As the nurses and interns went through the building, looking in all the rooms, Santa Rosenda watched them, thinking that they were behaving like idiots. She could not imagine what they wanted of her, but she mistrusted their intentions. As she floated around the building, observing the turmoil she had caused, she came upon a cloakroom where the nurses left their street clothes before donning their uniforms. This was the stroke of good luck she had been hoping for. Dresses, sweaters and coats hung on hooks along the wall, and many of the lockers were open, disclosing more garments for her examination. It took her only about ten minutes to choose the pieces of clothing she wanted. There were shoes in which her feet were comfortable, and she discovered a large Italian silk kerchief to wind around her head in place of the rag. Now, it seemed to her, she could move through any street without attracting attention. To test her anonymity she walked out of the main entrance gate of the hospital, and passed unnoticed.

The city resembled no city she had ever seen. Its streets were thronged with people, and although they did not appear to be in a festive mood, she assumed they were celebrating a holiday of some sort. The automobiles (which she thought of as wagons) all emitted an unpleasant smoke as they passed. A few minutes of contact with the crowd to persuade her that she was truly anonymous, and then she would leave for a quiet spot in the country, and would not set foot again in a city.

All at once, mixed with the smells of the street, she recognized the faint odour of resin burning in a censer. To her left a doorway opened into a church. Santa Rosenda turned and entered.

Immediately she knew that everything was wrong. The illumination within was almost like sunlight, and it did not come from candles. The music was not what it should have been. She listened until the priest began to speak. She could not understand the words. Suddenly she realized with horror that he was speaking, not in Latin, but in the language of the street.

Without a thought in her head save that of reaching the man and stemming the flow of sacrilege, Santa Rosenda began to run toward the altar. The few who noticed her did not try to stop her. Even when she was in front of the priest and he was staring into her face, he continued mechanically to intone the hateful words.

With both hands she pushed him in the chest, and for an instant they grappled, as peopled hurried in their direction. In the momentary struggle the silk kerchief was pulled from Santa Rosenda's head, and before the eyes of everyone the circle of light shone above her hair. She did not wait to see the reaction of the priest or the congregation, but resumed her normal state of invisibility. The degradation of the mass was one metamorphosis she was not prepared to accept, and she no longer had any desire to be on earth. In a few more centuries she might return; she hoped that by then matters would have been set straight.

Tea on the Mountain

The mail that morning had brought her a large advance from her publishers. At least, it looked large to her there in the International Zone where life was cheap. She had opened the letter at a table of the sidewalk café opposite the Spanish post office. The emotion she felt at seeing the figures on the cheque had made her unexpectedly generous to the beggars that constantly filed past. Then the excitement had worn off, and she felt momentarily depressed. The streets and the sky seemed brighter and stronger than she. She had of necessity made very few friends in the town, and although she worked steadily every day at her novel, she had to admit that sometimes she was lonely. Driss came by, wearing a spotless mauve *djellaba* over his shoulders and a new fez on his head.

'*Bonjour, mademoiselle*,' he said, making an exaggerated bow. He had been paying her assiduous attention for several months, but so far she had been successful in putting him off without losing his friendship; he made a good escort in the evenings. This morning she greeted him warmly, let him pay her check, and moved off up the street with him, conscious of the comment her action had caused among the other Arabs sitting in the café.

They turned into the rue du Télégraphe Anglais, and walked slowly down the hill. She decided she was trying to work up an appetite for lunch; in the noonday heat it was often difficult to be hungry. Driss had been Europeanized to the point of insisting on aperitifs before his meals; however, instead of having two Dubonnets, for instance, he would take a Gentiane, a Byrrh, a Pernod and an Amer

85

Picon. Then he usually went to sleep and put off eating until later. They stopped at the café facing the Marshan Road, and sat down next to a table occupied by several students from the Lycée Français, who were drinking *limonades* and glancing over their notebooks. Driss wheeled around suddenly and began a casual conversation. Soon they both moved over to the students' table.

She was presented to each student in turn; they solemnly acknowledged her '*Enchantée*', but remained seated while doing so. Only one, named Mjid, rose from his chair and quickly sat down again, looking worried. He was the one she immediately wanted to get to know, perhaps because he was more serious and soft-eyed, yet at the same time seemed more eager and violent than any of the others. He spoke his stilted theatre-French swiftly, with less accent than his schoolmates, and he punctuated his sentences with precise, tender smiles instead of the correct or expected inflections. Beside him sat Ghazi, plump and Negroid.

She saw right away that Mjid and Ghazi were close friends. They replied to her questions and flattery as one man, Ghazi preferring, however, to leave the important phrases to Mjid. He had an impediment in his speech, and he appeared to think more slowly. Within a few minutes she had learned that they had been going to school together for twelve years, and had always been in the same form. This seemed strange to her, inasmuch as Ghazi's lack of precocity became more and more noticeable as she watched him. Mjid noticed the surprise in her face, and he added:

'Ghazi is very intelligent, you know. His father is the high judge of the native court of the International Zone. You will go to his home one day and see for yourself.'

'Oh, but of course I believe you,' she cried, understanding now why Ghazi had experienced no difficulty in life so far, in spite of his obvious slow-wittedness.

'I have a very beautiful house indeed,' added Ghazi. 'Would you like to come and live in it? You are always welcome. That's the way we Tanjaoui are.'

'Thank you. Perhaps some day I shall. At any rate, I thank you a thousand times. You are too kind.'

'And my father,' interposed Mjid suavely but firmly, 'the

poor man, he is dead. Now it's my brother who commands.'

'But, alas, Mjid, your brother is tubercular,' sighed Ghazi.

Mjid was scandalized. He began a vehement conversation with Ghazi in Arabic, in the course of which he upset his empty *limonade* bottle. It rolled on to the sidewalk and into the gutter, where an urchin tried to make off with it, but was stopped by the waiter. He brought the bottle to the table, carefully wiped it with his apron, and set it down.

'Dirty Jew dog!' screamed the little boy from the middle of the street.

Mjid heard this epithet even in the middle of his tirade. Turning in his chair, he called to the child: 'Go home. You'll be beaten this evening.'

'Is it your brother?' she asked with interest.

Since Mjid did not answer her, but seemed not even to have heard her, she looked at the urchin again and saw his ragged clothing. She was apologetic.

'Oh, I'm sorry,' she began. 'I hadn't looked at him. I see now . . .'

Mjid said, without looking at her: 'You would not need to look at that child to know he was not of my family. You heard him speak . . .'

'A neighbour's child. A poor little thing,' interrupted Ghazi.

Mjid seemed lost in wonder for a moment. Then he turned and explained slowly to her: 'One word we can't hear is tuberculosis. Any other word, syphilis, leprosy, even pneumonia, we can listen to, but not that word. And Ghazi knows that. He wants you to think we have Paris morals here. There I know everyone says that word everywhere on the boulevards, in the cafés, in Montparnasse, in the Dôme . . .' he grew excited as he listed these points of interest – 'in the Moulin Rouge, in Sacré Coeur, in the Louvre. Some day I shall go myself. My brother has been. That's where he got sick.'

During this time Driss, whose feeling of ownership of the American lady was so complete that he was not worried by any conversation she might have with what he considered schoolboys, was talking haughtily to the other students. They were all pimply and bespectacled. He was telling them about the football games he had seen in Málaga. They had never been across to Spain, and they listened, gravely sipped their *limonade*, and spat on the floor like Spaniards.

'Since I can't invite you to my home, because we have sickness there, I want you to make a picnic with me tomorrow,' announced Mjid. Ghazi made some inaudible objection which his friend silenced with a glance, whereupon Ghazi decided to beam, and followed the plans with interest.

'We shall hire a carriage, and take some ham to my country villa,' continued Mjid, his eyes shining with excitement. Ghazi started to look about apprehensively at the other men seated on the terrace; then he got up and went inside.

When he returned he objected: 'You have no sense, Mjid. You say "ham" right out loud when you know some friends of my father might be here. It would be very bad for me. Not everyone is free as you are.'

Mjid was penitent for an instant. He stretched out his leg, pulling aside his silk *gandoura*. 'Do you like my garters?' he asked her suddenly.

She was startled. 'They're quite good ones,' she began.

'Let me see yours,' he demanded.

She glanced down at her slacks. She had espadrilles on her feet, and wore no socks. 'I'm sorry,' she said. 'I haven't any.'

Mjid looked uncomfortable, and she guessed that it was more for having discovered, in front of the others, a flaw in her apparel, than for having caused her possible embarrassment. He cast a contrite glance at Ghazi, as if to excuse himself for having encouraged a foreign lady who was obviously not of the right sort. She felt that some gesture on her part was called for. Pulling out several hundred francs, which was all the money in her purse, she laid it on the table, and went on searching in her handbag for her mirror. Mjid's eyes softened. He turned with a certain triumph to Ghazi, and permitting himself a slight display of exaltation, patted his friend's cheek three times.

'So it's set!' he exclaimed. 'Tomorrow at noon we meet here at the Café du Télégraphe Anglais. I shall have hired a carriage at eleven-thirty at the market. You, dear mademoiselle,' turning to her, 'will have gone at ten-thirty to the English grocery and bought the food. Be sure to get Jambon Olida, because it's the best.'

'The best ham,' murmured Ghazi, looking up and down the street a bit uneasily.

'And buy one bottle of wine.'

'Mjid, you know this can get back to my father,' Ghazi began.

Mjid had had enough interference. He turned to her. 'If you like, mademoiselle, we can go alone.'

She glanced at Ghazi; his cowlike eyes had veiled with actual tears.

Mjid continued. 'It'll be very beautiful up there on the mountain with just us two. We'll take a walk along the top of the mountain to the rose gardens. There's a breeze from the sea all afternoon. At dusk we'll be back at the farm. We'll have tea and rest.' He stopped at this point, which he considered crucial.

Ghazi was pretending to read his social correspondence textbook, with his *chechia* tilted over his eyebrows so as to hide his hopelessly troubled face. Mjid smiled tenderly.

'We'll go all three,' he said softly.

Ghazi simply said: 'Mjid is bad.'

Driss was now roaring drunk. The other students were impressed and awed. Some of the bearded men in the café looked over at the table with open disapproval in their faces. She saw that they regarded her as a symbol of corruption. Consulting her fancy little enamel watch, which everyone at the table had to examine and study closely before she could put it back into its case, she announced that she was hungry.

'Will you eat with us?' Ghazi inquired anxiously. It was clear he had read that an invitation should be extended on such occasions; it was equally clear that he was in terror lest she accept.

She declined and rose. The glare of the street and the commotion of the passers-by had tired her. She took her leave of all the students while Driss was inside the café, and went down to the restaurant on the beach where she generally had lunch.

There while she ate, looking out at the water, she thought: That was amusing, but it was just enough, and she decided not to go on the picnic.

She did not even wait until the next day to stock up with provisions at the English grocery. She bought three bottles of ordinary red wine, two cans of Jambon Olida, several kinds of Huntley and Palmer's biscuits, a bottle of stuffed olives and five hundred grams of chocolates full of liqueurs. The English lady made a splendid parcel for her.

At noon next day she was drinking an *orgeat* at the Café du Télégraphe Anglais. A carriage drove up, drawn by two horses loaded down with sleighbells. Behind the driver, shielded from the sun by the beige canopy of the victoria, sat Ghazi and Mjid, looking serious and pleasant. They got down to help her in. As they drove off up the hill, Mjid inspected the parcel approvingly and whispered: 'The wine?'

'All inside,' she said.

The locusts made a great noise from the dusty cliffs, beside the road as they came to the edge of town. 'Our nightingales,' smiled Mjid. 'Here is a ring for you. Let me see your hand.'

She was startled, held out her left hand.

'No, no! The right!' he cried. The ring was of massive silver; it fitted her index finger. She was immensely pleased. 'But you are too nice. What can I give you?' She tried to look pained and helpless.

'The pleasure of having a true European friend,' said Mjid gravely.

'But I'm American,' she objected.

'All the better.'

Ghazi was looking silently towards the distant Riffian mountains. Prophetically he raised his arm with its silk sleeve blowing in the hot wind, and pointed across the cracked mud fields.

'Down that way,' he said softly, 'there is a village where all the people are mad. I rode there once with one of my father's assistants. It's the water they drink.'

The carriage lurched. They were climbing. Below them the sea began to spread out, a poster blue. The tops of the mountains across the water in Spain rose above the haze.

Mjid started to sing. Ghazi covered his ears with his fat dimpled hands.

The summer villa was inhabited by a family with a large number of children. After dismissing the carriage driver and instructing him not to return, since he wanted to walk back down, Mjid took his guests on a tour of inspection of the grounds. There were a good many wells; Ghazi had certainly seen these countless times before, but he stopped as if in amazement at each well as they inspected it, and whispered: 'Think of it!'

On the rocky elevation above the farm stood a great olive tree. There they spread the food, and ate slowly. The Berber woman in charge of the farm had given them several loaves of native bread, and olives and oranges. Ghazi wanted Mjid to decline this food.

'A real European picnic is what we should have.'

But she insisted they take the oranges.

The opening of the ham was observed in religious silence. It was no time before both cans were consumed. Then they attacked the wine.

'If my father could see us,' said Ghazi, draining a tin cup of it. 'Ham and wine!'

Mjid drank a cup, making a grimace of distaste. He lay back, his arms folded behind his head. 'Now that I've finished, I can tell you that I don't like wine, and everyone knows that ham is filthy. But I hate our severe conventions.'

She suspected that he had rehearsed the little speech.

Ghazi was continuing to drink the wine. He finished a bottle all by himself, and excusing himself to his companions, took off his *gandoura*. Soon he was asleep.

'You see?' whispered Mjid. He took her hand and pulled her to her feet. 'Now we can go to the rose garden.' He led her along the ledge, and down a path away from the villa. It was very narrow; thorny bushes scraped their arms as they squeezed through.

'In America we call walking like this going Indian fashion,' she remarked.

'Ah, yes?' said Mjid. 'I'm going to tell you about Ghazi. One of his father's women was a Senegalese slave, poor thing. She made Ghazi and six other brothers for her husband, and they all look like Negroes.'

'Don't you consider Negroes as good as you?' she asked.

'It's not a question of being as good, but of being as beautiful,' he answered firmly.

They had come out into a clearing on the hillside. He stopped and looked closely at her. He pulled his shirt off over his head. His body was white.

'My brother has blond hair,' he said with pride. Then confusedly he put the shirt back on and laid his arm about her shoulder. 'You are beautiful because you have blue eyes. But even some of us have blue eyes. In any case, you are *magnificent*!' He started ahead again, singing a song in Spanish.

> '*Es pa' mi la más bonita,*
> *La mujer que yo más quiero. . . .*'

They came to a cactus fence, with a small gate of twisted barbed wire. A yellow puppy rushed up to the gate and barked delightedly.

'Don't be afraid,' said Mjid, although she had given no sign of fear. 'You are my sister. He never bites the family,' Continuing down a dusty path between stunted palms which were quite dried-up and yellow, they came presently to a primitive bower made of bamboo stalks. In the centre was a tiny bench beside a wall, and around the edges several desiccated rose plants grew out of the parched earth. From these he picked two bright red roses, placing one in her hair and the other under his *chechia*, so that it fell like a lock of hair over his forehead. The thick growth of thorny vines climbing over the trellises cast a shadow on the bench. They sat a while in silence in the shade.

Mjid seemed lost in thought. Finally he took her hand. 'I'm thinking,' he said in a whisper. 'When one is far away from the town, in one's own garden, far from everyone, sitting where it is quiet, one always thinks. Or one plays music,' he added.

Suddenly she was conscious of the silence of the afternoon. Far in the distance she heard the forlorn crow of a cock. It made her feel that the sun would soon set, that all creation was on the brink of a great and final sunset. She abandoned herself to sadness, which crept over her like a chill.

Mjid jumped up. 'If Ghazi wakes!' he cried. He pulled her arm impatiently. 'Come, we'll take a walk!' They hurried down the path, through the gate, and across a bare stony plateau towards the edge of the mountain.

'There's a little valley near by where the brother of the caretaker lives. We can go there and get some water.'

'Way down there?' she said, although she was encouraged by the possibility of escaping from Ghazi for the afternoon. Her mood of sadness had not left her. They were running downhill, leaping from one rock to the next. Her rose fell off and she had to hold it in her hand.

The caretaker's brother was cross-eyed. He gave them some foul-smelling water in an earthen jug.

'Is it from the well?' she inquired under her breath to Mjid.

His face darkened with displeasure. 'When you're offered something to drink, even if it's poison, you should drink it and thank the man who offers it.'

'Ah,' she said. 'So it *is* poison. I thought so.'

Mjid seized the jug from the ground between them, and taking it to the edge of the cliff, flung it down with elegant anger. The cross-eyed man protested, and then he laughed. Mjid did not look at him, but walked into the house and began a conversation with some of the Berber women inside, leaving her to face the peasant alone and stammer her dozen words of Arabic with him. The afternoon sun was hot, and the idea of some water to drink had completely filled her mind. She sat down perversely with her back to the view and played with pebbles, feeling utterly useless and absurd. The cross-eyed man continued to laugh at intervals, as if it provided an acceptable substitute for conversation.

When Mjid finally came out, all his ill-humour had vanished. He put out his hand to help her up, and said: 'Come, we'll climb back up and have tea at the farm. I have my own room there. I decorated it myself. You'll look at it and tell me if you have as pleasant a room in your house in America for drinking tea.' They set off, up the mountain.

The woman at the villa was obsequious. She fanned the charcoal fire and fetched water from the well. The children were playing a mysterious, quiet game at a far end of the enclosure. Mjid led her into the house, through several dim rooms, and finally into one that seemed the last in the series. It was cooler, and a bit darker than the others.

'You'll see,' said Mjid, clapping his hands twice. Nothing happened. He called peevishly. Presently the woman entered. She smoothed the mattresses on the floor, and opened the blinds of the one small window, which gave on to the sea. Then she lit several candles which she stuck on to the tile floor, and went out.

His guest stepped to the window. 'Can you ever hear the sea here?'

'Certainly not. It's about six kilometres away.'

'But it looks as though you could drop a stone into it,' she objected, hearing the false inflexion of her voice; she was not interested in the conversation, she had the feeling that everything had somehow gone wrong.

'What am I doing here? I have no business here. I said I wouldn't come.' The idea of such a picnic had so completely coincided with some unconscious desire she had harboured for many years. To be free, out of doors, with some young man she did not know – *could* not know – that was probably the important part of the dream. For if she could not know him, he could not know her. She swung the little blind shut and hooked it. A second later she opened it again and looked out at the vast expanse of water growing dim in the twilight.

Mjid was watching her. 'You are crazy,' he said at last despairingly. 'You find yourself here in this beautiful room. You are my guest. You should be happy. Ghazi has already left to go to town. A friend came by with a horse and he got a ride in. You could lie down, sing, drink tea, you could be happy with me . . .' He stopped, and she saw that he was deeply upset.

'What's the matter? What's the matter?' she said very quickly.

He sighed dramatically; perhaps it was a genuine sigh. She thought: There is nothing wrong. It should have been a man, not a boy, that's all. It did not occur to her to ask herself: But would I have come if it had been a man? She looked at him tenderly, and decided that his face was probably the most intense and beautiful she had ever seen. She murmured a word without quite knowing what it was.

'What?' he said.

She repeated it: 'Incredible.'

He smiled inscrutably.

They were interrupted by the sound of the woman's bare feet slapping the floor. She had a tremendous tray bearing the teapot and its accessories.

While he made the tea, Mjid kept glancing at her as if to assure himself that she was still there. She sat perfectly still on one of the mattresses, waiting.

'You know,' he said slowly, 'if I could earn money I'd go away tomorrow to where I could earn it. I finish school this year anyway, and my brother hasn't the money to send me to a Medersa at Fez. But even if he had it, I wouldn't go. I always stay away from school. Only my brother gets very angry.'

'What do you do instead? Go bathing?'

He laughed scornfully, sampled the tea, poured it back into the pot, and sat up on his haunches. 'In another minute it will be ready. Bathing? Ah, my friend, it has to be something important for me to risk my brother's anger. I make love those days, all day long!'

'Really? You mean all day?' She was thoughtful.

'All day and most of the night. Oh, I can tell you it's marvellous, magnificent. I have a little room,' he crawled over to her and put his hand on her knee, looking up into her face with an eagerness born of faith. 'A room my family knows nothing about, in the Casbah. And my little friend is twelve. She is like the sun, soft, beautiful, lovely. Here, take your tea.' He sipped from his glass noisily, smacking his lips.

'All day long,' she reflected aloud, settling back against the cushions.

'Oh, yes. But I'll tell you a secret. You have to eat as much as you can. But that's not so hard. You're that much hungrier.'

'Yes, of course,' she said. A little gust of wind blew along the floor and the candles flickered.

'How good it is to have tea and then lie down to rest!' he exclaimed, pouring her more tea and stretching out beside her on the mattress. She made a move as if to spring up, then lay still.

He went on. 'It's curious that I never met you last year.'

'I wasn't in town very much. Only evenings. And then I was at the beach. I lived on the mountain.'

He sat up. 'On this mountain here? And I never saw you! Oh, what bad luck!'

She described the house and, since he insisted, told him the rent she had paid. He was ferociously indignant. 'For that miserable house that hasn't even a good well? You had to send your Mohammed down the road for water! I know all about that house. My poor friend, you were robbed! If I ever see that dirty bandit I'll smash his face. I'll demand the money you paid him, and we'll make a trip together.' He paused. 'I mean, I'll give it to you of course, and you can decide what you want to do with it.'

As he finished speaking he held up her handbag, opened it, and took out her fountain-pen. 'It's a beautiful one,' he murmured. 'Do you have many?'

'It's the only one.'

'Magnificent!' He tossed it back in and laid the bag on the floor.

Settling against the pillows he ruminated. 'Perhaps some day I shall go to America, and then you can invite me to your house for tea. Each year we'll come back to Morocco and see our friends and bring back cinema stars and presents from New York.'

What he was saying seemed so ridiculous to her that she did not bother to answer. She wanted to ask him about the twelve-year-old girl, but she could find no excuse for introducing the subject.

'You're not happy?' He squeezed her arm.

She raised herself to listen. With the passing of the day the countryside had atttained complete silence. From the distance she could hear a faint but clear voice singing. She looked at Mjid.

'The *muezzin*? You can hear it from here?'

'Of course. It's not so far to the Marshan. What good is a country house where you can't hear the *muezzin*? You might as well live in the Sahara.'

'Sh. I want to listen.'

'It's a good voice, isn't it? They have the strongest voices in the world.'

'It always makes me sad.'

'Because you're not of the faith.'

She reflected a minute and said: 'I think that's true.' She was about to add: 'But your faith says women have no souls.' Instead she rose from the mattress and smoothed her hair. The *muezzin* had ceased. She felt quite chilled. 'This is over,' she said to herself. They stumbled down the dark road into town, saying very little on the way.

He took her to her small hotel. The cable she had vaguely expected for weeks was there. They climbed the stairs to her room, the concierge looking suspiciously after them. Once in the room, she opened the envelope. Mjid had thrown himself on to the bed.

'I'm leaving for Paris tomorrow.'

His face darkened, and he shut his eyes for an instant. 'You must go away? All right. Let me give you my address.' He pulled out his wallet, searched for a piece of paper, and finding none, took a calling card someone had given him, and carefully wrote.

'Fuente Nueva,' he said slowly as he formed the letters. 'It's my little room. I'll look every day to see if there's a letter.'

She had a swift vision of him, reading a letter in a window flooded with sunshine, above the city's terraced roofs, and behind him, in the darkness of the room, with a face wise beyond its years, a complacent child waiting.

He gave her the card. Underneath the address he had written the word 'Incredible', enclosed in quotation marks and underlined twice. She glanced quickly to see his face, but it betrayed nothing.

Below them the town was blue, the bay almost black.

'The lighthouse,' said Mjid.

'It's flashing,' she observed.

He turned and walked to the door. 'Goodbye,' he said. 'You will come back.' He left the door open and went down the stairs. She stood perfectly still and finally moved her head up and down a few times, as if thoughtfully answering a question. Through the open window in the hallway she heard his rapid footsteps on the gravel in the garden. They grew fainter.

She looked at the bed; at the edge, ready to fall to the floor, was the white card where she had tossed it. She wanted more than anything to lie down and rest. Instead, she went downstairs into the cramped little salon and sat in the corner looking at old copies of *L'Illustration*. It was almost an hour before dinner would be served.

The Successor

In the middle of the afternoon, lying on his mat, Ali sneezed. A hen that had been drowsing near him screeched and rushed out of the room to a circle of bare dusty ground under the fig tree, where she settled. He listened a while to the distant intermittent thunder in the mountains to the south of the town; then, deciding that he would be able to sleep no more until night, he sat up.

Beyond the partition of upright reeds his brother was talking to El Mehdi, one of the drivers of the carriages that brought people up from the town. From the terrace of the café the eye could wander over the tortured red earth with its old olive trees to the dark caves that lay just below the walls of the town.

The view was something visitors usually considered worth seeing. They would take one of the ancient carriages that waited down in the town and be driven up along the winding road that baked all day in the sunlight; it took less than an hour to reach the café. There they would sit under the trellis in the shade of the vines and drink their tea or their beer. The driver would give the horses water and before twilight they would start back.

On Sundays many carriages and cars came; the café was full all day. His brother, who owned the café and kept the accounts and the money, claimed that he made more on a Sunday than during all the rest of the week. Ali was sceptical of that, not because the statement seemed incredible, but simply because his brother had made it. There was the overwhelming fact that his brother was older than he and therefore had inherited the café from their father. In the face of such crushing injustice there was nothing to be done. Nor was anything his brother had to say of interest to him. His brother was like the weather: one watched it and was a victim to its whims. It was written, but that did not mean it could not change.

He leaned against the wall matting and stretched. His brother and El Mehdi were drinking beer; he was certain of it by the way their voices died down when there was any sound outside the room. They wanted to be able to hide the glasses swiftly if someone should come near the door, so they were listening as they talked. The idea of this childish secrecy disgusted him; he spat on the floor by his feet, and began to rub his bare toe back and forth in the little white mass of saliva.

The thunder rolled in the south mountains, no louder but longer than before. It was a little early in the season for rain, but the rain might come. He reached for the water jug and drank lengthily. Then he sat quite still for a while, his eyes fixed on the framed portrait of the Sultan that hung on the opposite wall.

The thunder came again, still scarcely any louder, but this time unmistakably nearer, the sound more intimate in its movements. It was like a person taking pains to conceal his approach. There was a clapping of hands on the terrace, and a man's voice called: '*Garçon!*' His brother went out, and heard El Mehdi gulp the rest of his beer and follow him. Presently a woman's voice remarked that it was going to rain. Then El Mehdi shouted: '*Eeeeee!*' to his horses, and the carriage began to creak as it started down the road.

After the customers had left, his brother remained outside. Ali went silently to the door, saw him standing by the parapet, his hands behind him, looking out over the town. At the other end of the terrace squatted the boy who washed the glasses and swept the floor. His eyes were closed. There was very little sound from the town below. Occasionally a bird flew out from the hill behind and let itself drop down towards the lower land. The sky was dark. His brother turned and saw him standing in the doorway.

'You slept?'

'Yes.'

'It's going to rain.'

'*Incha' Allah.*'

'Listen.' His brother's hand went up and he turned his face sideways. Very faintly from the town came the sound of the small boys' voices as they ran though the streets chanting the song to Sidi Bou Chta, the song they always sang just before the rain.

'Yes.'

Now the thunder was over the nearest mountains. His brother came towards the door and Ali stepped aside to let him pass.

'We'll close up,' said his brother. He called to the boy, who began to carry the chairs and tables into the room where they were kept piled. Ali and his brother sat on the mattress and yawned. When the boy had finished he closed the door, snapped the padlock and came into the front part of the room, where he set to fanning the fire with the bellows. Presently he brought them each a glass of tea.

'Go to the house. We'll eat early,' said his brother. The boy went out.

A crash of thunder directly above them made them look at each other. Ali said: 'I'll close the house. The boy is an idiot.'

The little house was behind the café, built against the low cliff, just beneath the road. When he got to the fig tree he heard his brother talking to someone. Surprised, he stopped and listened. Great drops of rain began to fall here and there on the dust. It was hard to hear what his brother was saying. He went on to the house.

No one lived there but the two of them and the boy, who slept outside. It was never very clean. If only his brother had been willing to get married, Ali would have had an excuse for going away. Until then, it would be impossible, because his father had told him to stay and help his brother with the café. All he got for staying was a dirty room and the bad food the boy cooked for them.

On the other hand, when his brother walked through the Moulay Abdallah *quartier* he was greeted by the women of every house. The money went on bracelets for them, and on wine and beer for his friends. Besides these women, with whom he spent most of his nights, there was always a young girl of good reputation whom he had hopes of seducing; usually he failed in these endeavours, but his setbacks only increased his interest.

At the moment it was Kinza, the daughter of a shopkeeper from Taza, whose favours he sought. She had granted him short conversations in unfrequented alleys, with a maidservant standing a few feet away; he had met her one twilight outside Bab Segma and put his arm around her (after persuading the servant to stand facing in the other direction), and he even had had a *tête-à-tête* alone with her in a room behind a café, when he had lifted her veil and kissed her. But she had refused any further intimacies, threatening, if he used force, to call the servant who was outside the door. After accepting a good many gifts she had promised him another such rendezvous, so he still had hopes.

Ali knew all about his brother's life and about Kinza, since, in spite of the fact that such subjects cannot be discussed between brothers, it is perfectly proper to talk about them with anyone and everyone else. He knew all about Kinza and he hoped his brother would have no luck with her.

The rain was falling more heavily now. He closed the windows so it would not come in. Then, out of boredom and because he was curious to know who had arrived at the café, he went across the open space between the two establishments, taking long strides, and re-entered the back room. Behind the partition the fire was being fanned again, this time by his brother.

'I'm very fond of your tea here in Morocco,' a man's voice was saying; they were speaking French.

His brother said: 'Me, I like beer best.'

'Have another bottle,' said the stranger magnanimously. 'Drink to the end of this damned rain. If it keeps up I won't get back to town before dark.'

Ali tried to look through the cracks to see what sort of person it was who would walk all the way up to the café, but the man was seated in the doorway looking out at the rain and he could see nothing but his back.

'We are glad to have the rain,' said his brother. 'Each drop is money. The *fellahin* give thanks.'

'*Oui, bien sûr*,' said the stranger without interest.

The thunder had passed over, but the rain was roaring; soon a stream of water burst throught the ceiling in a corner of the room and spattered on to the earthen floor. The added noise made it more difficult to hear their talk. He put his ear close to the reeds.

'Isn't Belgium near France?' his brother asked.

'Next door.'

'It's a good country?'

'Oh, yes.'

His brother handed the stranger a glass of tea.

'Have another bottle of beer,' the stranger suggested.

Ali heard the bottle being opened and the cap fall on to the stone door-sill.

'What's that?' said his brother, his voice bright with interest.

'Just a pill. If I'm nervous I take one. It makes me feel better. If I can't sleep I take two.'

'And then you sleep?'

'Like a child.'

There was a pause. Then his brother asked: 'And would they do that to anyone?'

The stranger laughed. 'Of course,' he said. 'Some people might have to take three, some only one.'

'And how long does it make you sleep?'

'All night.'

'If someone touched you, you'd wake up?'

'Why, yes.'

'But if you took four or five?'

'*Oh, là, là!* You could ride a horse over me then, and I wouldn't know it. That's too many.'

This time there was a long silence, and Ali heard only the noise of the rain all around. The water leaking through the roof had made a channel in the mud to the back door. Now and then a distant growl of thunder came from the hills on the north. The air that moved in through the door was cold and smelt of earth.

Presently his brother said: 'It's getting dark.'

'I suppose you want to close.'

'*Oh, ne t'en fais pas!*' said his brother cordially. 'Stay until it stops raining.'

The stranger laughed. 'It's very kind of you, but I'm afraid I'm going to get wet anyway, because it's not going to stop.'

'No, no!' his brother cried, an anxious note creeping into his voice. 'Wait a few minutes. Soon it will stop. Besides, I enjoy talking with you. You aren't like a Frenchman.'

The man laughed again; he sounded pleased and flattered.

Then Ali heard his brother saying timidly: 'Those pills. Where could I buy a bottle?'

'My doctor in Belgium gave them to me, but I imagine you could get a doctor here to prescribe some.'

'No,' said his brother hopelessly.

'Why do you want them? You don't look as though you had trouble sleeping.'

His brother squatted down beside the stranger. 'It's not that,' he said, almost whispering.

Ali peered intently between the reeds, making an effort to follow the movements of his brother's lips. '*C'est une fille.* I give her everything. She always says no. I was thinking, if just once I could . . .'

The man interrupted him. 'You give her enough of these and she won't be able to say anything.' He chuckled maliciously. 'Here. Hold out your hand.'

With a few inarticulate phrases of thanks, his brother rose to his feet, probably to get a box or an envelope for the pills.

Quickly Ali went out of the door through the rain to the house, where he changed his shirt and spread the wet one over the pillows, and lighted the lamp. Then he sat reading, with some difficulty, a newspaper that a customer had left behind the day before. A few minutes later his brother came in, looking pleased and a little mysterious.

It rained most of the night. At dawn, however, when they got up, the sky was clear. His brother drank his coffee hurriedly and went out, saying he would be back about noon.

Two couples came to the café during the morning, but

since they took beer the boy did not have to light the fire.

Somewhat later than twelve his brother returned. Ali looked up at his face as he came in the door, and said to himself: 'Something has happened.' But he pretended to have noticed nothing and turned away unconcernedly after greeting him. Whatever it might be, he knew his brother would never tell him anything.

This afternoon was exceptionally fine. A good many visitors came, as they always did when the weather was clear and the view good. His brother's face did not change. He carried the trays of tea glasses out to the tables like a man walking in his sleep, and he kept his eyes averted from the customers' faces. Each time someone arrived and walked under the arbour on to the terrace, Ali's brother looked as though he were about to run and jump off the edge of the parapet. Once when Ali saw him smoking, he noticed his hand trembling so violently that he had difficulty in getting the cigarette to his lips, and he looked away quickly so his brother would not see him watching.

When the evening call to prayer was over and the last carriage had rattled away down the road, the boy brought the tables and chairs in and swept the floor of the terrace. Ali stood in the doorway. His brother sat on the parapet, looking down over the olive trees in the dimming light, while the town below sank deeper into the gulf of shadow between the hills. An automobile came along the road, stopped. Against the sky Ali saw his brother's head jerk upward. There were the two sounds of a car's doors being shut. His brother rose, took two hesitant steps, and sat down again.

Ali moved backwards into the room, away from the door. It was not yet too dark for him to see that the two men walking across the terrace were policemen. Without slipping into his babouches he ran barefoot through the inner room of the café, across the open space to the house. He lay down on his mattress, breathing rapidly. The boy was in the kitchen preparing the evening meal.

For a long time Ali lay there, thinking of nothing, watching the cobwebs that dangled from the ceiling move slowly in the breeze. It seemed so long to him that he thought the two men must have gone away without his having heard them. He tiptoed to the door. The boy was still in the kitchen. Ali stepped outside. The crickets were singing all around and the moonlight looked blue. He heard voices on the terrace. Without making a sound he crept into the café's back room and lay down on the mat.

The policemen were making fun of his brother, but not pleasantly. Their voices were harsh and they laughed too loud.

'A Belgian, no less!' cried one with mock surprise. 'He fell out of the sky like an angel, *bien sûr*, with the veronal in one hand. But nobody saw him. Only you.'

Ali caught his breath, sprang up. Then very slowly he lay down again, scarcely breathing now, still listening. 'Nobody,' said his brother, his voice very low. It sounded as though he had his hands over his face. 'He said she'd just go to sleep.'

They thought this very funny. 'She did that, all right,' said one at length. Then their speech became abrupt, the tone brutal: '*Allez, assez! On se débine!*' They rose, yanking him up with them.

As they pushed him into the car, his brother was still saying: 'I didn't know. He didn't tell me.'

The motor started up; they turned the car around and drove down the road. Soon the distant sound of its motor was covered by the song of the crickets.

For a while Ali lay very still. Then, being hungry, he went to the house and had his dinner.

The Hours after Noon

If one could awaken all the echoes of one's memory simultaneously, they would make a music, delightful or sad as the case might be, but logical and without dissonances. No matter how incoherent the existence, the human unity is not affected.

– Baudelaire

1

'Oh, you're a *man*! What does a man know about such things? I can tell you how much: absolutely nothing!' When she argued with her husband at mealtimes, Mrs Callender often sought the support of the other diners in the room. In this instance, however, her appeal was purely formal, since at the moment she was the only woman present, and thus assumed she had their attention anyway. Her bright eyes flashed indignantly from one male diner to the next, and she even turned around in her chair to include old Mr Richmond, the teller in the Bank of British West Africa. He looked up from his food and said: 'Eh? Oh, yes. I dare say.'

The Pension Callender was surprisingly empty these days – empty even for the hot season. Besides old Mr Richmond, who had been with them since they had started eleven years ago, there was Mr Burton down from London to write a book; he had come last autumn and as yet had given no indication of being ready to leave. Mr Richmond and Mr Burton were the only true residents of the pension. The others either came and went irregularly, like Mr Van Siclen the archaeologist and Clyde Brown who was in business in Casablanca, or were merely there for a few days waiting for money or visas before they continued southward or northward, like the two young Belgians who had left that morning.

'A young girl – any young girl – is unbelievably sensitive. Like a thermometer, or a barometer. She catches hold of whatever's in the air. It's true, I tell you.' Mrs Callender looked around at each one defiantly; her black eyes flashed.

Mr Callender was in a good humour. 'That may be,' he said indulgently. 'But I wouldn't worry about Charlotte. And anyway, we don't even know for sure whether Monsieur Royer's coming or not. You know how he is, always changing his mind. He's probably on his way to Marrakesh right now.'

'Oh, he *will* come. You know he will! You simply don't want to face facts.' (Sometimes this was true of Mr Callender. When it was obvious that one of the Muslim servants was systematically stealing foodstuffs from the pantry, he would make no effort to discover who the culprit was, preferring to wait until he might possibly catch him red-handed.) 'You hope that somehow he won't get here. But he will, and he's a filthy, horrible man, and he's going to be sitting opposite your own daughter at every meal. I should think that might mean something to you.'

Her husband looked around at the other diners, an expression of amusement on his face. 'I don't think sitting opposite to him at mealtimes'll bring about her downfall, do you?'

'Abdallah! *Otra taza de café!*' The boy who had been standing by the fireplace trying to follow the conversation stepped forward and filled her cup. 'Silly boy!' she cried, sipping the coffee. 'It's quite cold.' He understood, and lifted the cup to carry it out. 'No, no,' she said sighing, reaching out for it. '*Déjalo, déjalo.*' And without pausing: 'He has a sinister personality. It has an effect on one. Women *feel* those things. I've felt it myself.'

Her husband raised his eyebrows. 'Aha! So now we come to the meat of the conversation. Gentlemen! Wouldn't you say that my wife is the one to watch? Don't you think *she* should be kept from Monsieur Royer?'

Mrs Callender simpered. 'Bob! You're positively appalling!' At the same time Mr Richmond raised his head in a startled fashion and said: 'Monsieur Royer? Oh?'

Clyde Brown was the only one of the four guests who had been following the conversation from the beginning. His watery blue eyes stared with interest. 'Who is this Monsieur Royer? A Latin Quarter Don Juan?'

There was a slight silence. The wind was blowing a blind outside the dining-room window back and forth; the distant sound of heavy waves pounding against the cliffs came up from below. 'Don Juan?' echoed Mrs Callender, laughing thinly. 'My dear, I wish you could see him! He looks like a furious lobster, one that's just been cooked. Absolutely hideous! And he's at least fifty.'

'You're treading on delicate ground,' said Mr Callender into his plate.

'I know, darling, but you don't go about annoying young girls and getting into messes. He gets into the most frightful messes. You haven't forgotten Señora Coelho's niece last year, when he . . .'

Mr Callender pushed back his chair; the scraping sound it made on the tile floor was very loud in the room. 'Probably does, and probably richly deserves whatever trouble he gets into,' he announced. Then impatiently, quickly, to his wife: 'I know all about him. What do you want me to do – wire him we're full up?'

He knew she would say no, and she did. There was always something in one of the stores in town which she coveted at the time: a silk scarf, a pair of shoes or gloves, and the only money which came in was that paid by the guests who stayed at the pension. 'But I should think you'd show more interest where your own daughter is concerned,' she added.

Mr Burton, who had just become aware that a discussion was in progress, raised his head from the book he had been reading and smiled affably at Mrs Callender. Old Mr

Richmond folded his napkin, stuffed it into its aluminium ring, and said: 'I expect it's time to be getting back into town.' Mr Callender announced that he was going to his cottage to take his afternoon siesta. Soon only Mr Van Siclen remained at his table by the window, sipping his coffee and looking distractedly out at the wind-blown landscape. He was a young man who had let his beard grow during the war when he had been stationed on some distant island in the Pacific; now finding that he looked more impressive with it (he was very young to be an archaeologist, people told him), he still wore it. Mrs Callender found herself watching him, wondering whether or not he would be better-looking without its black decoration: he would be less romantic, she decided, perhaps even a little frail of face. As he turned to look at her she felt a tiny thrill of excitement, but his expression swiftly effaced it. He always seemed pleasantly preoccupied; the cynical smile that flickered about his lips made him more remote than if there had been no smile at all. His way of being friendly was to look up from his book and say: 'Good morning. How are you today?' in a very firm voice; then by the time you had replied he would be buried again in the book. She considered his behaviour insufferably rude, but then she never had met an American who did not impress her as wanting in courtesy. It was more their attitude than it was anything they did or failed to do. She herself had been born in Gibraltar of an English father and a Spanish mother, her school days had been passed in Kent, and, although Mr Callender was an American, she considered herself English through and through. And Charlotte was going to be a typical English girl, a wholesome, simple lass without the ridiculous attitudes and feather-brained preoccupations of most American girls. Nor would she be granted the freedom so many American mothers allowed their daughters. Mrs Callender had enough of the Mediterranean in her to believe that while a boy should have complete liberty, a girl should have none at all. The wind continued to bang the shutter.

'I see. Trying to get rid of old Royer,' said Mr Van Siclen lazily, shaking his head with mock disapproval. 'Poor old Royer who never did any harm except ruin a girl's life here and there.'

'Oh, I'm so glad!' she cried; the force of her emotion
startled him. He glanced at her suspiciously.

'Glad about what?'

'Glad that you agree with me about Monsieur Royer.'

'That he's a useless old rake who'll be up to no good
until the day he dies? Sure I agree.'

'Of course you do,' she assured him; she did not see that
he was baiting her.

'But I don't agree with you about keeping him away
from anybody. Why? *Sauve qui peut*, I always say. And the
devil take the hindmost.'

She was genuinely indignant. 'How can you talk that
way? I'm being perfectly serious, even if you're not.'

'I'm perfectly serious, too. After all, a girl's education has
to start somewhere, some time.'

'I think you're quite revolting. Education, indeed!' Her
eyes looked beyond his face, through the window, to the
stunted cypresses below, at the top of the cliff. She could
remember some experiences she would have liked to avoid,
or at least have put off until later, when she might have
been ready for them. Her aunt in Málaga had been far too
lenient, otherwise it never would have been possible for her
to meet the sailor from the *Jaime II*, much less to have made
an appointment with him in the Alameda for the following
day. And the two students she had gone on the picnic with
to Antequera, who had thought they could take advantage
of her because she was not Spanish. I must still have had a
slight accent, she thought. She was sure it was because of
such memories as these that she now had 'sad days', when
she felt that life would never be right again. There were
many things a girl should not know until she was married,
and they were the very things it seemed every man was
determined to impart to her. Once she was married and it
all mattered so much less, precisely then the opportunities
for learning were cut down to a minimum. But of course
it was better that way.

Slowly her expression was changing from indignation to
wistfulness. Voluptuous memories burned in the mind like
fire in a tree stump: they were impossible to put out, and

they consumed from within, until suddenly nothing was
left. If she had a great many memories instead of only a
few, she reflected, she would surely be lost.

'You wouldn't talk that way, so playfully, if you knew
the hazards of bringing up a girl in this place,' she said
wearily. 'With these Moors all about, and strange new
people coming to the pension every day. Of course, we try
to get the good Moors, but you know how they are –
utterly undependable and mad as hatters, every one of them.
One never knows what any of them will take it into his
head to do next. Thank God we can afford to send Charlotte
to school in England.'

'I'm chilly,' said Mr Van Siclen. He rose from the table
rubbing his hands together.

'Yes, it's cool. It's the wind. Mind, I have absolutely
nothing personal against Monsieur Royer. He's always been
a model of fine behaviour with me. It isn't that at all. If he
were a young man' – she almost added: 'like you' – 'I'd
think it was amusing. I don't object to a young man who's
sowing his wild oats. That's to be expected. But Monsieur
Royer is at least fifty. And he goes after such mere children.
A young man is more likely to be interested in older women,
don't you think? That isn't nearly so dangerous.' She
followed him with her gaze, turning her head as he went
towards the door. 'Not nearly.'

He paused in the doorway, the same inexpressive smile
on his lips. 'Send him out to El Menar.' He had a little
native house at El Menar, where he was digging through
the Roman and Carthaginian layers of rubble, trying to get
at the earlier material. 'If he chases the girls around out
there they'll find him in a couple of days behind a rock
with a coil of wire around his neck.'

'Such brutes!' she cried. 'How can you stay out there all
alone with those wild men?'

'They're fine people,' he said, going out.

She looked around the empty room, shivered, and went
out on to the terrace, feeling unpleasantly nervous. The
wind was near to being a gale, but the clouds, which until
now had covered the sky, were breaking up, letting the
hard blue backdrop of the sky show through in places. In

the cypresses the wind whistled and hissed, and when it hit her face it took her breath away. The air was sharp with the odour of eucalyptus, and damp from the fine spray of the breaking waves below. Then, when the landscape was least prepared for such a change, the sun came out. In all these years of living in Morocco she never had ceased wondering at the astonishing difference made by the sun. Immediately she felt the heat seeping in through her pores, the wind was warm, no longer hostile; the countryside became greener, smiled, and slowly the water down there turned to a brilliant blue. She breathed deeply and said tentatively to herself that she was happy. She was not sure it was true, for it seldom happened, but sometimes she could bring it about in this way. It seemed to her that long ago she had known happiness, and that the brief moments of it she found now were only faint memories of the original state. Now, she always felt surrounded by the ugliness of humanity; the scheming little human mind was always present. A certain unawareness of what went on around her was essential if she were to find even normal contentment.

She saw a Moroccan coming towards her from the driveway. Vaguely she knew that his arrival would entail something unpleasant, but for the moment she refused to think about it. She ran her hand through her hair which the wind had blown awry, and tried to bring her mind back to the pension. There was Mr Richmond's mirror which was broken, Brahim needed a new electric bulb in the pantry, she had to look in the laundry for an undershirt of Bob's that was missing, she must catch Pedro before he drove the station-wagon into town, to remind him to stop at the Consulate and pick up Miss Peters whom she had invited for tea.

The Moroccan, his ragged *djellaba* whipping in the wind, emerged from the shadows of the nearest eucalyptus. She exclaimed with annoyance and turned to face him. He was old and he carried a basket. Suddenly she remembered him from last year: she had bought mushrooms from him. And as she remembered, she glanced involuntarily at the withered hand holding the basket and saw the six dark fingers that she knew would be there. 'Go away!' she cried passionately.

'*Cir f'halak!*' She wheeled about and began to run down the path to her cottage in the garden below. Without looking behind she went in and slammed the door behind her. The room smelt of damp plaster and insecticide. She stood a moment at the window looking apprehensively up the path through the bushes. Then, feeling slightly absurd, she drew the curtains across and began to remove her make-up. As a rule the mornings took care of themselves; it was the hours after noon that she had to beware of, when the day had begun to go towards the night, and she no longer trusted herself to be absolutely certain of what she would do next, or of what unlikely idea would come into her head. Once again she peered between the curtains up the sunlit path, but there was nobody.

2

The months in Spain had been not at all relaxing; he was fed-up with the coy promises of eyes seen above fans, furious with mantillas, crucifixes and titters. Here in Morocco, if love lacked finesse, at least it was frank. The veils over the faces did not disturb him; he had learned long ago to decipher the features beneath. Only the teeth remained a hazard. And the eyes he could read as easily as words. When they showed any interest at all, they expressed it clearly, with no hint of the prudishness he so hated.

Above a bank of thick clouds the twilight sky burned with a fierce blueness. He turned into the crowded native quarter. He had sent his luggage to the Pension Callender by taxi and had arranged to take Mr Callender's station-wagon when it started up from the market just before dinner. That left him free to wander a half-hour or so in the Casbah, nothing on his mind, nothing in his hands. He turned into the rue Abdessadek. The hooded figures in the street moved from stall to stall, their hands making the decorative oriental gestures, their voices strident with disagreement over prices. It was all familiar to Monsieur Royer, and very comforting. He felt he could again breathe easily. Slowly he ascended the hill, trying to recall a passage of something he once had read and loved: '*Le temps qui coule ici n'a plus d'heures, mais . . .*' He could not get beyond this point into the other thought. Turning into a smaller street, he was suddenly met by an overpowering odour of jasmine; it came from behind the wall beside him. He stood still a moment beneath the overhanging branch of a fig tree on the other side of the wall, and inhaled slowly, deliberately, still hoping to get beyond that part of the thought which had to do with time. The jasmine would help. It was coming to him: '*mais, tant le loisir . . .*' No.

A child brushed against him, and he had the impression that it had done so purposely. He glanced down: sure enough, it was begging. In a cajoling, unnatural little voice that set his nerves on edge it was asking alms, raising a tiny cupped hand towards him. He began to walk quickly, still sniffing the jasmine, feeling the elusive phrase he sought moving a little further away from him. The child hurried along beside him, continuing its odious chant. 'No!' he cried explosively, without looking down at it again, and forcing his legs to take enormous strides in the hope of escaping its singsong voice.

'*Le temps qui coule ici n'a plus d'heures, mais tant . . .*' he murmured aloud, to cover the sound beside him. It was impossible. Now his mood was irrevocably shattered. The child, growing bolder, touched his leg with a tentative finger. '*Dame una gorda,*' it whined. With a suddenness and ferocity which astonished him even as he acted, he dealt it a savage blow in the face, and a fraction of a second later heard it moan. Then he watched it duck and run to the side of the street where it stood against the wall holding its hand to its face and staring at him with an expression of reproach and shocked disbelief.

Already he was feeling a sharp pang of regret for his behaviour. He stepped towards the cowering child, not aware of what he was about to say or do. The child looked up; its pinched face was pale in the light of the arc-lamp that swung above. He heard himself say in a tremulous voice: '*Porqué me molestas así?*' It did not answer, and he felt its silence making an unbridgeable abyss between them. He took hold of its thin arm. Again, without stirring, it made its absurd, animal moan. In a new access of rage he struck it again, much harder. This time it made no sound; it merely stood. Completely unnerved and miserable, Monsieur Royer turned and walked off in the direction from which he had just come, colliding with a shrouded woman who was emptying garbage from a pan into the middle of the street. She called after him angrily, but he paid no attention. The idea that the Moroccan urchin must consider him with the same dread and contempt it felt for any other Christian interloper was intolerable to him, for he considered himself a particularly understanding friend of the Muslims. He hurried back through the town to the market, found the station-wagon, and got into it. By the light of the many flares in the vegetable stands opposite, he recognized old Mr Richmond of the Bank of British West Africa sitting on the seat facing him.

'Good evening,' said Monsieur Royer, feeling that any kind of conversation at all would help him to recover from the ill-humour induced by his walk.

Mr Richmond grunted a reply, and after a pause said: 'You're Royer, I believe?'

'Aha, you remember me,' smiled Monsieur Royer. But Mr Richmond said no more.

Presently Pedro arrived, his arms full of bundles which he piled on the floor between them. He greeted Monsieur Royer ceremoniously, and explained that they would not be going directly to the pension because they had to stop by the airport to call for Miss Charlotte, who was coming down from London. As they drove slowly through the crowded market, several times Monsieur Royer saw Mr Richmond glance across at him with a surreptitiousness which bordered on the theatrical. *Pauvre vieux*, he thought. He's losing his grip.

3

It had been a nerve-racking flight down, through clouds most of the way, with sudden terrifying exits into regions of pitiless burning sunlight against which the softness of the clouds seemed a protection. She was not afraid of flying; the uneasiness had begun long before she had left school. Each morning on waking she had smelt the freshly cut grass, heard the birds' familiar chirping in the bushes, and said to herself that she did not want to leave.

Of course there was no question of her not going home to visit her family; although her mother had come to England the year before to spend the vacation months with her, she had not seen her father for two years, and she really cared more for him than she did for her mother. He was quiet, he looked at her in a strange, appraising manner that enormously flattered her and, above all, he let her alone, refrained from making suggestions for the betterment of her appearance or character, which ostensibly meant that he considered her a fully formed individual. And while she had to admit that her mother was sweet, at the same time she could not help thinking her silly and something of a nuisance: she was so laden with advice and so eternally ready to bestow it. And the more one took, the more of it she attempted to unload upon one. There was no end to the chain of suggestions and admonitions. She told herself that this constant watching was a very common misapplication of maternal love, but that did not make it any easier to bear.

Her last two days at school she had spent packing slowly, automatically; they had been filled with a particular anguish which she finally brought herself to diagnose. It was sheer apprehensiveness at the prospect of being again with her mother. Other years she had prepared to go home without feeling this tremulous dread. It was as they left London Airport and she was bracing herself against the plane's banking that the reason came to her; without realizing it she already had determined to resist. The discovery was a shock. For a moment she felt like a monster. I can't go home feeling like this, she thought. But as the plane righted itself, and, soaring higher, broke through the pall of fog into the clarity above, she sighed and sat back to read, reflecting that after all the decision was purely private and could scarcely be read in her face. However, throughout the flight, as the plane moved onward from sunlight into shadow and out again, she continued from time to time to be plagued by the feeling that she had become disloyal; and with this suspicion went the fear that in some way she might hurt her mother.

It was a small airport. Before the plane had landed Charlotte had sighted the station-wagon, standing in the glare of the floodlights near the shack which served as waiting-room and customs office. She was not surprised to find that her father had not come to meet her; he left the pension only when he was forced to. Pedro piled her luggage on top and helped her into the back of the car.

'Pleasant journey?' Mr Richmond asked when they had greeted each other and she was seated beside him.

'Yes, thank you,' she said, waiting to be presented to the other gentleman sitting opposite them. He was obviously from the Continent and of a rather distinguished appearance, she thought. But Mr Richmond looked unconcernedly out at the lights of the airport, and so she spoke with the gentleman anyway.

They chatted about the weather and the natives. The car climbed the steep road; at each turn its headlights swept the white walls along the sides, crowned with masses of trailing flowers and vines. High in the dark trees a few cicadas continued to rasp their daytime song. She and the gentleman were still talking when the station-wagon pulled into the garage. Mr Richmond, however, had not said another word.

4

At the pension nothing had changed since her last visit. Her mother looked younger and prettier than ever, and seemed, if possible, still more scatter-brained and distraught – so much so that she too forgot to introduce her to the French gentleman. However, since he was seated in the farthest corner of the dining-room by the window, and was already finishing when the family sat down to eat, it did not matter much.

Her father looked at her across the table and smiled.

'So there you are,' he said with satisfaction. He paused

and turned to his wife: 'Better get Señorita Marchena busy on a dress.' And to Charlotte: 'There's a big shindig Saturday night at the Country Club.'

'Oh, but I have plenty of things to wear!' she objected.

'Yes, but this is very special. And calls for something very special. Señorita Marchena'll be equal to the occasion.' He looked at her carefully. 'And all I can say is, the Ramirez girls had better look to their laurels.'

She felt herself blushing. The Ramirez girls were three sisters who held the reputation of having a local monopoly on beauty.

'The Ramirez girls!' cried Mrs Callender, a note of scorn in her voice.

'What's the matter with them?' demanded her husband. 'They're nice girls.'

'Oh, they're pretty, yes, Bob, but they're scarcely what one would call nice girls.' (For Mrs Callender all Spaniards by definition were inclined to dubious morality.)

'Mother! How can you say that!' Charlotte exclaimed.

Mrs Callender looked about uneasily; it seemed to her that Monsieur Royer was listening to their conversation. She had purposely delayed sitting down to dinner until she thought he would be finished eating, but he was still toying with his fruit. 'I'll tell you about them later,' she said *sotto voce* to Charlotte, and changed the subject, fervently hoping that in a moment he would leave and go down to his cottage.

In the middle of the meal the door from the terrace opened and Mr Van Siclen burst in, fresh from El Menar, dressed in earth-stained overalls. He had a way of appearing unannounced at any hour of the day or night. Sometimes it was inconvenient for the servants, but since he paid full pension and ate few meals there, the Callenders never remarked upon his inpromptu arrivals. He shut the door carefully so the wind sweeping through the room from the kitchen would not slam it.

'Hello, everybody!' he said, running his hand through his hair. Mrs Callender glanced towards the window where Monsieur Royer was slicing an apple into paper-thin sections. 'Oh, how terrible! Monsieur Royer has your table! Do sit here with us. *Abdallah! Trae otra silla!*' She moved her own chair up a bit and indicated the space beside her. 'Before you sit down, this is my daughter Charlotte.' He acknowledged the introduction dryly, with a minimum of civility, and seated himself, sighing mightily.

'What a night!' he exclaimed as his soup was placed before him. 'An ocean breeze, a full moon, and big clouds. I just came in from El Menar in my jeep,' he told Charlotte. (She had decided he was pretentious, with that beard.)

'How enchanting!' cried Mrs Callender. 'Now, do tell us. Have you stumbled on something fantastic out there? Gold coins? Lapis lazuli cups?'

As he spoke, Charlotte watched his face, complacent and slightly mocking. It summed up all the things she disliked most in men: conceit, brashness, insensitivity. Still, he could not be as bad as he looked, she thought; some of it must be the beard. No one his age had a right to such decoration.

From time to time she stole a glance at her mother, who was following his dull discourse as if it were of the greatest interest, punctuating it with little cooing sounds and exclamations of rapture. Somehow she had expected to find her less silly this time (perhaps because of her determination to resist) and instead, here she was, worse than ever. It must be her age, she decided. At some point she would probably change suddenly, overnight. And now, becoming aware that it was precisely this quality of superficiality to which she most objected, she no longer felt even a twinge of guilt at her own rebelliousness. Trying to manage other people's lives was a definite thing. It had its limits. But the kind of irresponsibility she saw in her mother amounted to a denial of all values. There was no beginning and no end; anything was equal to anything else.

Two nurses on leave from the hospital in Gibraltar pushed back their chairs and walked across the room to the door. 'Good nayt,' they said. Both wore glasses; both were dressed in execrable taste. Charlotte watched them and thought: To have reached thirty and to look like that . . . !

Someone laid a hand lightly on her shoulder. She twisted her head around. The French gentleman was standing behind her chair, smiling at her mother.

'I wish to compliment you, madame. A lovely girl like this could only be the daughter of so charming a mother as you.'

He bowed low, from behind her, so that for a second his head was level with hers; his hand remained on her shoulder. A short silence fell upon the table. To Mr Van Siclen Monsieur Royer said: 'Good evening, my dear fellow! How are you? Have you made any remarkable discoveries recently?'

'Hello, Royer. I was just telling the Callenders a little about the new wall I came to yesterday.'

'But it's splendid! Only yesterday! I want to hear about it.'

'Sit down,' said Mr Van Siclen. Mrs Callender flashed him a furious glance.

'I'm afraid it'll be rather crowded,' she said, scraping her chair back and forth on the tiles as noisily as possible, and failing to move it an inch.

'Oh, no. There's room,' objected Charlotte. 'Here beside me.'

'No, no! You are very kind and I want very much to hear about the latest developments of this prodigious excavating. Perhaps tomorrow, Mr Van Siclen?' Ceremoniously he kissed the hands of Mrs Callender and Charlotte, and went out.

Mrs Callender rolled her eyes at her husband. 'One needs the patience of Job,' she said. 'What an insufferable fool!'

Charlotte hesitated an instant before saying: 'Why? I think he's rather sweet.'

Her mother gave a little shriek, part giggle, and looked at Mr Callender as if seeking support. Then she said very seriously: 'I'm sorry to hear it, darling, because it only shows what faulty judgement you have. The man's an utter cad, a complete bounder. They don't come lower.'

Charlotte in turn looked at her father. 'Is that really true?' she asked.

'He's a bad egg, all right,' he said.

They sat a while over coffee exchanging news. The dining-room was empty now save for their table. Abdallah leaned by the fireplace more asleep than awake. Mr Van

Siclen had ceased taking part in the talk, and tilted his chair back, puffing on a pipe. From time to time the wind shook the house. Slowly the conversation had centred itself upon Charlotte. She was telling her parents about school, about her classes and friends; she had almost forgotten Mr Van Siclen was present. Suddenly she stopped short.

'This must all be the most frightful bore for Mr Van Siclen,' she said apologetically.

'Nonsense; go on,' said her father. 'If he doesn't like it he can leave.'

Mr Van Siclen smiled sleepily through the smoke. 'I'm not bored at all,' he assured her. 'It's very instructive.'

She was convinced he was making fun of her, and grew hot with anger.

'I'm dreadfully tired. I think I should go to sleep.' It was the only way to avoid going on with it; now that she was conscious of his amused eyes she could not possibly continue talking.

Her mother jumped up. 'Of course she's tired, poor baby. Come along. You must get to bed immediately.' She tried to take her arm, to pull her towards the door, but Charlotte could not allow that. Gently she disengaged herself and went over to kiss her father good-night; she took leave of Mr Van Siclen with more civility than she felt; then, back at the door, she seized her mother's arm and led her down the steps through the garden to the cottages below. Mrs Callender went in and sat on the bed while she unpacked, gossiping about the servants. Hassan's eleven-year-old brother had been put in prison for reaching in through the open window into Mr Burton's room and taking a hundred-peseta note which lay on the table.

'But, Mother! that's terribly young to be in prison.'

'Darling, I've said for years that the child was a thief. I've told Hassan to watch him, or we should have trouble. Isn't that the bathrobe Mrs Grey gave you? It's rather pretty, but it seems a bit long.' Eventually she went out, leaving Charlotte wide awake in the dark, listening to the rhythmical roar of the waves. They were not very loud tonight; she could remember many nights when they had seemed right in the room. But tonight the wind was from the west.

5

It was not long before she realized how foolish of her it had been to drink coffee after dinner; she would not be sleepy for hours. And since her mother generally read for an hour or so before going to sleep, and could see across to her cottage, she could not very well get up. Directly she turned on her light, her mother would be over to see what was wrong. She wanted to take a walk – perhaps down on the beach. But it would mean getting dressed in the dark and stealing out quietly at the risk of meeting her father. She had not yet heard him go into his own cottage. If she waited, it would be safer, but she did not feel like waiting. As she groped about cautiously for her skirt she heard him shut his door. She sighed with relief. Now that everyone was in, it would be much easier.

It all went very smoothly; she did not make a sound. Under the grape-arbour, through the vegetable garden, down across the open field towards the promontory where the cypresses and rocks overlooked the water beneath. The low clouds scudding overhead made waves of shadow that moved slowly across the moonlit country. She hummed happily as she walked along. To the right, under the big bent cypresses, through the little ravine, up again; she knew the way perfectly. What she had not counted on was meeting Mr Van Siclen sitting on a rock directly in the path, as she reached the edge of the cliff. He sat there looking out to sea; at her involuntary 'Oh!' he turned and smiled at her in the moonlight.

The sight of him there had so thoroughly disrupted her state of mind that she merely stood still and looked at him.

'I *thought* you'd be out,' he said with satisfaction.

She could only say, stupidly: 'Why?'

'I didn't think you were sleepy.'

She said nothing. Her impulse was to be unfriendly, but she decided it would be childish. 'I thought I'd go for a walk down on the beach for a bit.'

He laughed. 'I saw you come sneaking out.' (Why did he have to be so objectionable?) 'Care to go for a little ride?'

'Oh, I don't think so, thank you,' she said politely,

conscious at the same time that her voice lacked forcefulness.

'Sure you would. Come on!'

He sprang up, seized her hand, and began to pull her along, back up the path. 'No, really! No! Listen to me!' She wanted to resist physically, but she was afraid of seeming a whining creature – a poor sport. Presently she was obliged to stop for a moment. 'Please!' she gasped. 'Not so fast!' This he appeared to construe as a tacit acceptance of his suggestion; he laughed, loosened his grip, and said: 'The jeep's in the upper driveway.'

And once she was in the car, going up the mountain with the night wind in her face, she thought that perhaps she had meant to accept from the moment he had invited her. There was a sharp, spicy odour in the air: they were in the eucalyptus forest. It was like going through a high dark tunnel. The sound of the motor reverberated overhead. A minute later the walls of Sultan Moulay Hafid's palace loomed, growing higher as they approached the entrance. In another moment there were no walls at all; the car was on the high, flat section of road leading through the olive-grove to Bou Amar. The rolling hills stretched away to the south in a vast misty panorama whitened by the moonlight. Here and there the uncertain shadow of a cloud moved up a slope, assuming a new form as it reached the summit and spread over the valley beyond. The clouds were low and moved swiftly. She wanted to say: 'It's lovely.' But he had turned the windshield horizontal, and her breath was cut by the onrushing blast of air. The little white native houses of Bou Amar flitted past, and again they were in the country, among the pines now. The road did not deviate from its straight line, but it rose and dipped like a roller-coaster over the hills. He closed the windshield.

'Shall I open her up?' he called.

'Don't go any faster, if that's what you mean.'

'That's what I mean.'

'No!'

'This thing can't go, anyway!' he yelled.

But it seemed to her he had increased the speed.

Now there were no more trees; it was a high, open, rocky region dotted with clumps of holly and heather that glistened under the moon. Far ahead the lighthouse on the cape sent out its recurrent message. All at once he brought the jeep to a stop. It was absolutely silent up here save for the wind: there were no insects and the sea was too far away to be heard. He lit a cigarette without offering her one, and looked at her sideways.

'Are you what's laughingly called a virtuous young lady?' Her heart sank.

'What?' (And it was so idiotic, in any case.) She waited, then said: 'I expect so. Why?'

'*Very* virtuous?'

'Did you bring me out here to inquire after my morals?'

'They don't mean a damn thing to me, if you want to know. I'm just asking to be polite. You know – how's your lumbago? How's your abscessed tooth?'

In spite of herself she said: 'You know, I think you're quite disgusting.'

He blew some smoke in her face. 'All disgust, my dear young lady, is nothing but lack of appetite – desire not to touch with the mouth.'

'What?'

'Eating an object. Kissing somebody. Same thing.'

'I don't know what you are talking about.' She began to be alarmed: it was like conversing with a madman.

'I'm just trying to tell you that I don't really disgust you.'

The lighthouse was flashing. How can I get him to go back? she thought.

'I should think I'd be the best judge of that,' she said a bit shakily.

'And yet you want me to kiss you.'

'What?' she cried shrilly. After a moment she said in a low voice: 'Why should I want you to kiss me?'

'I'm damned if I know. But you do.'

'It's not true. I don't.'

He tossed his cigarette away. 'I think we've argued enough about this little thing,' he said, turning towards her.

She had never been treated this way before. When he seized her, she could do nothing. When with all her might she tried to pull her head away, he caught hold of her lip with his teeth, so that she cried out with pain. After a prolonged struggle he let go and sat grinning at her. She tried to speak, but sobbed and choked.

'Have a handkerchief,' he said. Automatically she accepted it and blew her nose. Then she dabbed at her lip and saw the dark blood on the white linen. For some reason this gave her the courage to raise her head and look at him.

'I . . .'

'Don't try to talk,' he said shortly.

She stared at him, overcome by her hatred of him, opened her mouth to speak, and choked afresh. When she had calmed herself sufficiently to be able to think: That was beastly rather than This is beastly, she handed him his handkerchief and said quietly: 'My mother was wrong. She said they don't come lower than Monsieur Royer.'

He laughed delightedly. 'Oh, he's much worse! *Mu-u-uch* worse!'

'If you don't mind, I'd prefer not to talk about it any more.'

'Ah, it wasn't as bad as all that,' he said.

She did not answer.

'As a matter of fact,' he pursued, 'this ride was good for you.'

'I don't think my father would agree,' she said somewhat primly.

'Probably not. But he'll never be asked his opinion, will he?'

Remembering her sigh of relief when she had heard her father shut the door of his cottage, she was silent. He started up the engine, turned the jeep around, and they went back over the road as quickly as they had come. When they arrived at the garage, she jumped out without speaking again, and hurried to her cottage. All the lights in the other cottages were out. She undressed in the dark, turning on the light over the wash-basin just long enough to put a drop of iodine on her lip. As she got into bed she noticed that she was trembling. Even so, it was not long before the sound of the waves had lulled her to sleep.

6

In the morning she awoke in rather a bad humour. Perhaps the trip was just having its effect, or perhaps the unpleasantness of last night had upset her nerves. Halima, the younger of Mustapha the cook's two wives, brought her breakfast. When she had finished eating, she got out of bed and looked in the mirror. Her lower lip was still swollen. Maybe by lunch-time it will be gone, she thought hopefully, and she put on her bathing-suit and rushed down to the beach where she spent the whole morning swimming and sunbathing. About noon she caught sight of Monsieur Royer coming around the point at the base of the cliffs. He was in white flannels and flourished a cane. She watched him approach, glad he was not Mr Van Siclen.

'Aha! A mermaid today!' he cried. 'Is the sea comfortable?'

'Oh, yes. It's lovely.'

He stood above her, making designs in the sand with the tip of his cane, and they talked. Finally he said: 'May I be seated?'

'Oh, please! Of course!' She felt rude for not having suggested it.

When he was beside her he continued to chat and plough up the sand with his cane. After a few minutes he turned and looked into her face, smiling in such a way that his eyes seemed to shine more brightly, and said: 'It is not too many times in his life that a man has the privilege of sitting with a real mermaid, you know. So you must forgive me if I enjoy this privilege.'

She did not know what she ought to say, but his manner amused her, and so she laughed and said: 'Thank you.'

He did not seem entirely satisfied. 'I don't want to embarrass you, my dear. You must realize that what I say is said quite sincerely. It is not meant to be flattery. If it seems comic, that is merely my English vocabulary.'

'But it's not comic at all,' she protested. 'It's very charming, really. And you speak English beautifully.'

His conversation consisted of very little else besides these elaborate compliments, but she found them inoffensive, a little touching, and on the whole enjoyable. As they talked, her sympathy for him increased, and she found herself wishing she could confide in him – not about anything in particular or anything serious, she thought – just about whatever came into her head at the moment. He was friendly, detached, sincere, and, she was sure, very wise. As a little fishing-boat rounded the point, bobbing up and down in the rough water, she suddenly said: 'Monsieur Royer, tell me your honest opinion. Do you think it's despicable for a man to kiss a girl against her will?' She was shocked to hear the words coming out; she had not known they would be exactly those words, but apparently she needed to say them, and there was no one else to say them to.

A cloud seemed to spread across Monsieur Royer's sunburned face. Slowly he said: 'Ah. I see that people have been talking to you about me.'

'No! No!' she cried, startled and then horrified.

'Naturally they have,' he said calmly. 'We have never even been presented one to the other. Do you realize that? Yes. Of course they have. Why not? They are quite right.' He paused. 'Luncheon will be ready soon, and I must first prepare. But I want to answer your question. Yes. I think such a thing is despicable. You used the words: "against her will". But there are a great many girls who have no will, like the natives here, or even the Spanish girls of the lower class. It is all the same to them, as long as they receive a gift. They have no wish one way or the other. And if they have no will, one can scarcely go against it, can one?'

She was silent. 'I wasn't talking about you,' she finally said.

He looked at her very seriously; he seemed not to have heard her. 'Do you see what I mean to say?'

'I'm not sure,' she said, letting the sand run between her fingers. 'But I really didn't mean . . .'

He had risen.

'Good morning, madame.'

She looked around: her mother stood there. She greeted Monsieur Royer crisply. Then she looked down.

'Charlotte, it's lunch-time. Come up and dress.' There was an edge of fury in her voice that recalled long-forgotten days of childhood misbehaviour and recrimination.

The upward climb was steep. Charlotte went first, with her mother panting behind her. 'Charlotte, I'm extremely angry with you. You're not a child any more, you know. . . .' Between each sentence she ceased speaking and took a breath. 'You father and I as much as told you to have nothing to do with Monsieur Royer. How explicit must one be? I was going to tell you all about him this morning. But of course you disappeared. I don't know why . . . I couldn't be more annoyed with you. You're thoroughly thoughtless and egotistical. . . .'

Charlotte listened with apathy to the diatribe, walking quickly so that her mother, in attempting to keep up with her, would have the maximum of difficulty in delivering it. At one point she had been about to protest that Monsieur Royer had only happened by a short while ago, and that she had been sitting with him only a few minutes, but she felt that this would seem to put her in the wrong; it would sound like an excuse, and she was determined to admit to no fault. Since she did not answer at all, her mother's voice softened tentatively as she continued: 'Don't you think it's time you changed, and thought of others?'

'I expect so,' she said vaguely, adding in a louder voice: 'But I can't see what you have against poor Monsieur Royer to say such horrid things about him.'

Mrs Callender snorted impatiently.

'Oh, good heavens, Charlotte! I know all about the man. Please believe me, he has a most unsavoury reputation. If only for that, he's no one for you to see. But I happen to know as well that his reputation is completely justified. He's a confirmed roué and a scoundrel. In any case, I don't intend to argue the point with you. It's an established fact. But what I do intend to have is your promise – your promise that you won't speak to him again unless either your father or I, one of us, is present.'

They were at the top of the cliff. Mrs Callender would have liked to stop a moment and catch her breath, but Charlotte hurried on. The path was less steep here, and her mother quickly caught up with her, breathing heavily. She sounded angrier now.

'I refuse to stand by and watch an old libertine like that try to ruin your life – I won't *have* you seeing him. Do you understand me?'

Charlotte spoke without looking around. 'Yes, of course I understand. But I don't agree.'

'It's of no interest to me whether you agree or not!' cried Mrs Callender shrilly. 'I expect you think it's brilliant and becoming to show spirit. . . .'

The had reached the vegetable garden. One of the nurses from Gibraltar was sitting on the porch of her cottage sunning herself. Mrs Callender lowered her voice and became cajoling. 'Darling, please don't ruin my pleasure in your stay by being stubborn and belligerent about this.'

'Do you want me to be rude to him?'

'It's not necessary. But if you disobey me I shall be the one to be rude. I shall simply ask him to leave. And I've never done that to anyone.'

'Then the only thing for me to do is to tell him in front of you that you've forbidden me to speak to him.'

They stood in the garden between their respective cottages.

'If that's the pleasantest way you can devise, do so by all means,' said her mother acidly. 'I'm sure I don't mind.' She went into her room and shut the door. Charlotte stood a moment looking after her.

In her mirror she examined her lip; the salt water had brought the swelling down. She dressed quickly and went up to the dining-room, noting to her immense relief that Mr Van Siclen was not there. During lunch she glanced out of the window and saw Monsieur Royer being served on the terrace in the sun; she wondered if he were eating outside because he liked it, or out of consideration for her. While her parents were still finishing their dessert she excused herself and went out. She paused an instant on the steps, and then walked casually towards the table where Monsieur Royer sat sipping his coffee. He rose and seized a chair from the next table for her. Knowing she was being watched through the window, she sat down with him. Hassan brought her a cup of coffee and they talked brightly for a quarter of an hour or so. She fully expected her mother to appear and precipitate a scene, but nothing happened. When she got up and went down to her cottage she thought: Now she'll come, but she lay awake a long time listening for her mother's footsteps, and they did not arrive. At last she sank into a heavy slumber.

7

In the rose garden behind the bar Mr and Mrs Callender walked back and forth, conversing in low tones.

'You saw it!' exclaimed Mrs Callender in an intense whisper. 'Pure infatuation, nothing else. It's not like Charlotte to behave this way. She'd never defy me like this. I admit it was pure provocation, the whole little act, yes. But she's never been this way before. The man has bewitched her, it's perfectly clear. We must do something. Immediately.'

Back and forth along the short, bordered path they walked. 'We've got to send him away," she said.

'Impossible,' said Mr Callender.

'Then I shall take Charlotte and go to a hotel until he leaves,' she declared.

Mr Callender grunted.

'All she needs', he said at length, 'is to meet some boys her own age. The ones she used to know here are mostly gone. Too bad the dance at the Club isn't tonight or tomorrow night. She'd forget about Royer in short order.'

Mrs Callender sighed. 'If he could only be put on ice until the dance,' she mused. Then she straightened and tried once more. 'Oh, Bob, we *must* get rid of him.'

Her husband stood still. 'The time to get rid of Monsieur Royer was before he came. You had your chance. I asked you if you wanted me to wire him there was no room, and you said no. It's one thing to tell someone the place is full up. And another to send a man away for no reason at all. You can't do it.'

'No reason at all, indeed!' she snorted.

Now she sat in her room on the edge of the bed and fidgeted. The long windswept afternoon depressed her. There was too intimate and mysterious a connection between what she felt, and the aspect of the countryside, now brilliant under the ardent sun, now sombre in shadow as the endless procession of separate clouds raced past. It was easy to say 'This is a sad day' and attribute it to the unfortunate coincidence which had brought Charlotte and Monsieur Royer here at the same time. But that did not really explain anything. The aching nostalgia for her own youth remained – the bright Andalusian days when each hour was filled to bursting with the promise of magic, when her life lay ahead of her, inexhaustible, as yet untouched. It was true that she had not always been happy then, but there had been the imminent possibility of it, at every moment. And the people around her had not had the strange faculty they now had of becoming suddenly sinister. Even her husband, when she looked at him quickly, sometimes seemed to be coming hurriedly back from somewhere not in the light. It disconcerted her, and if she ever had dwelt on it for very long at a time, it would have terrified her.

A *rhaïta* was being played fairly far away on the mountain, announcing a wedding. It would probably go on for several days and nights. She put her hands over her ears. As if that could help! Whenever she took them away, the slippery little sound would be there, twisting thinly around itself like a tree-snake. She pressed her palms more tightly against her head, until the vacuum hurt her eardrums. But the images had been awakened: the donkeys laden with blankets and painted wooden chests, the procession of lanterns, the native women in white with their drums. . . . She jumped up, looked at her watch, stepped to the mirror and powdered her face. Then she went down to Mr Van Siclen's cottage. He had had lunch in town with the American Vice-Consul, saying that he would be back early as he was returning to El Menar before dark. She knocked; there was no answer. She went up to the bar where he often sat thumping out old tunes with one finger on the piano. He was talking with the barman.

'Mr Van Siclen, I must speak with you.'

'Sure.' He followed her outside.

'I know all this won't interest you in the least, but it's the only favour I shall ever ask of you. Monsieur Royer has his eye on Charlotte. No, don't laugh. It's most serious. I'm counting on you. You *must* help me.'

'Well, well!' he said. And after a bit: 'OK. What do you want me to do?'

'I thought if you could invite him out to El Menar. . . . Just for a few days . . .' she hastily added as he frowned.'. . . Just for two or three days. At least until I've had the opportunity of talking with her. You see, for some mad reason *she* seems quite taken with *him* as well. There's no explaining these things. But one must act. I shall be eternally grateful to you.'

'Well,' he said slowly, smoothing his hair, 'I'm willing to extend the invitation, but how do I know he'll accept?'

'I think you can make it attractive to him if you really try,' she said, smiling significantly. 'Playing up the native life a bit . . . ? You know him, after all. You know what amuses him.'

'Damn it!' he cried, suddenly annoyed. 'I don't want him out there trailing me around all day while I work.'

And seeing her face, he added resignedly: 'But I'll ask him, I'll ask him.'

'You *are* a darling,' she said.

It was done. For some reason she felt no doubt that Monsieur Royer would accept. Fittingly, the sun was shining as she went through the garden to her cottage. It was almost an anticlimax when at tea-time Monsieur Royer came to announce his departure.

'We shall miss you,' she smiled. 'I expect you'll want to keep your cottage.' And when he said that he did, she generously suggested: 'We'll put you on demi-pension for those days. That way you'll only be paying a little more than the price of the room.'

'No, no,' he protested politely, but she saw that he was pleased.

A little while later she watched her two guests drive off in the open jeep into the twilight.

At dinner Mr Callender looked around the room. 'Where's everybody?' he said.

'Oh, Mr Van Siclen's gone back to El Menar and taken Monsieur Royer along with him.'

'*What?*' He was incredulous.

Charlotte said nothing. Several times during the meal Mrs Callender glanced across at her, but if she was feeling any emotion she did not betray it.

'She's rather a little sneak,' said Mrs Callender to herself, disappointed; she had expected a little more reaction than this.

Charlotte was thinking: He's gone, thank Heavens. But she meant Mr Van Siclen. She went to bed immediately after dinner, slept soundly, and awoke early with a desire to see Gloria Gallego, a friend from her *lycée* days. She breakfasted, dressed, and in the fresh of the morning set out on foot for town. It was not a great walk; she could make it in an hour. The moving air was a tonic. The sun had not yet begun to weight it down with its heat, nor the flowers with their noonday scent, nor the insects with their droning. When she arrived in the market she was startled to see Mr Van Siclen's jeep parked by the Ciné Régis. She kept her face averted as she passed, lest he should be in it. But she came face to face with him at the corner.

'Hi there!' he said, grasping her arm, quite, she thought, as if nothing had ever occurred between them.

She was not effusive in her greeting. The crowd of Berbers passing pushed them this way and that.

'Where are you off to so early?' he demanded.

'Just up to the Boulevard,' she said coldly.

'It's quite a walk. Let me take you up.'

'I enjoy walking.'

'Come on, be a good sport. Don't go on having hard feelings. You'll get old before your time.'

He did not let go of her arm; the easiest way out was to accept. She let him lead her back to the jeep and help her in. As they went around the north end of the market they met the pension's station-wagon which had just deposited Mr Richmond at the bank. She waved to Pedro, who waved back.

'Am I forgiven?' asked Mr Van Siclen.

'Only if you don't go on talking about it,' she replied.

'That's the spirit,' he said approvingly. 'I had to come in for kerosene. There wasn't even enough for the lamps last night. Poor old Royer had to go to bed by moonlight, I guess. I didn't hear him come in.'

He let her out at the Boulevard. At lunch-time she tried to telephone her mother to tell her that she was eating at the Gallegos', but the line was having one of its frequent bad days, and she was unable to reach the pension.

'Bob, I *am* worried about Charlotte,' Mrs Callender was saying at lunch. (If the telephone had not been out of order it would have rung at that instant.) 'She was already gone at eight when I went in to see her. It's not like her to go out so early. Where can she be?'

'Don't get so wrought up,' said Mr Callender gently. 'Quit thinking she's a kid. She's in town somewhere and she can't get through on the phone, that's all.'

Mrs Callender pouted. 'She's been intolerable since the moment she arrived. Inconsiderate and perverse. I've done nothing all morning but worry about her.'

'I know.'

'And I've a fearful migraine as a result. It's that *beastly* Monsieur Royer,' she added with vehemence.

At the next table Mr Burton laid aside his book and feebly inquired: 'I expect your daughter is pleased to be back home?'

Mrs Callender turned to face him. 'Oh, yes! She adores it here. Of course it's ideal for young people.'

'Oh, quite! Yes, indeed.'

After lunch she took more aspirin. Now she felt a slight nausea as well. She lay on her bed, the curtains drawn, reflecting with a dim satisfaction that at least Charlotte would know she had made her mother ill. The wind still blew, the trees still swayed and roared, and through their sound from time to time crept the shrill, tiny notes of the distant *rhaïta*. She dozed, woke, dozed. At tea-time Halima knocked to ask if she wanted tea in her room. She inquired if Señorita Charlotte had returned. Halima had not seen her.

Although she wanted Charlotte to find her ill in bed when she returned, she disliked having tea in her cottage alone and, deciding to run the risk of rising, went up to the salon in the main house for her tea. Only the nurses were there, but she sat down anyway. Soon she heard Pedro's voice in the hall and excused herself. '*Oiga, Pedro*,' she called, running out. 'You haven't seen Señorita Charlotte this afternoon, have you?'

'*Esta tarde? Nó, señora*. Not since this morning in the market, riding with Señor Van Siclen in his car.'

'*Cómo!*' she cried; the word was like an explosion. Her eyes had become very large. Pedro looked at her and thought that perhaps Señora Callender was about to faint.

'Get the *camioneta*,' she said weakly. '*Vamos a El Menar.*'

'Now?' he asked, surprised.

'Immediately.'

8

She sat in front with Pedro, her head pounding so hard that it was merely an enormous and imprecise pain she carried with her. The familiar landmarks as they passed made no sense. She could not have identified one. Nor did she know which of the three enraged her most: Charlotte, for her effrontery and disobedience, Mr Van Siclen for his perfidy, or Monsieur Royer, for existing at all.

As long as she was sitting in the moving car her anger remained at fever pitch. But when Pedro stopped in the wilderness, pointing to a road strewn with large stones, and remarking that they would have to walk up it to get to the village, her annoyance at this unexpected obstacle somewhat calmed her. It was quite dark by this time, and the faint light from Pedro's torch wavered uncertainly. Out here the wind came directly off the Atlantic; it was violent and damp.

The road led upward, zigzagging among huge boulders. Each minute the sound of the sea became more audible. She had never been here before; the idea of this absurd village perched on the crags above the ocean filled her with terror. They met a Berber on his way down, and by the flashlight's feeble glimmer she saw him, stocky and dark-skinned, and carrying a shepherd's crook. '*Msalkheir*,' he said as he passed. He was in the darkness back of them before they could ask him how far the village was. Suddenly they came to a hut.

There was a flickering light inside, and the sound of many goats and sheep. A little farther on Pedro spied the jeep. She caught herself thinking, How does he ever drive up that trail? and quickly remembered the seriousness of her errand.

'*Pregúnteles*,' she whispered to Pedro, indicating a group of dark figures at the right. The barnyard odours were overwhelming. As Pedro left her side to approach the men, she glanced up and saw the sky, uniformly black. Not a star showed through the huge curtain of cloud. Yes, far out over the invisible sea she thought she saw one shining, but it could have been a boat. She had neglected to bring a wrap, and she was shivering.

The house was up ahead, at the top of the village. She could see the lamp through the open door, the brightest light in the landscape. Several dogs went slinking away into the dark as they approached the house. Pedro called out: '*Señor!*' and Mr Van Siclen appeared.

'Good God!' he cried when he saw them standing in the doorway. 'What are you doing here?'

She pushed past him into the tiny room. There was a chair, a table littered with papers, and a mattress on the floor in the corner. And there were large native baskets everywhere, full of pieces of stone. The light hurt her eyes.

'Where's my daughter?' she said, going to the door of the adjoining room and peering in.

'What?'

She looked at him; for the first time since she had known him he seemed really perturbed – even frightened.

'Charlotte. Where is she?'

The expression on his face did not change. Her question seemed not to have reached it. 'I have no idea. I let her off early this morning on the Boulevard by the French Consulate.'

Mrs Calender hesitated, not completely sure he was telling the truth. He took the initiative. 'It'd be more to the point to ask where Monsieur Royer is. You haven't seen *him* by any chance? I don't mind telling you I'm worried.'

'Monsieur Royer? Certainly not! Isn't he here with you?'

He shrugged his shoulders helplessly. 'I'm afraid not. I don't know what's up. But it doesn't look good to me.'

She sat down sideways on the straight-backed chair. For a second she heard the sea much closer than it should have been.

'He went out last night right after supper. There were some drums beating.'

She had her hand to her head. And as so often happens in moments of great fatigue, she felt that the scene was one whose outcome she knew by heart, that although she was in it, it would go on and play itself through to the end without her participation. Mr Van Siclen would reach into his hip-pocket, pull out a packet of cigarettes, extract one, light it, and hold the match a moment before blowing it out, just as he did do each of these things a fraction of a second after she had known he would. And he would go on speaking.

'. . . but I don't quite know what the hell to do. The worst thing about it is that the natives all claim not to have seen him, ever. They don't know there is such a person. I know damned well they're lying. It's too unanimous. I don't think he ever came back at all. The blankets on his mattress in there', he indicated the next room, 'haven't been touched. I didn't notice that until I got back from town this morning. I thought he was asleep.'

She said nothing because she felt she was getting much too far ahead of him now. At the moment this bare room with the wind outside was the less strong of two realities. The other was a spoken sentence, a dreadful image, but she could recall neither the sentence nor the image it had evoked – only the brief horror she had felt at the time.

She was standing up, walking towards the door.

'I feel a bit ill.' To say the words demanded a monstrous effort.

Outside, the sea-wind battered her face. She breathed deeply several time. Mr Van Siclen's voice came from the door, solicitous. 'Are you all right?'

'Yes,' she said.

'Be careful out there. There's barbed wire strung along the edge where you are.'

Now it was complete. Everything had been said. All she had to do was go on breathing deeply, facing the sea. Of course. A coil of wire around his neck. Behind a rock. A minute or two later she went back in.

'Better?'

'If I could have a drink,' she said wanly. (She could not say to him: 'It's not my fault. You yourself put the idea into my head', because to admit that much would establish her guilt firmly, for all time.)

'Whisky, you mean? Or water?'

'I think whisky.'

As she drank it he said: 'We'll have a searching party out looking for him the first thing in the morning. That is, if he doesn't turn up tonight. I'll drive you back now so you won't have to walk down the hill. And I think it might be a good idea to call the *comisaría* tonight, anyway.'

She smiled ruefully. 'The police won't be of much use, will they?'

'Never know,' he said, slipping into his jacket. 'He may be lying only a half mile from here with a broken leg.'

Again she smiled: she was so sure it was not that. And so was he, she thought, but now that she was upset too he could afford to pretend.

'Well, shall we get going?' he asked her.

The wind blew, the great black cloud from the sea had covered everything. He put his arm about her waist as they stumbled downward. She thought of nothing, let herself bump against him as they avoided rocks.

The were in the jeep. At the foot of the hill Pedro got out. 'Do you want to go in your own car?' said Mr Van Siclen. 'It'd be more comfortable, I guess.'

'No. This air is just what I need.'

Swiftly they left El Menar behind in the darkness.

9

From the spot where he lay, he could have heard the two motors grow fainter and be drowned by the vaster sound of the sea; he could have seen the two little red tail-lights moving away across the empty countryside. Could have, if all that had not been decided for him twenty-one hours earlier. In the bright moonlight he had sat with the child on his knee (for she was really no more than a child) letting her examine his watch. For some reason – probably the sight of this innocent animal holding the thin gold toy in her tattooed hands – he was put in mind of the phrase he had not been able to recall the evening of his arrival. He began to murmur it to himself, even at the moment her expression changed to one of terror as, looking up over his shoulder, she saw what was about to happen.

'*Le temps qui coule ici n'a plus d'heures, mais, tant l'inoccupation de chacun est parfaite. . . .*'

This time he might have completed it.

The Frozen Fields

The train was late because the hot-box under one of the coaches had caught fire in the middle of a great flat field covered with snow. They had stayed there about an hour. After the noise and rushing of the train, the sudden silence and the embarrassed stirrings of people in their seats induced a general restlessness. At one point another train had shot by on the next track with a roar worse than thunder; in the wake of that, the nervousness of the passengers increased, and they began to talk fretfully in low voices.

Donald had started to scratch pictures with his fingernail in the ice that covered the lower part of the window-pane by his seat. His father had said: 'Stop that.' He knew better than to ask 'Why?' but he thought it; he could not see what harm it would do, and he felt a little resentful toward his mother for not intervening. He could have arranged for her to object to the senseless prohibition, but experience had taught him that she could be counted on to come to his defence only a limited number of times during any given day, and it was imprudent to squander her reserve of good will.

The snow had been cleared from the station platform when they got out. It was bitter cold; a fat plume of steam trailed downwards from the locomotive, partially enveloping the first coach. Donald's feet ached with the cold.

'There's Uncle Greg and Uncle Willis!' he cried, and he jumped up and down several times.

'You don't have to shout,' said his father. 'We see them. And stand still. Pick up your bag.'

Uncle Willis wore a black bearskin coat that almost

141

touched the ground. He put his hands under Donald's arms and lifted him up so that his head was at a level with his own, and kissed him hard on the mouth. Then he swung him over into Uncle Greg's arms, and Uncle Greg did the same thing. 'How's the man, hey?' cried Uncle Greg, as he set him down.

'Fine,' said Donald, conscious of a feeling of triumph, because his father did not like to see boys being kissed. 'Men shake hands,' he had told him. 'They don't kiss each other.'

The sky was crystal clear, and although it was already turning lavender with the passing of afternoon, it still shone with an intense light, like the sky in one scene at the Russian Ballet. His mother had taken him a few weeks earlier because she wanted to see Pavlova; it was not the dancing that had excited him, but the sudden direct contact with the world of magic. This was a magic sky above him now, nothing like the one he was used to seeing above the streets of New York. Everything connected with the farm was imbued with magic. The house was the nucleus of an enchanted world more real than the world that other people knew about. During the long green summers he had spent there with his mother and the members of her family he had discovered that world and explored it, and none of them had ever noticed that he was living in it. But his father's presence here would constitute a grave danger, because it was next to impossible to conceal anything from him, and once aware of the existence of the other world he would spare no pains to destroy it. Donald was not yet sure whether all the entrances were safely guarded or effectively camouflaged.

They sat in the back of the sleigh with a brown buffalo robe tucked around them. The two big grey horses were breathing out steam through their wide nostrils. Silently the white countryside moved past, its frozen trees pink in the late light. Uncle Greg held the reins, and Uncle Willis, sitting beside him, was turned sideways in his seat, talking to Donald's mother.

'My feet hurt,' said Donald.

'Well, God Almighty, boy!' cried Uncle Willis. 'Haven't

you got 'em on the bricks? There are five hot bricks down there. That's what they're there for.' He bent over and lifted up part of the heavy lap-robe. The bricks were wrapped in newspaper.

'My feet are like blocks of ice, too,' said Donald's mother. 'Here, take your shoes off and put your feet on these.' She pushed two of the bricks towards Donald.

'He just wants attention,' said Donald's father. But he did not forbid him to have the bricks.

'Is that better?' Uncle Willis asked a moment later.

'It feels good. How many miles is it to the farm?'

'Seven miles to The Corner, and a mile and a half from there.'

'Oh, I know it's a mile and a half from The Corner,' said Donald. He had walked it many times in the summer, and he knew the names of the farms along the road. 'First you come to the Elders, then the Landons, then the Madisons . . .'

His father pushed him hard in the ribs with his elbow. 'Just keep quiet for a while.'

Uncle Willis pretended not to have heard this. 'Well, well. You certainly have a good memory. How old are you now?'

Donald's throat had constricted; it was a familiar occurrence which did not at all mean that he was going to cry – merely that he felt like crying. He coughed and said in a stifled voice: 'Six.' Then he coughed again; ashamed, and fearful that Uncle Willis might have noticed something amiss, he added: 'But I'll be seven the day after New Year's.'

They were all silent after that; there were only the muffled rhythm of the horses' trot and the soft, sliding sound of the runners on the packed snow. The sky was now a little darker than the white meadows, and the woods on the hillside beyond, with their millions of bare branches, began to look frightening. Donald was glad to be sitting in the middle. He knew there were no wolves out there, and yet, could anybody be really certain? There had been wolves at one time – and bears as well – and simply because nobody had seen one in many years, they now said there weren't any. But that was no proof.

They came to The Corner, where the road to the farm turned off from the main road. Seven rusty mailboxes stood there in a crooked row, one for each house on the road.

'R.F.D. Number One,' said Uncle Willis facetiously. This had always been a kind of joke among them, ever since they had bought the farm, because they were townspeople and thought the real farmers were very funny.

Now Donald felt he was on home ground, and it gave him the confidence to say: 'Rural Free Delivery.' He said the words carefully, since the first one sometimes gave him difficulty. But he pronounced it all right, and Uncle Greg, without turning round, shouted: 'That's right! You go to school now?'

'Yes.' He did not feel like saying more, because he was following the curves in the road, which he knew by heart. But everything looked so different from the way he remembered it that he found it hard to believe it was the same place. The land had lost its intimacy, become bare and unprotected. Even in the oncoming night he could see right through the leafless bushes that should have hidden the empty fields beyond. His feet were all right now, but his hands in their woollen mittens under the buffalo skin were numb with cold.

The farm came into view; in each downstairs window there was a lighted candle and holly wreath. He bent over and put his shoes on. It was hard because his fingers ached. When he sat up again the sleigh had stopped. The kitchen door had opened; someone was coming out. Everyone was shouting: 'Hello!' and 'Merry Christmas!' Between the sleigh and the kitchen he was aware only of being kissed and patted, lifted up and set down, and told that he had grown. His grandfather helped him take off his shoes again and removed a lid from the top of the stove so he could warm his hands over the flames. The kitchen smelt, as in summer, of woodsmoke, sour milk and kerosene.

It was always very exciting to be in the midst of many people. Each one was an added protection against the constant watchfulness of his mother and father. At home there were only he and they, so that mealtimes were periods of torture. Tonight there were eight at the supper table.

They put an enormous old leather-bound dictionary in a chair so he would be high enough, and he sat between his grandmother and Aunt Emilie. She had dark brown eyes and was very pretty. Uncle Greg had married her a year ago, and Donald knew from many overheard conversations that none of the others really liked her.

Gramma was saying: 'Louisa and Ivor couldn't get down till tomorrow. Mr Gordon's driving them down as far as Portersville in his car. They'll all stay in the hotel tonight, and we've got to go in first thing in the morning and bring them out.'

'Mr Gordon, too, I suppose,' said his mother.

'Oh, probably,' Uncle Greg said. 'He won't want to stay alone Christmas Day.'

His mother looked annoyed. 'It seems sort of unnecessary,' she said. 'Christmas is a *family* day, after all.'

'Well, he's part of the family now,' said Uncle Willis with a crooked smile.

His mother replied with great feeling: 'I think it's terrible.'

'He's pretty bad these days,' put in Grampa, shaking his head.

'Still on the old fire-water?' asked his father.

Uncle Greg raised his eyebrows. 'That and worse. You know. . . . And Ivor too.'

Donald knew they were being mysterious because of him. He pretended not to be listening, and busied himself making marks on the tablecloth with his napkin ring.

His father's mouth had fallen open with astonishment. 'Where do they get it?' he demanded.

'Prescription,' said Uncle Willis lightly. 'Some crooked Polack doctor up there.'

'Oh, honestly,' cried his mother. 'I don't see how Louisa *stands* it.'

Aunt Emilie, who had been quiet until now, suddenly spoke. 'Oh, I don't know,' she said speculatively. 'They're both very good to her. I think Mr Gordon's very generous. *He* pays the rent on her apartment, you know, and gives her the use of the car and chauffeur most afternoons.'

'You don't know anything about it,' said Uncle Greg in a gruff, unpleasant voice which was meant to stop her from talking. But she went on, a bit shrilly, and even Donald could hear that they were in the habit of arguing.

'I *do* happen to know that Ivor's pefectly willing to give her a divorce any time she wants it, because she told me so herself.'

There was silence at the table; Donald was certain that if he had not been there they would all have begun to talk at that point. Aunt Emilie had said something he was not supposed to hear.

'Well,' said Uncle Willis heartily, 'how about another piece of cake, Donald, old man?'

'How about bed, you mean,' said his father. 'It's time he went to bed.'

His mother said nothing, helped him from his chair and took him upstairs.

The little panes of his bedroom window were completely covered with ice. Opening his mouth, he breathed on one pane until a round hole had been melted through and he could see the blackness outside. 'Don't do that, dear,' said his mother. 'Gramma'll have to clean the window. Now come on; into bed with you. There's a nice hot brick under the covers so your feet won't get cold.' She tucked the blankets around him, kissed him, and took the lamp from the table. His father's voice, annoyed, came up from the foot of the stairs. 'Hey, Laura! What's going on up there? Come on.'

'Won't there be any light in my room at all?' Donald asked her.

'I'm coming,' she called. She looked down at Donald. 'You never have a light at home.'

'I know, but home I can turn it on if I need it.'

'Well, you're not going to need it tonight. Your father would have a fit if I left the lamp. You know that. Now just go to sleep.'

'But I won't be able to sleep,' he said miserably.

'Laura!' shouted his father.

'Just a *minute*!' she cried, vexed.

'Please, Mother . . . ?'

Her voice was adamant. 'This cold air will put you to sleep in two shakes of a lamb's tail. Now go to sleep.' She went to the doorway, the lamp in her hand, and disappeared through it, closing the door behind her.

There was a little china clock on the table that ticked very loud and fast. At infrequent intervals from below came a muffled burst of laughter which immediately subsided. His mother had said: 'I'll open this window about an inch; that'll be enough.' The room was growing colder by the minute. He pushed the sole of one foot against the heated brick in the middle of the bed, and heard the crackle of the newspaper that enfolded it. There was nothing left to do but go to sleep. On his way through the borderlands of consciousness he had a fantasy. From the mountain behind the farm, running silently over the icy crust of the snow, leaping over the rocks and bushes, came a wolf. He was running towards the farm. When he got there he would look through the windows until he found the dining-room where the grown-ups were sitting around the big table. Donald shuddered when he saw his eyes in the dark through the glass. And now, calculating every movement perfectly, the wolf sprang, smashing the panes, and seized Donald's father by the throat. In an instant, before anyone could move or cry out, he was gone again with his prey still between his jaws, his head turned sideways as he dragged the limp form swiftly over the surface of the snow.

The white light of dawn was in the room when he opened his eyes. Already there were bumpings in the bowels of the house: people were stirring. He heard a window slammed shut, and then the regular sound of someone splitting wood with a hatchet. Presently there were nearer noises, and he knew that his parents in the next room had got up. Then his door was flung open and his mother came in, wearing a thick brown flannel bathrobe, and with her hair falling loose down her back. 'Merry Christmas!' she cried, holding up a gigantic red mesh stocking crammed with fruit and small packages. 'Look what I found hanging by the fireplace!' He was disappointed because he had hoped to go and get his stocking himself. 'I brought it up to you because the house is as cold as a barn,' she told him. 'You stay put right here in bed till it's warmed up a little.'

'When'll we have the tree?' The important ritual was the

tree: the most interesting presents were piled under it.

'You just hold your horses,' she told him. 'You've got your stocking. We can't have the tree till Aunt Louisa gets here. You wouldn't want her to miss it, would you?'

'Where's my present for Aunt Louisa and Uncle Ivor? Uncle Ivor's coming, too, isn't he?'

'Of course he's coming,' she replied, with that faintly different way of speaking she used when she mentioned Uncle Ivor. 'I've already put it under the tree with the other things. Now you just stay where you are, all covered up, and look at your stocking. I'm going to get dressed.' She shivered and hurried back into her room.

The only person he had to thank at breakfast was his grandfather, for a box of coloured pencils which had been jammed into the foot of the stocking. The other gifts had been tagged: 'For Donald from Santa.' Uncle Willis and Uncle Greg had eaten an early breakfast and gone in the sleigh to the hotel in Portersville to fetch Aunt Louisa and Uncle Ivor. When they got back, Donald ran to the window and saw that Mr Gordon had come. Everyone had talked so mysteriously about Mr Gordon that he was very eager to see him. But at that moment his mother called him upstairs to help her make the beds. 'We all have to do as much as we can for Gramma,' she told him. 'Lord knows she's got all she can manage with the kitchen work.'

But eventually he heard Aunt Louisa calling up the staircase. They went down: he was smothered in kisses, and Aunt Louisa asked him: 'How's my boy? You're *my* boy, aren't you?' Then Uncle Ivor kissed him, and he shook hands with Mr Gordon, who was already sitting in Grampa's armchair, where nobody else ever sat. He was plump and pale, and he wore two big diamond rings on one hand and an even bigger sapphire on the other. As he breathed he wheezed slightly; now and then he pulled an enormous yellow silk handkerchief out of his breast pocket and wiped his forehead with it. Donald sat down on the other side of the room and turned the pages of a magazine, from time to time looking up to observe him. He had called Donald 'my lad', which sounded very strange, like someone talking in a book. At one point he noticed Donald's attention, and beckoned to him. Donald went and stood beside the armchair while Mr Gordon reached into his pocket and pulled out a fat watch with a little button near the stem. 'Push it,' he said. Donald pushed the button, and tiny chimes struck inside the watch. A few minutes later he signalled to him afresh; Donald bounded over to him and pressed the button again. The next time, his mother told him to stop bothering Mr Gordon.

'But he *asked* me to,' objected Donald.

'Sit down right there. We're all going in and have our tree in a little while. Uncle Ivor's going to be Santa Claus.'

Presently Uncle Willis came into the room. 'Well, everybody,' he said, rubbing his hands together, 'I think the parlour's warm enough now. How about our tree?'

'It's about time,' said Aunt Emilie. She was wearing a red taffeta dress which Donald had heard his mother discussing with his father earlier. '*Most* inappropriate,' she had said. 'The girl doesn't seem to realize she's living on a farm.' Aunt Emilie reached down and took Donald's hand. 'Would you care to accompany me, sir?' she said. They walked into the parlour holding hands. The fire in the fireplace roared and crackled.

'Where's Ivor?' said Uncle Greg. 'Has everybody got a seat?'

'Here he is,' said Uncle Ivor, coming in from the hallway. He had put on an old red knitted skull-cap and a red dressing-gown, and he had a wreath of green fluted paper around his neck. 'This is all Santa Claus could find,' he announced.

Aunt Louisa began to laugh. 'Look at your Uncle Ivor,' she told Donald.

'I am,' said Donald. But he was really looking at the tree. It was a tall hemlock that reached to the ceiling, and underneath it was piled the most enormous assortment of packages he had ever seen.

'Look at that!' they all cried.

'What *do* you suppose is in them all?' said Aunt Louisa.

'I don't know,' he replied.

Uncle Ivor sat down on the floor as near the tree as he could get, and lifting up a large crate he passed it to Uncle

Greg, who stood in the middle of the room. 'Let's get this out of the way first,' he said. Then Uncle Greg intoned: 'To Donald from the Folks at Rutland.'

While Uncle Ivor went on passing out packages, Donald struggled with his box. He was vaguely aware of the little cries that were being uttered around him: 'How lovely! But it's too much!' 'Oh, you shouldn't have!' 'Why did you do it?' as the others opened their gifts, but he was too preoccupied to notice that most of the exclamations were being addressed to Mr Gordon, who sat in the window looking very pleased.

It was too good to believe: a fire-engine three feet long, with rubber tyres and a bell and a siren and three ladders that shot upward automatically when it stopped. Donald looked at it, and for a moment was almost frightened by the power he knew it had to change his world.

'Oh . . . isn't . . . that . . . lovely!' said his mother, her annoyance giving a sharp edge to each word. 'Louisa, why did you do it?' Donald glanced up quickly and saw Aunt Louisa indicate Mr Gordon with a jerk of her head, as if she were saying: 'Everything is his fault.'

His mother moved along the floor towards the crate and fished out the greeting-card. 'I want you to keep each card in with the present it came with,' she told Donald, 'because you'll have a lot of thank-you notes to write tomorrow, and you don't want to get them mixed up. But you can thank Aunt Louisa and Uncle Ivor right now.'

He hated to be told to thank a person in that person's presence, as though he were a baby. But he said the words bravely, facing Mr Gordon: 'Thank you so much for the beautiful fire-engine.'

'There's more there, my lad,' beamed Mr Gordon; the diamonds flashed in the sunlight.

Aunt Emilie was holding out her arm in front of her, loooking at her new wrist-watch. Grampa had put on a black silk dressing-gown and was smoking a cigar. He looked perfectly content as he turned to Mr Gordon and said: 'Well, you've spoiled us all.' But Donald's mother interpreted his phrase as a reproach, and added in explanation: 'We're not used to getting such *elaborate* gifts, Mr Gordon.'

Mr Gordon laughed, and turning to Donald, told him: 'You've barely started, my lad. Tell your Uncle Ivor to get on with it.'

Now it seemed as though nearly every package was for Donald. He opened them as fast as he could, and was freshly bewildered by the apparition of each new marvel. There were, of course, the handkerchiefs and books and mufflers from the family, but there was also a Swiss music-box with little metal records that could be changed; there were roller-skates, a large set of lead soldiers, a real accordion, and a toy village with a street-car system that ran on a battery. As Donald opened each package, the little cries of admiration made by his parents came closer to sounding like groans. Finally his father said, in a voice loud enough for Mr Gordon to hear him above the general conversation: 'It's bad business for one kid to get so much.'

Mr Gordon had heard him. 'You were young once yourself,' he said airily.

Aunt Emilie was trying on a fur jacket that Uncle Greg had given her. Her face was flushed with excitement; she had just planted a big kiss on Uncle Greg's cheek.

'The little Astor baby got five thousand dollars' worth of toys on its last birthday,' she said to Donald's father, running her hand back and forth along the fur.

Donald's father looked at her with narrowed eyes. 'That', he said, enunciating very clearly, 'is what might be called an *asinine* remark.'

Save for the crackling of the fire there was silence for a moment in the room. Those who had not heard knew that something had happened. Uncle Greg looked quickly at Donald's father, and then at Aunt Emilie. Maybe there would be a quarrel, thought Donald, with everyone against his father. The idea delighted him; at the same time he felt guilty, as though it were his doing.

Uncle Ivor was handing him a package. Automatically he untied the ribbon, and pulled out a tan cashmere sweater. 'That's Mother's and Daddy's present to you,' his mother said quietly. 'It's a little big for you now, but I got it big purposely so you could grow into it.' The small crisis had passed; they all began to talk again. Donald was relieved and disappointed. 'How about christening that bottle of brandy?' cried Uncle Willis.

'You menfolk sit here,' Gramma told them. 'We've got to get out into the kitchen.'

'I'll bring yours out to you,' said Uncle Ivor to Aunt Louisa as she got up.

On her way out of the room Donald's mother bent over and touched his shoulder. 'I want you to put every present back into its box just the way it was. After that you carry them all up into our room and stack them carefully in the corner under the window. You hear me?'

She went out. Donald sat a moment; then he jumped up and ran after her to ask if he might save out just one thing – the fire-engine, perhaps. She was saying to Gramma: '. . . quite uncalled-for. Besides, I don't know how we're *ever* going to get it all back to New York. Owen can take the big things at least with him tomorrow, I suppose.'

He stopped running, and felt peace descend upon him. His father was leaving the farm. Then let him take everything with him, fire-engine and all; it would not matter. He turned and went back into the parlour, where he meticulously packed the toys into their boxes, put the covers on, and tied them up with lengths of ribbon and string.

'What's all this?' exclaimed Mr Gordon suddenly, noticing him. 'What are you doing?'

'I have to take everything upstairs,' said Donald.

His father joined the conversation. 'I don't want to find those boxes lying all over the place up there, either. See that you pile 'em neatly. Understand?'

Donald continued to work without looking up.

After a moment Mr Gordon said under his breath: 'Well, I'll be damned.' Then to Donald's father: 'I've seen some well-behaved kids in my time, but I don't mind telling you I never saw one like *that*. Never.'

'Discipline begins in the cradle,' said his father shortly.

'It's sinister,' murmured Mr Gordon to himself.

Donald glanced up and saw his father looking at Mr Gordon with hatred.

In the kitchen his grandmother, his aunts and his mother were busy preparing dinner. Donald sat by the window mashing potatoes. The blue of the sky had disappeared behind one curtain of cloud, uniformly white. 'We'll have more snow before night,' said Gramma, looking out of the window above the sink.

'Want to smell something good?' Donald's mother asked him. He ran across to the stove and she opened the oven door: the aroma of onions mingled with that of the roasting turkey. 'He's coming along beautifully,' she announced. She shut the oven door with a bang and hung the pot-holders on their hooks. Then she went into the pantry. Donald followed her. It was very cold in here, and it smelt of pickles and spices. His mother was searching for something along the shelves, among the jars and tin boxes.

'Mother,' he said.

'Hmm?' she replied distraughtly, without looking down at him.

'Why does Mr Gordon live at Uncle Ivor's?'

Now she did look at him, and with an intensity that startled him. 'What was that?' she demanded sharply. Then, before he could repeat his question, she went on in a suddenly matter-of-fact voice: 'Dear, don't you know that Uncle Ivor's what they call a male nurse? Like Miss Oliver, you remember, who took care of you when you had influenza? Only a man. A man nurse.'

'Is Mr Gordon sick?'

'Yes, he is,' she said, lowering her voice to little more than a whisper. 'He's a very sick man, but we don't talk about it.'

'What's he got?' He was conscious of being purposely childish at the moment, in the hope of learning more. But his mother was already saying: 'I don't know, dear. You go back into the kitchen now. It's too cold for you in here. Scoot! Out with you!' He giggled, ran back into the kitchen, satisfied for having definitely established the existence of a mystery.

During dinner his father looked across at him and, with the particular kind of sternness he reserved for remarks which he knew were unwelcome, said: 'You haven't been outside yet today, young man. We'll take a walk down the road later.'

Aunt Louisa had brought a large glass of brandy to the table with her, and was sipping it along with her food. 'It's too cold, Owen,' she objected. 'He'll catch his death o' cold.' Donald knew she was trying to help him, but he wished she had kept quiet. If it became an issue, his father would certainly not forget about the walk.

'Too cold!' scoffed his father. 'We have a few basic rules in *our* family, and one of them is that he has to get some fresh air every day.'

'Couldn't you make an exception for Christmas? Just for one day?' demanded Aunt Louisa.

Donald did not dare look up, for fear of seeing the expression on his father's face.

'Listen, Louisa,' he said acidly. 'I suggest you just stay on your side of the fence, and I'll stay on mine. We'll get along a lot better.' Then as an afterthought he snapped: 'That all right with you?'

Aunt Louisa leaned across Grampa's plate towards Donald's father and spoke very loud, so that everyone stopped eating. 'No, it's not all right with me!' she cried. 'All you do is pick on the child from morning till night. It's shameful! I won't sit by and watch my own flesh and blood plagued that way!'

Both Gramma and Donald's father began to speak at once. Gramma was saying: 'Louisa,' trying to soothe her. Donald's father shouted: 'You've never *had* a kid. You don't know the first thing *about* raising kids.'

'I know when a man is selfish and plain cussed,' Aunt Louisa declared.

'Louisa!' cried Gramma in a tone of surprise and mild reproof. Donald continued to look at his plate.

'Have I ever come up to Rutland and stuck my nose in your affairs and criticized? Have I?' demanded Donald's father.

'Now come on,' said Uncle Willis quickly. 'Let's not spoil a beautiful Christmas.'

'That's right,' Grampa said. 'We're all happy. Let's not say anything we'll be sorry for later.'

But Aunt Louisa would not retreat. She took a fast gulp of brandy and almost choked on it. Then, still leaning towards Donald's father, she went on: 'What do you mean, come to Rutland and criticize? What've you got to criticize in Rutland? Something wrong there?'

For an instant Donald's father did not reply. During that instant it was as though everyone felt the need to say something without being able to say it. The one who broke the short silence was Donald's father, using a peculiar, soft voice which Donald recognized immediately as a vicious imitation of Uncle Ivor. 'Oh, *no*! There's nothing wrong in *Rut*land!'

Suddenly, with two simultaneous motions, Donald's mother slapped her napkin into her plate and pushed her chair back violently. She rose and ran out of the room, slamming the door. No one said anything. Donald sat frozen, unable to look up, unable even to breathe. Then he realized that his father had got up, too, and was on his way out.

'Leave her alone, Owen,' said Gramma.

'You keep out of this,' his father said. His footsteps made the stairs creak as he went up. No one said anything until Gramma made as if to rise. 'I'm going up,' she declared.

'For God's sake, Abbie, sit still,' Grampa told her. Gramma cleared her throat, but did not get up.

Aunt Louisa looked very red, and the muscles of her face were twitching. 'Hateful,' she said in a choked voice. 'Just hateful.'

'I felt like slapping his face,' confided Aunt Emilie. 'Did you hear what he said to me when we were having our presents?'

At a glance from Uncle Greg, Aunt Emilie stopped. 'Why, Donald,' she exclaimed brightly, 'you've scarcely touched your dinner! Aren't you hungry?'

In his mind's eye he was seeing the bedroom upstairs, where his father was twisting his mother's arm and shaking her to make her look at him. When she wouldn't, he punched her, knocking her down, and kicked her as hard as he could, all over her body. He looked up. 'Not very,' he said.

Without warning Mr Gordon began to talk, holding his glass in front of him and examining it as he turned it this way and that. 'Family quarrels,' he sighed. 'Same old thing. Reminds me of my boyhood. When I look back on it, it seems to me we never got through a meal without a fight, but I suppose we must have once in a while.' He set the glass down. 'Well, they're all dead now, thank God.'

Donald looked quickly across at Mr Gordon as if he were seeing him for the first time.

'It's snowing!' cried Gramma triumphantly. 'Look, it's snowing again. I knew we'd have more snow before dark.' She did not want Mr Gordon to go on talking.

Aunt Louisa sobbed once, got up, and went out into the kitchen. Uncle Ivor followed her.

'Why, Donald! You've got the wishbone!' cried Aunt Emilie. 'Eat the meat off it and we'll hang it up over the stove to dry, and tomorrow we'll wish on it. Wouldn't that be fun?'

He picked it up in his fingers and began to chew on the strips of white meat that clung to it. When he had carefully cleaned it, he got down and went out into the kitchen with it.

The room was very quiet; the tea-kettle simmered on the stove. Outside the window the falling snowflakes looked dark against the whiteness beyond. Aunt Louisa was sitting on the high stool, doubled over, with a crumpled handkerchief in her hand, and Uncle Ivor was bending over her talking in a very low voice. Donald laid the wishbone on the sink shelf and started to tiptoe out, but Uncle Ivor saw him. 'How'd you like to go up to the henhouse with me, Donald?' he said. 'I've got to find us a dozen eggs to take back to Rutland.'

'I'll get my coat,' Donald told him, eager to go out before his father came back downstairs.

The path up the hill to the henhouse had been made not by clearing the snow away, but by tramping it down. The new snow was drifting over the track; in some places it already had covered it. When Uncle Ivor went into the henhouse Donald stood still, bending his head back to catch some snowflakes in his mouth. 'Come on in and shut the door. You'll let all the heat out,' Uncle Ivor told him.

'I'm coming,' said Donald. He stepped through the

doorway and closed the door. The smell inside was very strong. As Uncle Ivor approached the hens, they set up a low, distrustful murmur.

'Tell me, Donald,' said Uncle Ivor as he explored the straw with his hands.

'What?' said Donald.

'Does your mother often run to her room and shut the door, the way she did just now?'

'Sometimes.'

'Why? Is your father mean to her?'

'Oh,' said Donald vaguely, 'they have fights.' He felt uncomfortable.

'Yes. Well, it's a great pity your father ever got married. It would have been better for everybody if he'd stayed single.'

'But then I wouldn't have been born at all,' cried Donald, uncertain whether Uncle Ivor was serious or not.

'At least, we *hope* not!' said Uncle Ivor, rolling his eyes and looking silly. Now Donald knew it was a kind of joke, and he laughed. The door was flung open. 'Donald!' roared his father.

'What is it?' he said, his voice very feeble.

'Come out here!'

He stumbled towards the door; his father was peering inside uncertainly. 'What are you doing in there?' he demanded.

'Helping Uncle Ivor look for eggs.'

'Hmph!' Donald stepped out and his father shut the door.

They started to walk along the road in the direction of the Smithson farm. Presently his father fell in behind him and prodded him the back, saying: 'Keep your head up. Chest out! D'you want to get round-shouldered? Before you know it you'll have curvature of the spine.'

When they had got out of sight of the house, in a place where the tangle of small trees came to the edge of the road on both sides, his father stopped walking. He looked around, reached down, picked up a handful of the new snow, and rolled it into a hard ball. Then he threw it at a fairly large tree, some distance from the road. It broke, leaving a white mark on the dark trunk. 'Let's see you hit it,' he told Donald.

A wolf could be waiting here, somewhere back in the still gloom of the woods. It was very important not to make him angry. If his father wanted to take a chance and throw snowballs into the woods, he could, but Donald would not. Then perhaps the wolf would understand that he, at least, was his friend.

'Go on,' said his father.

'No, I don't want to.'

With mock astonishment his father said: 'Oh, you don't?' Then his face became dangerous and his voice cracked like a whip. 'Are you going to do what I told you?'

'No.' It was the first time he had openly defied him. His father turned very red.

'Listen here, you young whippersnapper!' he cried, his voice tight with anger. 'You think you're going to get away with this?' Before Donald knew what was happening, his father had seized him with one hand while he bent over and with the other scooped up as much snow as he could. 'We'll settle this little matter right now,' he said through his teeth. Suddenly he was rubbing the snow violently over Donald's face, and at the same time that Donald gasped and squirmed, he pushed what was left of it down his neck. As he felt the wet, icy mass sliding down his back, he doubled over. His eyes were squeezed shut; he was certain his father was trying to kill him. With a desperate lunge he bounded free and fell face downward into the snow.

'Get up,' his father said disgustedly. He did not move. If he held his breath long enough he might die.

His father yanked him to his feet. 'I've had just about enough of your monkeyshines,' he said. Clutching him tightly with both hands, he forced him to hobble ahead of him, back through the twilight to the house.

Donald moved forward, looking at the white road in front of him, his mind empty of thoughts. An unfamiliar feeling had come to him: he was not sorry for himself for being wet and cold, or even resentful at having been mistreated. He felt detached; it was an agreeable, almost voluptuous sensation which he accepted without understanding or questioning it.

As they advanced down the long alley of maple trees in

the dusk his father said: 'Now you can go and cry in your mother's lap.'

'I'm not crying,' said Donald loudly, without expression. His father did not answer.

Fortunately the kitchen was empty. He could tell from the sound of the voices in the parlour that Aunt Louisa, Uncle Ivor and Mr Gordon were getting ready to leave. He ran upstairs to his room and changed his clothes completely. The hole he had breathed in the ice on the window-pane had frozen over thickly again, but the round mark was still visible. As he finished dressing his mother called him. It was completely dark outside. He went downstairs. She was standing in the hallway.

'Oh, you've changed your clothes,' she said. 'Come out and say goodbye to Aunt Louisa and Uncle Ivor. They're in the kitchen.' He looked quickly at her face to see if there were signs of her recent tears: her eyes were slightly bloodshot.

Together they went into the kitchen. 'Donald wants to say goodbye to you,' she told Mr Gordon, steering Donald to Aunt Louisa. 'You've given him a wonderful Christmas' – her voice became reproachful – 'but it was *much* too much.'

The thick beaver collar of Mr Gordon's overcoat was turned up over his ears, and he had on enormous fur gloves. He smiled and clapped his hands together expectantly; it made a cushioned sound. 'Oh, it was a lot of fun,' he said. 'He reminds me a little of myself, you know, when I was his age. I was a sort of shy and quiet lad, too.' Donald felt his mother's hand tighten on his shoulder as she pushed him towards Aunt Louisa. 'Mm,' she said. 'Well, Auntie Louisa, here's somebody who wants to say goodbye to you.'

Even in the excitement of watching Uncle Willis and Uncle Greg drive the others off in the sleigh, Donald did not miss the fact that his father had not appeared in the kitchen at all. When the sleigh had moved out of sight down the dark road, everyone went into the parlour and Grampa put another log on the fire.

'Where's Owen?' Gramma said in a low voice to Donald's mother.

He must be upstairs. To tell the truth, I don't care very much where he is.'

'Poor child,' said Gramma. 'Headache a little better?'

'A little.' She sighed. 'He certainly managed to take all the pleasure out of *my* Christmas.'

'A mean shame,' said Gramma.

'It was all I could do to look Ivor in the face just now. I mean it.'

'I'm sure they all understood,' said Gramma soothingly. 'Just don't you fret about it. Anyway, Owen'll be gone tomorrow, and you can rest up.'

Shortly after Uncle Willis and Uncle Greg got back, Donald's father came downstairs. Supper was eaten in almost complete silence; at no time did his father speak to him or pay him any attention. As soon as the meal was over his mother took him upstairs to bed.

When she had left him, he lay in the dark listening to the sound of the fine snow as the wind drove it against the panes. The wolf was out there in the night, running along paths that no one had ever seen, down the hill and across the meadow, stopping to drink at a deep place in the brook where the ice had not formed. The stiff hairs of his coat had caught the snow; he shook himself and climbed up the bank to where Donald sat waiting for him. Then he lay down beside him, putting his heavy head in Donald's lap. Donald leaned over and buried his face in the shaggy fur of his scruff. After a while they both got up and began to run together, faster and faster, across the fields.

Sylvie Ann, the Boogie Man

Sylvie Ann woke up early. There was a sweet smell in the air. It wasn't flowers, because nobody had much room to plant flowers there in that neighbourhood where she lived, by the railroad tracks. It was the special smell of dirt, the way black dirt smells some early mornings in May, even better than roses or lilacs. She flexed her toes back and forth several times, and suddenly remembered that today was her birthday. Yesterday she had been forty-nine, but today she was fifty. Then she thought of something bad. She saw the white children playing in the empty lot next door to Mrs Hofstetter's, where she worked on Mondays, and heard their sharp hateful voices singing: 'Sylvie Ann, the boogie man.' And that mean little Jason had squealed: 'She's a hundred and ten.' Remembering it, she snorted and turned over.

The bed was much too short for her to lie out straight in, but she was proud of being six feet one, and although she knew that was part of the reason why people laughed – her own people behind her back and the white people practically in her face – she was never sorry to be so tall. Sometimes she said to the Lord: 'And thank you for make me like I am. If ever I tell you different, don't you pay me no mind.'

She washed clothes for three ladies who lived on the hill: Mrs Fairchild, Mrs Lauder and Mrs MacElroy. She had two other ladies as well, but they lived downtown and paid her less. Best of all she liked going to Mrs Lauder's because it was the cleanest house. At least, the cellar and the back part of the house were; she hadn't seen the rest of it, but she was sure it was the cleanest. When Mrs Lauder's maid set the table for Sylvie Ann in the breakfast nook, she used the same doilies and dishes that they used in the dining-room, and Mrs Lauder herself usually came out to ask her if she wanted a second helping of food. She didn't accept it very often, but she liked being asked.

Mrs Lauder was the only one of the three ladies on the hill who hadn't laughed when Sylvie Ann had first carried her umbrella out with her to hang up clothes. Mrs MacElroy had said: 'But Sylvie Ann, it's not raining. Look, the sun's out.' And when Sylvie Ann had explained that the sun was bad for her skin, Mrs MacElroy had laughed so hard that she'd had to cover her face with her apron. And later Sylvie Ann had heard her telling the lady next door: 'You'll die. She's afraid of getting sunburned. Isn't it rich?' She had felt like calling out from under the clothes-line where she was and telling Mrs MacElroy that sunburn was just as painful if you had dark skin as it was if you had white skin, but then she thought that if Mrs MacElroy was all that ignorant, she would be the sort of lady who would just laugh in her face and the next minute get angry and tell her she'd better not bother to come back to work any more if she was going to be so fresh. Then there would be only two ladies on the hill, and she would have to take on somebody else who lived downtown, like Mrs Hofstetter. This she did not want at all, because it had taken her four years to get these three regular places on the hill.

The first thing Sylvie Ann did each morning when she got up was to pour a pail of cold water over her head and scrub herself hard with Ivory soap and a brush. Today, as she stood there shivering and rubbing her long thin legs, she thought: 'Fifty years old and stronger than Mrs Lauder.' Then she thought how lucky it was that going to Mrs Lauder's came on the same day as her birthday this year. It was almost like a sort of celebration. As she ate her breakfast she debated with herself as to whether she ought to tell Mrs Lauder about her birthday. She wanted to, because fifty somehow seemed an important number, but it would be awful if Mrs Lauder thought she was fishing for a present. Last year she had mentioned her birthday a week or so later, and Mrs Lauder had said: 'Why didn't you tell me sooner?'

By quarter-past seven, when she started out to walk up to Mrs Lauder's, some of the morning's sweet smell had gone because there were cars in the streets. The sun was already quite hot, and Sylvie Ann was glad she had brought her umbrella because she would need it later.

At the stationer's opposite the lumber-yard she stopped to buy a box of menthol cough-drops. He opened early because people in this neighbourhood got up early. 'Thank you kindly, Mr Schwartzman,' she said, snapping her change purse shut and hoping she could get out before he asked her the same stupid question he nearly always asked her. But as she pushed against the screen door he said it. 'So you still ain't got a boy-friend yet?'

'Mr Schwartzman,' she said distinctly, 'you know I got no boy-friend. What I want a boy-friend for anyway? I got more important things on my mind than such foolishness.' She stepped outside, taking care not to let the door slam, so Mr Schwartzman wouldn't think she was really cross with him.

The clock over the bandstand in the park was supposed to say twenty minutes to eight when she passed it. It did, and that meant that she would arrive at Mrs Lauder's exactly at eight. It was a good idea to get there on time, since if she was even ten minutes late Mrs Lauder, who was always sitting in the breakfast nook and couldn't fail to see her come up the back steps into the kitchen, would greet her by exclaiming: 'Mercy, Sylvie Ann, you're late! What happened to you?' Then she would sit back with such an air of concentration that Sylvie Ann felt she had to tell her something, had to give her some good reason why she hadn't arrived at eight sharp. She hated this because at such moments it seemed to her that Mrs Lauder looked as though she were only pretending to believe her, as though she knew that Sylvie Ann couldn't tell the truth even if she tried, so that Sylvie Ann, who ordinarily told things exactly as they had happened, found herself seizing on details of her walk across the town and transforming them into little incidents which had somehow held her up and kept her from getting there on time. The trouble was that she liked Mrs Lauder, and since Mrs Lauder so clearly expected explanations, she felt she had to provide them for her. It was certainly better to be on time.

Today when she got to the house she could see it was a special day. The upstairs windows were open and Ingrid was hanging the small rugs out across the sills. Several larger rugs lay on the back lawn, where Whiskers d'Alessio, an Italian boy who mowed the lawn and did other outside jobs, was beating them hard with a rug-beater. Whiskers joked too much; there was joking in his eyes now as he called: 'Hi, Sylvie Ann!' She nodded her head at him. 'Hello, how you this morning?' she said. Then she went quickly into the kitchen without giving him a chance to say anything else.

Mrs Lauder was in the breakfast nook as usual. Dr Lauder had finished his breakfast and gone; there were cigarette ashes in the saucer under his coffee-cup. 'Good morning, Sylvie Ann,' said Mrs Lauder, rising. 'I was just wondering if you were going to get here on time.'

'Morning, Mrs Lauder,' said Sylvie Ann, and she added: 'It's just eight o'clock now', in case Mrs Lauder thought she was late. But Mrs Lauder paid no attention. 'We're busy as bees this morning,' she said. 'I've got my club ladies coming for luncheon and I want to get all the sheets and bigger things dry and inside before they get here. There's a glorious sun and they'll dry fast.' If Mrs Lauder used the word *luncheon*, it meant automatically that there were going to be guests; otherwise she said *lunch* like everybody else.

Sylvie Ann saw her eyes straying as usual to the umbrella under her arm, but she knew she would never say anything about it because it was natural for Mrs Lauder to be the sort of lady who minded her own business. 'Mrs Lauder is the nicest lady I got,' Sylvie Ann would tell her friends, sometimes adding, if she felt happier than usual: 'The prettiest, too, I declare.' Mrs Lauder's hair was beginning to turn silver, and it made her china-blue eyes even brighter and her cheeks pinker. To Sylvie Ann she looked rather like a grown-up doll. Her niceness wasn't exactly the sort that gave Sylvie Ann an easy feeling, but then, in her life she had met very few white people who could give her that feeling, and it had always been on buses or in stores or just walking in the street, and she never saw them again after they had been easy and pleasant just for a few seconds, so that she wondered whether, if somehow she'd got to know them, their niceness wouldn't have turned out to be of the same stiff and unsure kind as Mrs Lauder's. But Mrs Lauder did mean well. There was only one small trouble with her, and that was that she was fussy. She was the only lady Sylvie Ann had who always went into the laundry with her and showed her exactly what she wanted done with everything – which pieces had to be washed first and with which kind of soap, and how hot the water ought to be for each separate pile of things. She even went outside with her to show her just where she wanted the laundry hung. And of course everything had to be done by hand; she would not have a washing-machine in the house. It was true that if Sylvie Ann did exactly what she was told, Mrs Lauder never found fault the way the other ladies so often did, but Sylvie Ann couldn't help wishing she would leave her alone. 'I know my washing,' she would say when her sister came to visit her. 'Why can't she just leave me be? Seem like almost she don't trust me.'

'It's the truth. That's the way they are,' said her sister.

'She's one mighty fine lady, though,' Sylvie Ann would always be sure to add.

Mrs Lauder brushed some toast crumbs from the table into her hand and dropped them on to a plate. 'Well,' she said heartily, 'let's go down and start our day.' She led the way towards the cellar stairs. Half-way through the kitchen she hesitated an instant, then continued walking. As they came to the door into the butler's pantry, she turned and said to Sylvie Ann: 'Would you like to see something beautiful, Sylvie Ann?'

Sylvie Ann opened her mouth to say 'Yes, Mrs Lauder,' but Mrs Lauder did not give her the chance. 'Come in here a minute and I'll show you,' she said impulsively, and she pushed open the swing door. On the shelf was a big leather chest with drawers in it. Some of the drawers were open. They were lined with purple satin, and they held rows of spoons, and fancy knives and forks, some with mother-of-pearl handles.

'Isn't it lovely?' Mrs Lauder murmured, and her voice sounded strange. Sylvie Ann glanced swiftly at her to see if she might be going to cry, for it sounded like it, but she wasn't.

'Sure is pretty,' Sylvie Ann agreed. Mrs Lauder's manner made her uneasy.

'You remember at Easter time I told you Dr Lauder's mother had passed away. All this beautiful silver was hers. Some of it dates back to Revolutionary times. Long, long ago.' Mrs Lauder's voice was still trembling.

'They got one like this at Kaminsky's,' said Sylvie Ann. 'Sure is mighty pretty, Mrs Lauder.'

Suddenly Mrs Lauder laughed. Sylvie Ann was startled and shocked. It was as though someone had tittered in front of the coffin at funeral.

'Oh, no, Sylvie Ann!' she exclaimed, smiling. 'This is priceless old silver! Sterling. Pure silver. And some of the spoons, these darker ones, are what they call coin silver. They used to melt the money down and make it into spoons. You couldn't buy these anywhere in town.'

Sylvie Ann's umbrella slid to the floor. She stooped and picked it up. 'Oh yes, Mrs Lauder,' she said earnestly. 'They got the same thing at Kaminsky's now. The big box with the drawers in and everything, same thing.' She had seen it in the show window only last week, and had stood admiring it a full five minutes.

'Sylvie Ann, don't be silly,' said Mrs Lauder reproachfully, and her voice sounded almost angry. 'They *couldn't* have anything *like* this at Kaminsky's. It's a hardware store, in the first place.' She seemed about to say more, then smiled and waited a second. 'Maybe it *looked* like this,' she added comfortingly. She sighed and turned towards the door. '*We've* got to get busy.'

Throughout the morning, as Sylvie Ann washed, her mind dwelt on the little scene, and she grew increasingly indignant. 'Make liar out of *me*,' she said under her breath, her movements giving rhythm to the words. 'So high and mighty with her knives and forks. Think she got something nobody got.' If any other one of her ladies had done this to her she wouldn't have minded so much, but with Mrs Lauder it was a serious betrayal of friendship. By noon the little phrase 'They all alike' had crept into her monologue. When Ingrid appeared and told her lunch was ready, she stood up straight, and mopping her face with a soiled dish-towel, sighed: 'It's God's truth.'

She sat in the breakfast nook, looking out at the lawn where under the pergola Mrs Lauder and Ingrid had set the table for the luncheon. There was a big bowl of white roses in the centre, and the tablecloth was striped black and white. Like the men on the chain-gang back home, she thought scornfully, stabbing the yolk of the poached egg that crowned her pile of hash. 'So high and mighty.' The sound of her own whispered words still echoed in the cellar of her mind.

When she was nearly finished, she heard Mrs Lauder come into the kitchen and say, a little breathlessly: 'Ingrid, can you fasten these hooks for me? I seem to be a real butterfingers today.' Presently she inquired: 'Is Sylvie Ann all provided for?' and an instant later she appeared in the breakfast nook carrying a cup and saucer, all dressed up and smelling very strongly of perfume.

'Here's your tea, Sylvie Ann. I know you like two slices of lemon. Are you getting on all right?' She set the cup and saucer down.

'Thank you, Mrs Lauder,' said Sylvie Ann.

'You eat about as much as a bird, Sylvie Ann,' Mrs Lauder told her. 'Just about as much as a canary.' This was what she always said when she came in and saw Sylvie Ann having her lunch. Sylvie Ann didn't reply.

More as if she were thinking out loud in front of Sylvie Ann than really talking to her, Mrs Lauder went on: 'I'm afraid I haven't done very much in the way of making things festive. I'm just not very good at giving parties, I guess. You should see some of the other ladies' tables when they give a luncheon party. Some of them are simply lovely.' She glanced out of the window at her own table under the wistaria vines. Sylvie Ann knew she wanted her to say how pretty it looked, but she sipped her tea and said nothing. She was being mean to Mrs Lauder, and that was what she wanted.

'Two of my club ladies have birthdays this week, so this is sort of a double birthday luncheon for them. Ingrid's made a perfectly beautiful cake. I'll see that you get a piece before you go home.'

Sylvie Ann set her cup down, and before she could stop herself she had said: 'Today's *my* birthday.' She hadn't wanted to say anything about it, but it was too late now.

'It *is*?' cried Mrs Lauder. 'Why, Sylvie Ann, you should have told me!'

Sylvie Ann could feel her heart beating fast and hard, and the doctor had told her she must not let herself get excited. The only thing to do was to get the whole thing over with as quickly as possible.

'I'm fifty,' she said, marvelling at the sound of the word. It was the first time she had said it aloud, and she was glad she had, because it made her feel in some way different, and calmed the pounding of her heart a little.

'You're fifty?' Mrs Lauder echoed unbelievingly, but also in a voice that sounded really interested, as though she had only now begun to pay attention and take part in the conversation, and Sylvie Ann thought fleetingly: She's fifty herself, that's why.

'Yes, Mrs Lauder, that's right.' Affirming this made her feel so much better that she added: 'You didn't know I was all that old, did you?'

Mrs Lauder hesitated. 'To tell the truth, I didn't,' she told her. 'I guess I just never thought about it.' She paused again, and then said: 'Well, well! Anyway, many happy returns of the day.'

At half-past three Ingrid came into the laundry with a glass of iced grape-juice and four thin cookies which she set on the table by the ironing-board without saying anything. Sylvie Ann knew Mrs Lauder had sent it down because today was her birthday, and for some reason this made her mad all over again.

The ladies in the garden had been talking and laughing

almost continuously ever since they had arrived; she wondered vaguely what they were talking about, but the laundry windows were too far away to let her hear. Each time she looked over at the tall glass with the beads of moisture coming out all over it, she felt resentful, and she slammed the iron down hard on the board. 'I'm not going to drink it,' she said to herself, and after a while she felt she couldn't have drunk it if her life had depended on it. When she finished the pyjamas she was ironing she took the cold glass in her hand and leaning over one of the' wash-tubs poured the grape-juice directly into the drain hole, looking guiltily over her shoulder as it ran down the pipe. She laid the cookies in a row along the window-sill above the tubs, and then she resumed her work, feeling somehow sad and disconnected from the bright afternoon.

Sylvie Ann always worked fast; today she seemed to be working faster than usual. Ordinarily when half-past four came there was still a good-sized pile of laundry to be ironed. Mrs Lauder would come down and show her just which pieces she wanted her to finish before she went at five, and which ones could be left for Ingrid, who had been known to scorch things and thus couldn't be trusted with anything 'good'. Perhaps today there had been less laundry than usual; in any case, at quarter to five Sylvie Ann had finished every last piece. She unplugged the iron from the overhead socket, unwrapped the bath-towel from around her head, and put on her hat. Then quietly she closed the windows, which were so high up that even she had to stand on tiptoe to do it. One of the cookies fell off the window-sill on to the floor behind a wash-tub. She left it there in the dark. The club ladies had already gone, and Dr Lauder stood by the messy table under the pergola talking to Mrs Lauder, who was hidden by the wistaria vine. When Sylvie Ann had locked both windows, she took her umbrella off the hook on the wall, and went upstairs to the clothes closet to get her coat, hoping that Ingrid would have put her money out for her on the kitchen table.

The window looking out on to the lawn here was the nearest one to the pergola; as she slipped her coat on she heard Mrs Lauder say: 'I'd have given her some little thing, but she only told me at lunch.'

Dr Lauder snickered. 'Like a compact full of stove polish?' he suggested. Sylvie Ann stood absolutely still, not breathing.

'Charles, for heaven's *sake*!' cried Mrs Lauder in an agitated voice. 'She's still here. I *told* you she hadn't gone yet.'

Neither one of them said anything for a moment. Sylvie Ann went on standing like a statue, listening. The closet smelled of naphthalene. Then Mrs Lauder continued in a very low but perfectly audible voice: 'She said she was fifty. How *could* she be, Charles? She must be older than that.'

'I hope you don't think she really knows her age,' replied Dr Lauder. 'They never do, that type, I mean. I bet she's got no idea how old she is.'

'How old would you guess?'

'How should I know? It's almost impossible to tell. She looks older than God.'

'You know, I was thinking, Charles, how nice it would be if you'd just drive her home for once.'

'You mean now? Have a heart, woman!' he protested. 'I've had a full day.'

'She'd appreciate it so much,' said Mrs Lauder. 'It'd give the poor old soul such pleasure, and it *is* her birthday, Charles.'

When Dr Lauder did not reply, Sylvie Ann's eyes grew large, for she was certain he had consented, and she knew she was not going to get into his car no matter what happened. Mrs Lauder's next words confirmed her fears. 'Stop in at Bohm's on the way back and get me a pound of peanut brittle, will you, dear? I feel like crunching on something.'

Sylvie Ann flung the door open and rushed into the kitchen, where Ingrid stood amazed by the sink. She had to get through the back door and down the steps before Dr Lauder started in, or she was lost. 'Oh, dear Jesus,' she moaned as she got to the door, for she saw him on his way across the lawn. She clattered down the steps and around the corner of the house without looking up again. She was aware of cries of 'Sylvie Ann!' and 'What's the matter?' in the air around her, and she felt that Dr and Mrs Lauder were very near her and might reach out and touch her, but somehow she got away from the house and into the street. Even then she kept running, taking great long steps like a sprinter. Her umbrella had fallen from under her arm, but she did not look back.

She was half-way down Union Street before the car, with Dr and Mrs Lauder in the front seat, drew up a little distance in front of her. She saw them out of the corner of her eye, and kept running, although she knew it was hopeless.

'Sylvie Ann!' called Mrs Lauder, leaning out of the car window. 'What is it? What on earth's the matter? Sylvie Ann!'

Sylvie Ann stopped and leaned against a tree for support. Her heart felt as though it would explode. She did not look at the Lauders.

Mrs Lauder opened her door without getting down. 'What happened, Sylvie Ann?' she cried, and waited.

When the breath had come back to Sylvie Ann's chest, she began to cough. Then, between coughs, she said without looking away from the ground: 'I'm not coming back to work for you no more, Mrs Lauder.'

'Oh, now, Sylvie Ann,' began Mrs Lauder, but she couldn't think of what to say after that.

'No, *ma'am*!' Sylvie Ann told her.

'Now, Sylvie Ann,' Mrs Lauder said more gently, 'why don't you just get in the car and we'll talk it over. I've got your umbrella here. You dropped it in the driveway. And I haven't even paid you for the day, you know. Come on, get in.' She reached around and opened the rear door for Sylvie Ann.

'If you want pay me and give me my umbrella, here I am,' said Sylvie Ann. 'I'm not going to get in. Other people got fancy knives too, you know. You not the only one.'

'Fancy what?' demanded Dr Lauder of his wife.

'I think she said knives,' she answered, and her voice sounded innocent, as if she didn't know what Sylvie Ann was talking about.

Now Dr Lauder called out the window loudly: 'Come around this side, Sylvie Ann.' It was a command. He held

her money out of the window and waved it in the air.
Sylvie Ann walked unevenly to within reach and took it
out of his hand. Then he thrust the umbrella out to her,
and she took that. 'Shut the door,' he told Mrs Lauder. She
did.

'I don't understand, Sylvie Ann,' said Mrs Lauder sadly,
leaning out again. 'We've always got on so well together.'

'Let her go, let her go for *God's sake!*' Dr Lauder cried.
'Can't you see she's . . .' He lowered his voice and muttered
something to his wife, and the car started ahead slowly.

Mrs Lauder leaned far out and looked back at Sylvie Ann
as they moved away. 'Well, you think it over and see how
you feel next week,' she called. 'I hope you'll change your
mind.' Then Dr Lauder turned his face towards Mrs Lauder
and began to talk angrily with her, and they drove away.

Sylvie Ann returned to the tree and stood against it for
a while, resting. Finally she started to walk again, not very
fast. It was half-past six by the time she got home.

The evening was so warm that she decided to sit out on
the front stoop a while before she went in to get supper.
There was one star in the still light sky, and when the sky
got dark, that one was brighter than the rest. She sat there
much longer than she'd intended, until that star and many
others had sunk out of sight. At first she was not aware
that the bright one was gone, and mistook others for it,
but when she realized it had disappeared, she stood up,
carried her chair inside, and shut the door.

Monologue, Tangier 1975

I first met her just after she'd bought the big villa overlooking
the valley Saudis have it now they've got most of the good
properties I remember she asked Anton and me to tea we
hadn't been married very long then she seemed very much
interested in him she'd seen him dance years ago in Paris
before his accident and they talked about those days it was
all very correct she had delicious petits fours strange how
that impressed itself on my mind of course at that time you
must remember we were frightfully poor living on the
cheapest sort of food fortunately Anton was a fantastic cook
or we should have starved he knew how to make a meal
out of nothing at all I assure you well it wasn't a fortnight
later that she invited us to lunch terribly formal a large staff
everything perfect and afterward I remember we were
having coffee and liqueurs beside the fireplace and she
suddenly offered us this little house she had on the property
there were several extra cottages hidden around you know
guest-houses but most of them were up above nearer the
big house this one was way down in the woods far from
everything except a duck pond I was absolutely stunned it
was the last thing I should have expected of her then she
took us down to see it very simple but charming tastefully
furnished and a rather primitive kitchen and bath but there
were heaps of flowers growing outside and lovely views
from the windows we were enchanted of course you
understand there was nothing to pay we were simply given
the use of the house for as long as we wished I admit it
was a very kind gesture for her to make although at the
time I suspected that she had her eye on Anton I was quite

wrong as it happened in any case having the house made
an enormous difference to us it was a gift from the gods
there was as a matter of fact one drawback for me Anton
didn't seem to mind them but there were at least twenty
peacocks in an enormous aviary in the woods not far away
and some nights they'd scream you know how hair-raising
the sound is especially in the middle of the night it took
me weeks to get used to it lying there in the dark listening
to those insane screams eventually I was able to sleep
through it well once we'd moved in our hostess never came
near us which was her privilege naturally but it did seem a
bit peculiar at least she wasn't after Anton the months went
by and we never caught sight of her you see we had a key
to the gate at the bottom of the estate so we always used
the lower road to come and go it was much easier than
climbing up past the big house so of course in order for us
to see her she'd have had to come down to our part of the
property but she never ventured near us time went on then
all at once we began to hear from various directions a
strange rumour that whenever she spoke of us she referred
to us as her squatters I was all for going up and having it
out with her on the spot is that why you invited us here
so you could ridicule us wherever you go but Anton said
I'd got no proof it could simply be the typical sort of
malicious gossip that seems to be everywhere in this place
he said to wait until I heard it with my own ears well clearly
she wasn't likely to say it in front of me then one morning
I went to take a little walk in the woods and what should
I see but several freshly painted signs that had been put up
along the paths all saying DEFENSE DE TOUCHER AUX FLEURS
obviously they'd been put there for us there was no one
else isn't it extraordinary the way people's minds work we
didn't want her beastly flowers we'd never touched them I
don't like cut flowers I much prefer to see them growing
Anton said best pay no attention if we have words she'll
put us out and he was right of course but it was very hard
to take at all events you know she had lovers always natives
of course what can one expect that's all right I'm not so
narrow-minded I'd begrudge her that dubious pleasure but
there are ways and ways of doing things you'd expect a

woman of her age and breeding to have a certain amount
of discretion that is she'd make everything as unnoticeable
as possible but no not at all in the first place she allowed
them to live with her quite as if they were man and wife
and that gave them command over the servants which is
unthinkable but worse she positively flourished those
wretched lovers of hers in the face of the entire town never
went out without the current incumbent if people didn't
include him she didn't accept the invitation she was the
sort of woman one couldn't imagine ever having felt
embarrassment but she could have managed to live here
without alienating half the Europeans you know in those
days people felt strongly about such things natives couldn't
even enter the restaurants it wasn't that she had lovers or
even that her lovers were natives but that she appeared with
them in public that was a slap in the face for the European
colony and they didn't forgive it but she couldn't be bothered
to care what anybody felt what I'm leading up to is the
party we never caught a glimpse of her from one month to
the next you understand and suddenly one day she came to
call on us friendly as you please she said she had a favour
to ask of us she was giving this enormous party she'd sent
out two hundred invitations that had to be surrendered at
the gate she said there were always too many gate-crashers
at her parties the tourists would pay the guides to get them
in and this time nobody was to get in excepting the ones
she'd invited what she wanted us to do was to stand in a
booth she'd built just outside the gate it had a little window
and a counter Anton was to examine the invitations and
give a sign to one of the policemen stationed outside to
admit the holder I had a big ledger with all the names
alphabetically listed and as Anton passed me the invitation
I was to make a red check opposite the name she wanted
to be sure later who had come and who hadn't I've got ten
servants she said and not one of them can read or write it's
discouraging then I thought of you and decided to ask this
great favour of you is everything all right in your little
house do you enjoy living here so of course we said oh yes
everything is lovely we'd be glad to help you what fools
we were it won't take long she said two hours at most it's

a costume party drinks dinner and dancing by moonlight in the lower garden the musicians begin to play at half-past seven after she'd gone I said to Anton two hundred invitations indeed she hasn't got twenty friends in this entire city well the night of the party came and we were up there in our little sentry-box working like coolies the sweat was pouring down my back sometimes a dozen people came all together half of them already drunk and they didn't at all like having to wait and be admitted one at a time they kept arriving on and on I thought they'd never stop coming at midnight we were still there finally I told Anton this is too much I don't care who comes I'm not going to stand here another minute and Anton said you're right and he spoke to the guard and said that's it no more people are coming don't let anybody else in and good night and so on and we went down to where the party was the costumes were very elaborate we stood for a few minutes at the end of the garden watching them dancing suddenly a tall man in robes with a false beard and a big turban came up to us I had no idea who he was but Anton claimed he recognized him at once anyway it was her lover if you please she'd sent him to tell us that if we were going to come to the party would we please go and put on our costumes as if we had any costumes to put on I was staggered after getting us to stand for almost five hours in a suffocating little box she has the infernal gall to ask us to leave yes and not even the common courtesy to come and speak to us herself no she sends her native lover to do it I was starved there was plenty of food on the buffet but it was a hundred feet away from us at the other end of the garden when we got back down to our house I told Anton I hate that woman I know it's wrong but I really hate her to make things worse the next day she came down to see us again not as you might think to thank us far from that on the contrary she'd come to complain that we'd let in people who had no invitations what do you mean I cried look at the cards and look at the book they tally what are you talking about and she said the Duchesse de Saint Somethingorother was missing her evening bag where she'd put her emerald ear-rings and I said just what has that got to do with us will you please tell me well she said we'd left our post our post she called it as though we were in the army and after we'd gone some other people had arrived and the police let them in Anton asked if they'd presented their invitations well she said she hadn't been able to get hold of that particular policeman so she didn't know but if we'd been there it wouldn't have happened my dear lady I said do you realize we were in that booth for five hours you told us it wouldn't take more that two I hope you're aware of that well it's most unfortunate she said I've had to call in the police that made me laugh eh bien madame I said since according to you it was the police who let the thief in it ought to be very simple I don't see that we have anything to do with it then she raised her voice all I can say is I'm sorry I was foolish enough to count on you I shall know better another time and she went out it was then that I said to Anton look we can't go on living in this woman's house we've got to find somewhere else he was earning a little at that time working in an export-import office practically nothing but enough to pay rent on a small cottage he thought we should hang on there and hope that things would return to normal but I began to go out by myself nearly every day to look for somewhere we could move to this turned out later to have been very useful at least I'd seen a good many houses and knew which ones were possible you see the party was only the prelude to the ghastly thing that happened less than a month afterward one night some teenage hoodlums got into the big house the lover had gone to Marrakesh for the weekend so she was alone yes she made the servants sleep in cabins in the upper garden she was alone in the house and you know these people they're always convinced that Europeans must have vast sums of money hidden about the premises so they tortured her all night long trying to make her tell where it was she was beaten and burned and choked and cut and both her arms were broken she must have screamed I should think but maybe they covered her face with pillows at all events no one heard a thing the maids found her in the morning she was alive but she died in hospital that afternoon we knew nothing about it until the police suddenly arrived two days later and said the property was being padlocked and everybody had to leave immediately meaning the servants and gardeners and us so out we went with all our things it was terrible but as Anton said at least we lived for more than a year without paying rent he always insisted on seeing the positive side of things in a way that was helpful later when I heard the details I was frightfully upset because you see the police traced the hooligans through a gold cigarette case and some other things they'd taken the night they tortured her and then it was discovered that they also had the Duchess's evening-bag one of the criminals had arrived late the night of the party and slipped in along with a group of Spaniards after Anton and I had left the gate and of course that gave him the opportunity of examining the house and grounds for the break-in later so I felt terribly guilty of course I knew it wasn't my fault but I couldn't keep myself from thinking that if we'd only stayed on a little longer she'd still have been alive I was certain at first that the lover had had some part in it you see he never left her side she wouldn't hear of it and all at once he goes off to Marrakesh for a weekend no it seemed too pat it fitted too well but apparently he had nothing to do with it besides he'd had every chance to make off with whatever he wanted and never had touched a thing so he must have been fairly intelligent at least he knew better than to bite the hand that was feeding him except that in the end he got nothing for his good behaviour poor wretch I've tried to think back to that night and sometimes it seems to me that in my sleep maybe I did hear screams but I'd heard those blasted peacocks so many times that I paid no attention and now it makes my blood run cold to think that perhaps I actually did hear her calling for help and thought it was the birds except that the big house was so far away she'd have had to be screaming from a window that looked over the valley so I keep telling myself I couldn't possibly have heard her they wouldn't have let her get near a window but it's upsetting all the same

Monologue, New York 1965

a dazzling accomplishment Kathleen Andrews has succeeded
in forging a language capable of bearing her to the highest
reaches of lyrical expressivity the poems soar above the
stratosphere what idiotic reviews they write you know her
mother has a certain amount of influence she's also very
rich so I wouldn't be surprised if there'd been a bit of quid
pro quo under the table publishers and critics are human
too no I'm afraid I'm unconvinced I've read her poetry you
see we were classmates at Sarah Lawrence I knew her well
she's not someone you'd forget easily either she was always
impossible writing poetry even back then and publishing it
right and left a lot of people were impressed she probably
did have some talent but what a waste it was she could be
held up as the classical example of the person who
systematically ruins her own life purely self-destructive in
college she would always go out of her way to say things
nobody could possibly have agreed with she'd explain I'm
for giving the world shock treatment that's what it needs
people enjoy being scandalized more than anything else yes
that may be Kathleen I'd tell her but don't you see that
every time you shock them they put a little more distance
between you and them can't you see that in the end they're
not going to take anything you say seriously you're going
to be some sort of freak as far as they're concerned have
you thought about it I used to argue with her almost plead
with her you know the way you do when you see a friend
doing everything wrong I took her seriously I thought I

179

could help her but her reaction was oh if they want to think I'm a freak what difference does it make well this childish attitude was all right then I suppose but later on it wasn't so amusing anyway as far as I could see she had no interest in men she was far too busy thinking about herself she did say she wanted the experience of having a child but wouldn't dream of marrying I told her she'd better think twice before doing anything so scatter-brained actually she was pregnant the first year after graduation but she didn't tell me I was about the only one of her old friends who kept on seeing her she simply shut herself off anyway as soon as she knew she was pregnant it seems she began holding long conversations with the baby she had this strange idea that she could influence it by talking to it all the time Kathleen I'd tell her come back to reality you can't go on this way you've got to be serious a baby's not an idea or a poem it's real and you're going to have to take care of it oh that's all right she said I've got my trust fund it ought to be enough that's not what I'm talking about I told her you're going to be a mother a flesh-and-blood mother do you know what that means what it involves oh of course I'll find out what it means all right when the time comes and I thought but will you and that poor child but she was stubborn she had an idea she liked and she was going to hold on to it come hell or high water she wouldn't listen she'd just smile her superior smile and say my life is my own to do with as I please yes I said but not the life of your child that isn't to do as you please with think about it and for God's sake try to make sense it's not a game Kathleen you know she was ashamed of being pregnant she didn't want anyone to see her she wouldn't go out at all she simply hid herself away in that little apartment in the Village month after month every two weeks or so I'd drop in to see her because we were really close friends practically everybody else was fed up with her nonsense but I guess I imagined I might be able to appeal to her common sense we always think we can help even when we ought to know better it would be sad if it hadn't been so funny I remember that winter there was a blizzard and I walked all the way from Gramercy Park to Bank Street one day so that by the time I got to her place I was half frozen and my feet were soaked Little Missy had all the lights out she was lying in bed with one candle burning on the table beside her and a book in her hand but she jumped up and turned on the lights she had only about a month to go I sat by the fireplace warming my feet while she brewed tea well she seemed to be making perfectly good sense but then she suddenly got back into bed and said excuse me I want to finish it'll only take a minute I'm reading the Analects of Confucius to Alaric isn't the name perfect isn't it precisely what you'd expect her to choose no one's been named Alaric for the past fifteen hundred years oh I love it and then my dear she began to read out loud looking down at herself the Master said this and the Master said that well it was grotesque it made my flesh crawl but I couldn't very well interrupt her her voice was so sepulchral so I sat twiddling my toes by the fire after a while she shut the book and spoke up in a normal voice you see while he's still with me I want to be as close to him as I can because once he's born there's no more I can do she said all this in such a reasonable tone of voice that I was suddenly furious Kathleen I said you ought to know by now you can't shock me I'm shockproof as far as you're concerned tell me what are you trying to prove but she simply opened her eyes wide and said I don't know what you mean well I said in the first place what makes you so sure it's going to be a boy oh of course it's a boy I decided that at the beginning the thing is I want to give him a good pre-natal education so when he's born he won't be so much at the mercy of outside negative influences it's the most important part of a child's upbringing but most mothers don't feel close to their babies until they can actually see them human stupidity as always and she began to tell me what was wrong with everybody look I said I don't suppose it's occurred to you that you might as well be reading to that table you know damned well it can't even hear much less understand what you're saying why do you insist on playing games with yourself can't you just relax and be natural for a while oh she said of course he understands how can he help it we're the same person I know once he's born he won't understand anything after all I'm not living in Fantasy Land so you see that's why I have to spend all my time with him until then because once he's left me he's on his own and I can't do anything more for him I must have had a strange expression on my face because she suddenly straightened up and said I'm sorry you feel so strongly about it I know most people think it's their duty to press their own ideas on others but I'd always imagined you were more tolerant and she looked at me as if I'd been a great disappointment to her well Kathleen all I can say is I hope the baby's healthy I have the feeling that when you've taken care of it for a while you'll see things differently and we talked a little and I told her Jack and I were off to Rio and I'd see her when I got back and not to worry worry she said what would I worry about I'm happy so I went out into the blizzard again and got a cab home thinking it would have been a lot better if I hadn't gone my God not living in Fantasy Land indeed and I thought then I'm not going to go on seeing her when I get back it's a lost cause and I really meant it but you know me curiosity killed a cat oh yes I looked her up again the next summer the baby must have been about five months old perfectly healthy as far as I could see although I noticed it didn't smile once what got me was her offhand attitude toward it when she first showed it to me she said there he is the little horror and I thought here comes more of the same but for once I'm not going to react he's lovely I said do you breastfeed him yes she said but once he's weaned I'm going to take him to my mother's in Lake Forest she'll find a good nanny for him she said she didn't ever want to have to correct or discipline him because it would destroy their relationship and it was so important for him to have confidence in her and she went on the whole thing getting more outrageous by the minute I should have realized long before that she was never going to change but somehow I'd thought having the baby might have done something of course I couldn't have been more wrong as the twig is bent baby or no baby that's it I thought well better for him to have a good nanny at least than to be left to the tender mercies of Kathleen seeing all this made me rather thankful that Jack and I had never had any children so she went off to her mother's but

the most incredible episode of all came several years later
by then I'd more or less stopped thinking about her once
in a while I did wonder what had become of her well one
fine day I got a letter covered with Moroccan stamps from
Kathleen she'd left her mother's and gone to Europe with
Alaric her mother paid for the trip probably to get rid of
her she'd been living here and there and had ended up in
Tangier being Kathleen she was in the native quarter of
course and Alaric was learning about life with his peers
playing with the Moroccan boys in the neighbourhood and
she thought it was wonderful and wanted to stay for ever
and hoped sometime I'd pass through Tangier it all sounded
suspiciously like a continuation of the pattern anyway a year
or so later when Jack and I were in Europe I decided to fly
down to Tangier for a weekend and look in on Kathleen I
was intrigued American girl living alone in the native quarter
well Jack didn't want to go so he stayed in London and I
went flying off down to Morocco I can't tell you it was
incredible the whole thing it took me hours to find her
house I finally had to go back to the hotel and get a guide
and we went through all the dark alleys eventually we came
to the door it was wide open to the street I told the guide
to wait ouside I'd never have found my way back to the
hotel well she was there dressed in some sort of flashy native
costume the place had no furniture in it just mats and
cushions and a big table in the middle of the room and
here's the pay-off on the table was an enormous pile a
mountain of marijuana I saw it from the street before I went
in without knowing what it was Kathleen I said that stuff
is forbidden you know that how can you leave it out in
plain sight like that anyone going past can see it my guide
must have seen it I was feeling damned nervous sitting
there can't you shut the door please she shrugged and went
to shut it I asked her where Alaric was I was curious to see
how he'd turned out she looked vague oh outside he has
lots of friends this made me think of the awful kids I'd just
seen playing in the street each time we saw a crowd of them
the guide would say hold on to your handbag madame it's
nice he has friends I said and you how are you I was
thinking how can she possibly live like this it smelt exactly

like a stable she began to walk back and forth looking preoccupied and once she stood and stared down at the table this stuff's not mine she said it's Todd's Todd's staying with me he's gone to the store, he'll be back in a minute oh I see I said and pretty soon Todd came in about six foot three and jet black this was interesting I thought it showed a new side of Kathleen not a very original one I admit but still something different from before anyway I was sitting there trying to make conversation with the two of them and suddenly there was this terrible gurgling animal sound in the next room it echoed my God what's that I asked her she was perfectly matter-of-fact about it it's just our sheep we've had it now a month fattening it up for the festival next week Alaric is all excited about it he lives for that sheep it's hard to get him away from it but in the house I said how can you stand it well the boy finally came in and he had a whole crew of other kids with him all jabbering in Arabic it must have been but at least he looked healthy through the dirt he was as filthy as the rest of them and hadn't had his hair cut in a year incredible they trooped in and all rushed to the room where the sheep was tied up and it began to make its awful bleat I decided this was a good moment to disappear I said I had to go because my guide was waiting but I'd come back the next day Kathleen looked at me as if it were the end of the world but you just got here she kept saying then the kids all went out all except Alaric and he climbed on to Todd's lap and began to hug him that kid was starved for affection I said to him Alaric it's nice you have the sheep he can be your friend and follow you around wherever you go and that kid looked straight at me and said oh no we're going to cut his throat next Tuesday I thought he was making it up but Kathleen said yes Tuesday's the day of the sacrifice as I went out she said she'd been writing lots of poetry and I thought I'll bet you have and what a blessing I don't have to read it I said goodbye see you tomorrow and I really meant to go back and try to talk with her just the two of us but it was all so abject and sordid and she was so childish it was really depressing I couldn't face looking for that alley again the next morning I got a plane out to London I've never heard

from her since what a waste I don't think she has any idea
of what she's done to herself I suppose I'm getting less
tolerant but I have no patience with people who refuse to
abide by the rules of the game and that boy of hers I'd be
willing to bet he ends up behind bars it's inevitable but she
has no one to blame she's brought it all on herself the sad
part is that she'll never realize how much harm she's caused
it'll never cross her mind that her life has been one great
mistake from the beginning pretty ridiculous isn't it

Monologue, Massachusetts 1932

just applejack little mint little lemon nothing better on a
hot afternoon you want more ice it's here I don't like ice
in my drink nor ice-cream either funny when I was a little
tyke they gave me some and I spit it out said it burned my
mouth yep that's thunder all right I figured we were about
due for a shower we get some bad ones here they come
rolling up the valley God you'd think it was bombs sit here
wondering where it's going to hit next got the barn out
there twice once two years ago didn't do any harm other
time oh fifteen years ago more than half of it burned down
got the horses out all right though had horses then that was
one time when the family was lucky we get some corkers
here generally come in August the worst ones my wife my
first wife that is as soon as she'd hear thunder she'd go to
pieces all white and start trembling couldn't do anything
with her lightning rods didn't mean a thing to her I'd tell
her Susan even if it hits the house it's not going to hurt
you when women get nervous no use trying to make 'em
listen to reason go right on with the same thing over and
over yep this is the house I was born in always lived here
didn't use to look like this it was my second wife brought
all this furniture here it doesn't belong in an old place like
this yes the house is pretty old seventeen ninety-six you can
see the numbers chiselled on the doorstep out front all these
old houses have little rooms there's no space for big chairs
and tables I told her the only room in this house big enough
to hold that grand piano is the kitchen but there it is takes

up half the room that was a loud one it's coming this way all right look at the sky out there over the top of the hill black as sin yep live here alone since my last wife died haven't even got a dog to keep me company I don't mind it too much never could stand a lot of commotion around anyway can't abide noise that radio there never turn it on except I want to hear the news how's that drink coming here I'll fix you another yes hits the spot but you know you can't use peppermint got to use spearmint funny the peppermint won't give it the flavour so you saw my ad came all the way here to see the place not much to see just the old house got a hundred and forty-five acres of woods down back there's a pretty good brook runs through got some fruit trees out on that side that's about all I keep busy got fifty-odd cord of wood stacked in the shed for cold weather too bad you didn't get here an hour sooner we could have gone down to the woods I presume you'd like to see the whole property well we can look around outside a little we'll have to stick close to the house though you can smell the rain in the air bring your drink along that's all right those four old maples were just as big when I was a boy I recall my grandfather told me he couldn't remember a time when they weren't there the two little windows upstairs well there's two bedrooms and a garret up there here it comes it's going to come down hard too bad well we didn't get wet this room on the right is the parlour I keep it shut off never come in here got plenty of room without it it's stuffy you can smell the dust come on in the other room and get a fresh drink the applejack glad you like it that's right make it myself down cellar I've got a little still down there my father had it before me it's real good stuff if you make it right Christ that was near must have been over by the Henderson farm hit something I've got to shut the windows the rain's coming in I make it every year God no I don't sell it that would be asking for trouble it's just for household consumption except I've got no household no no more marriage for me I've tried it twice and both times it turned out bad tragic awful they were both of them very refined and sensitive the first one had a little money the second was as broke as I am a few shares of Tel and Tel but she did have all this furniture well it's nigh on ten years since I married my first wife my old man died and the place was up to here in mortgages she wanted to get them cleared up first thing so I got that off my mind yes I did say tragic terrible I'm coming to that after about a year I begin to notice that Susan isn't in such good shape she's sort of going to pieces I don't know nervous as a witch and can't sleep and I have to put up with her nagging nag nag day and night night most of all wouldn't let me sleep so finally I slept on a sofa we used to have in here I don't know if you noticed this shot-gun in the corner in the parlour I always keep it there ready for action so I can get at it fast maybe a woodchuck in the garden or a red squirrel can't leave them around tear your house to pieces anyway Susan knew it was there only she never even touched it when she dusted she was afraid of it well she'd been going from bad to worse finally she just clammed up on me wouldn't say a word that was all right with me I had this new Ford truck I used to drive into town every few days stock up on food it's only eighteen miles if you go straight through by the back road some of it's pretty rough didn't bother me any in the truck though I generally went in the morning so I'd be back by noon but this day I didn't start out till after lunch about two it took me longer than usual in town got home a little after sundown went into the house looked around for Susan no sign of her when I went into the room across the hall there the parlour I found her dead yes she'd shot herself she sat down in a chair rested the stock on the floor leaned way over put the barrel into her mouth and pulled the trigger a terrible thing you don't want to hear all this how did I start on it don't see so many people these days somebody comes I open up I guess can I make you another no not even a small one you're right it packs a wallop well you don't mind if I help myself I don't have to drive anywhere well this awful thing damn near broke me up after the funeral I went down to New York took in a few shows Christ I'd have gone crazy if I'd stayed here it was down there I first met Laura didn't see much of her that year the next year I went to New York again and we saw a lot more of each other wasn't till

the year after that we got married she was wild about the
house always wanted to live in one just like this we got rid
of the old tables and chairs weren't any great shakes anyhow
and she shipped all her stuff here Laura she was very delicate
high-strung used to having her own way she loved the
country she'd walk for hours in the woods at least she did
the first year or so she was artistic too set up her easel out
in the orchard and paint the trees she didn't do anything
with the pictures she just liked to paint 'em there's a whole
stack up in the garret she was a good sport we used to go
berrying up on Hawk Mountain fix sandwiches stay there
all day don't know how many quarts we'd bring back could
hardly carry it all between us it's letting up a little going
on down the valley still coming down all right though the
trouble was my fault ought to have told her about Susan I
mean how she died I ought to have told her right off might
have known she'd hear about it somehow you know
women's gossip so she wants to know all about it and why
I didn't tell her in the first place instead of letting her find
out she kept asking questions how Susan could have reached
the trigger with such a long barrel figure it out for yourself
I told her she thought there was something I was trying to
hide she got so she wanted to talk about it all the time she'd
say oh sometimes I get to thinking about Susan and it makes
me feel so blue I wonder what she was feeling and how she
could have done that to herself I'd tell her for Christ's sake
you never even met Susan how can you think about her
that's why I didn't want to tell you because I knew you'd
take it this way it wasn't long before I see we were never
going to get on together she didn't exactly nag but she was
sarcastic and she had her own ideas anyway too late now I
thought just have to make the best of it well one way of
making the best of it was to get out of the house whenever
she started playing the piano it's stopped going to open the
windows no air in here sure you don't want another I'm
helping myself again hope you don't mind don't drink much
when I'm alone don't enjoy it no fun to drink if you've got
nobody to talk to right and worse to drink with somebody
who won't drink and doesn't want you to drink either Laura
couldn't drink claimed it gave her a headache so she took

exception to it when I drank even wanted me to get rid of the still said it made her nervous knowing it was down there did my drinking out in the tool shed you know it's a bad thing when a man can't do as he's a mind to in his own house we were getting on each other's nerves something terrible and she was spending more and more time at the piano what kind of music God I don't know but it was always loud I didn't stay to listen I got out she'd be pounding there all afternoon long I put up with it till one day I told her look we've got to have an understanding about that piano right now it seems to me an hour in the morning and an hour in the afternoon's enough for anybody and by God that's all you're going to play I'm going to time you and if you go on after your time's up I'm going to come in and drag you out of here by force you hear well that didn't go down with her after that she wouldn't play at all said I'd ruined it for her you see this was just part of her nervous breakdown cutting off her nose to spite her face but she held it against me right up to the end I even tried once in a while to get her to play but she wouldn't wouldn't even come into this room any more sat in the kitchen by the big window mooning I didn't know then but she must have had Susan on her mind the whole time I think even if I'd told her myself instead of her finding out from the neighbours the way she did I think it would have been the same anyway one morning I was out in the field hoeing and I heard a funny noise in the house by God I said she's playing with that shot-gun and I started to run well I found her in the parlour she'd done it the same way as Susan both of them I couldn't believe it couldn't believe it things like that don't happen I mean twice exactly the same way no well it was terrible I asked Doc Synder about it later if he thought it was my interfering with her piano but he said no she was melancholic and would have done the same thing anyway so I mustn't feel to blame but I still did he told me Caleb when a woman like your wife gets an idea into her head you might as well give up you're not going to get it out he didn't help Laura any he'd joke with her but she just nodded her head Doc said he wasn't much surprised at what she'd done he'd sort of been expecting

something bad well it was a pleasure talking to you come
back if you still want to see the place in good weather be
glad to see you any time a pleasure take it easy on the road
you won't get back before dark anyway

In Absentia

(sent to Pamela Loeffler)

I'll try to keep this short so it won't take you too much time to read it. I know how women worry when they have to settle into a new house, with new servants to take charge of, and when they're faced with all those terrible decisions about how to place the furniture and where to store things.

This is a beautiful sunny day for a change. It's been raining on and off this past week, so that the sudden appearance of bright sunlight is a tonic. And the sun made me think of you, who have always loved it as much as I. Do you still sunbathe, out there where you are, or is it too hot? I gave up the practice years ago. Too many of my friends developed skin cancer from it.

So this morning I woke up thinking: I shall write to Pamela today. I know it's been a long time since we saw each other or communicated, but I've followed your activities from afar via what are admittedly unreliable sources: *Time* and the *International Herald Tribune*. And I can now congratulate you. (Nothing is sacred; everyone knows how much you got. But even that amount won't ruin old Loeffler, so don't ever feel guilt.) I can only remark that occasionally the scale tips in favour of justice, and I'm happy that you've been able to experience the phenomenon concretely.

I now have a vague concept of where you are: on the north shore of Maui. I've even found Kahului and Paukokalo. As I studied the map I couldn't help noticing that the entire west coast of the island of Hawaii is decorated with lava

192

flows, as you no doubt know. What amuses me is that each one is named after the year the stuff slid down the mountainside, so that you get *Lava Flow of 1801, Lava Flow of 1859, Lava Flow of 1950.* It puts me in mind of the streets in Latin American countries, named after important dates. 'He lives on the corner of the Fourth of April and the Nineteenth of October.'

I remember, when people used to ask me what Pamela was doing, I'd reply: Oh, she's busy being beautiful. I remember, also, being taken to task for my flippant answer. But what's wrong with it? Isn't it true? You *are* beautiful (as we know) and you've remained beautiful thanks to your determination to do so. That requires concentration and effort. How otherwise would there have been a Loeffler?

Now I'm trying to imagine you in the un-American decor of our fiftieth state. Do you wear jodhpurs, like Karen Blixen in Kenya? When you have a moment, send a snapshot. I'll be waiting for it.

(sent to Pamela Loeffler)

No, a three-month silence is quite forgivable. I wonder you were able to find the time even when you did. Most of the matters I felt like asking you about in my last, but refrained from mentioning out of tact, seem to have been arranged more or less happily: plumbing, staff, provisions, neighbours. The last named would be rather important, I should think. Great that you should have discovered the Hollywood people only six miles up the road. I don't remember ever having seen his name. But then, he could have been the most famous director in the US and I still wouldn't have heard of him. As you know, I was never a film enthusiast. Anyway, it's nice that they're there, and companionable to boot. They sound *echt* Beverly Hills, but that may be only because I'm relying on your description.

Above all I was happy to hear that a few old friends will be visiting you soon. If Florence actually arrives (does she ever know what she's doing?) give her my love. I can see her getting to San Francisco and deciding to go to Carmel instead of Honolulu, and then two months later suddenly arriving at your place without a word of warning, just when the house is *archicomplet*. I remember one winter when she kept the house in Turtle Bay open, with the housekeeper in residence, to take care of her cat while she was away (but for six months or more) because she believed that cats grow fond of places rather than people, and the cat would have been too unhappy if it had been taken away from the house. Then as soon as she got back home she gave the cat to somebody who lived in Connecticut.

Tell me – you ought to know this by now, being surrounded by exotic flora – is frangipani the same tree which is known in the Philippines as ylang-ylang, and in India as champak? I'm not trying to test you; I don't know myself, and there's no reason why I should expect you to. And yet it's just the sort of thing you might know. If you don't, perhaps one of your friends from Boston will. Bostonians often know the most unlikely things. At least, they used to. Or are there no true Bostonians left?

I see you understand the pleasure that can be got from writing letters. In other centuries this was taken for granted. Not any longer. Only a few people carry on true correspondences. No time, the rest tell you. Quicker to telephone. Like saying a photograph is more satisfying than a painting. There wasn't all that much time for writing letters in the past, either, but time was found, as it generally can be for whatever gives pleasure.

And when *you* find the time, send me a few recent snapshots of yourself and the place. I imagine they'll have to be Polaroids, since from what you write you haven't easy access to what we like to call the amenities of civilization. It sounds to me as though most of your supplies had to be flown over from Honolulu. That's all too reminiscent of the situation here. 'We're waiting for a new shipment. Maybe in three or four months.' Those are the honest baqals; the others say: 'Next week, incha'Allah', knowing it's untrue. You may, or you may never, get your saucepan or your powdered milk or your trowel or your broom or your Gruyère or your spatula. More likely you never will, for such things are not allowed entry into the country these days. *Tant pis et à bientôt.*

(sent to Pamela Loeffler)

Thank you for the year-old photo of the house-in-progress. Even without its finishing touches I can see how handsome it must be now. It's really very sumptuous, very grand. You must have room for a dozen visitors, in case you ever should feel afraid of succumbing to melancholia. But I see no sign of *you*, nor of anyone else. Incredibly fine vegetation.

What makes you think I should be able to interpret your dream? In the first place, I don't believe X can explain to Y what Y dreamed. How do I know what the act of running along a pier represents to you, or what your usual reaction to seaweed is? I don't understand my own dreams, much less those of others. I do notice that people have a tendency to recount dreams in which there is action, to such an extent that I often wonder if they don't unconsciously supply the action in the telling. Because I can't ever recall any narrative content in my own dreams. They're more like a succession of unrelated still photographs, rather than a film. But dream tellers go right on saying: 'And then. And then.' I'd like to know if it's really that way with them, or if they only feel that it should be that way.

And besides, why interpret a dream? If it's a warning from your unconcious mind, you'll get the message eventually in any case. Tell me, can you force a dream to recur? I can't. Anyway, good dreaming.

(sent to Pamela Loeffler)

Still at me about dreams? Why do you say that I 'of all people' should know about them? I don't think about them in the way you do. For me they're a psychic barometer, useful only to the person who does the dreaming, in the way a clinical thermometer is useful to the one running a fever. It seems a mistake to attach particular importance to one image rather than another (no matter how significant it may seem at the time of dreaming) since the images themselves are only delegates for other, unformulated images. How can you expect anyone to give you the 'meaning' of masses of red seaweed floating in the water? Seaweed means seaweed. You also claim that there was total lack of affect connected with the sight of it. Then why in God's name are you interested in discovering its 'meaning'? If it meant nothing to you in the dream, how can it mean anything in retrospect?

You ask if the Muslims here have a system for explaining dreams. They have, of course, as they have (theoretically) a system for everything, but it's divination using approved religious symbology. I can't see that it's in any sort of agreement with Freudian theory. (How could it be?) It all might have come out of a little book called *Ali Baba's Dream Almanac*. But they believe it, just as the Hindus believe in that idiotic zodiac with its twelve signs. (And not only the Hindus, alas.)

Dear Pamela, the value of a letter can't be measured quantitatively. If you haven't time to write what you call a 'real' letter, then write a few lines. I don't expect anyone to compose long-winded epistles, as I sometimes do. I write letters because I enjoy doing it. It doesn't even matter too much whether the recipient takes pleasure in reading what I write: I've had my pleasure.

So don't decide not to write merely because you know it can be only a few lines. You could send me a note that read: ' A muggy day and I'm depressed. I had baked ham and fruit salad for lunch.' And I'd be delighted. But if you send nothing at all, you leave the field to the imagination, which is always ready with its angst. I want to hear how you feel about the house, as well as about the guests who are staying with you. You wouldn't need much time to tell me that, would you?

(sent to Pamela Loeffler)

I think Tangier is getting less and less liveable. One of the principal reasons why I've continued to stay here has been the good air that we breathe. But the traffic has increased tenfold in the past five years, and with practically all the recent cars equipped with diesel engines, the streets are full of smoke. The buses and trucks constantly whoof out fat black columns of it. At home it doesn't bother me, because I live high up. It's walking in the street that's troublesome. Apart from the pollution, the sidewalks are crowded with obstacles: cars parked in the middle, groups of students sitting along the curb, and beggars installed against the walls. If you mention the beggars to a Moroccan, he'll tell you: Not one of them is from Tangier. They're all down from the mountains. Don't give them anything.

You underestimate the intelligence of the Moroccans at your peril. They know when you're lying and when you're only exaggerating, they know when you mean what you say and when you're only talking, and these things they know directly and not as a result of deduction. It's true that they sometimes scent deceit where there is none. I've argued with Moroccans who refuse to believe that anyone has been to the moon. 'Just America advertising.' Others, admitting the moonwalk, think the money should have been spent feeding hungry people. 'What good did it do?' They're not fascinated or excited by the idea of exploring space, because they have no concept of historic movement or growth; for them time is an eternal stasis. Everything is as it always has been, and will remain thus for ever. A comforting philosophy, if you can subscribe,

(*sent to Pamela Loeffler*)

Your letter about the Palmers very amusing, I thought. Surely you're not encouraging Dick to look for property in your vicinity? That would be catastrophic, wouldn't it? I agree that it's nice to have acquaintances living only fifteen or twenty miles away, if your first reaction each time you see them doesn't express itself as a sudden sinking sensation. It takes such a lot of energy to fight that. I've got to the point of preferring solitude to being under that sort of stress.

Of course Ruth was always a negative quantity, even

before she married Dick. Collecting potsherds, pieces of quartz and crinoids, when I knew her. So the butterfly business is quite in line. It must be marvellous to see her bounding around as she wields the net! Hyperthyroid and graceless. Dick is merely obstinate and dictatorial; that's how I remember him. (I haven't seen him in fifteen years, more or less, but I feel pretty certain that he hasn't changed much. Perhaps extra years have decreased his energy, but it doesn't take much energy to be egotistical if that's one's nature.) When he had a flat here he was completely wrapped up in the Rolling Stones, who were friends he'd known in London. The name meant nothing to me, but Dick insisted they were the greatest rock group in existence. He got me out of bed one night at one o'clock, came pounding on my door, very excited. I must go with him to his flat because he had the Stones there. I, sleepy: 'What stones?' He explained, and I went. A man named Jagger, dressed for a costume party, reclined on the bed, gnawing on a leg of lamb. A girl lay face down at his feet, and there were other people spread out asleep on the floor. It wasn't bright enough in the room for me to see their costumes in detail. Mr Jagger said nothing. His muzzle was shiny with lamb fat. Dick saw my surprise at the sight of the inert bodies on the floor, and confided that everyone had taken a new drug which apparently induced a comatose state. It's strange: Dick has this air of breathless enthusiasm. It's a physical attribute which ought to be contagious, but isn't. Instead, it comes across as sales talk, and creates next to no empathy.

After about an hour I thanked him and said I was off to bed. This didn't go down at all well. He took it as an offence, assuming, quite correctly, that I hadn't appreciated my great opportunity of meeting the Stones. I considered that I had been patient, but as I went out and turned to thank Dick again, he drew himself up and, pretending to be a very proper English governess, said: 'Oh, urfty turfty wiffy bibben bibben, oh yes!' and slammed the door.

If the moment seems right, you may mention this episode to Dick, and see if he remembers it. What he's sure to remember is that they all went to Marrakesh the next morning at seven o'clock, Dick included. That was in the pre-Ruth days.

I'm not surprised that Florence postponed her visit; in fact, I predicted it. What does strike me as strange is that you should have Dick and Ruth Palmer there, because I know they're not the ones you'd most like to have staying with you. But of course, that's what happens when one has a large house in a remote place. Still, it's certainly better for you to have guests than to be alone. This next guest of yours, Fronda Farquhar, who is she and what is she? And that name, at the far end of credibility! You speak of her as if I should know who she is, but I don't. What does she do? Or is she another Ruth, searching for arrowheads and shells?

Well, it all sounds like fun.

(sent to Susan Choate)

Now what? Hippocrates strikes again. I wondered at your long silence and now I understand. Hepatitis B is not so amusing. What astonishes me is that you got rid of it in a hospital, which I thought was a place where one contracted it rather than cured it. Do you think it's really gone? I must say I hope so. That hospital bill you enclosed is staggering. How can you be sure that I'll be able to pay it? Clearly I can't keep sending larger and larger amounts. All your expenses grow like weeds. I realize that you can't help it; money has less and less value, but that simply means that people like me can buy less and less. I'm not lecturing; I'm just bewailing this hospital bill. It's surprising they let you out of the institution without some sort of guarantee that it would be paid. Naturally you took it for granted that I could pay it, without considering the possibility that I might be short of funds. And I can pay it, yes, but not with pleasure. How did you ever get hepatitis? Did they have any theories as to the origin? I hope they gave you some pointers as to how to avoid it in the future.

Did you get the caftan? It should be ideal for dressy occasions in New York or Boston, if indeed there are any more such things. (Although I'm told that girls are becoming interested once more in clothes, and can conceive of wearing something besides those proletarian blue jeans they've been affecting for the past few decades.) Anyway, the caftan is a museum piece. That very heavy silk brocade is no longer woven – not even by Fortuny. I bought it from a Moroccan friend in whose family it had been since the turn of the century. I know you'll look superb in it, and I only hope you'll wear it. (Not in a hospital, however!) I hope to hear from you.

(sent to Susan Choate)

Glad to hear you've had no further trouble with your liver. But good God, Suky, no wonder you came down with hepatitis. Haiti, of all insane places to go, even for a short holiday. I'm not surprised you didn't mention it to me. You must have known I'd do my best to discourage you. You seem to think it was all right because you were invited, so that it cost you nothing. But it did cost you six weeks of classes, not to mention that it cost me a fortune to pay for it.

You say Haiti was picturesque, and I'm sure it is. But it's precisely in this sort of poverty-induced picturesqueness that diseases are rampant. I myself have spent plenty of time enjoying the poverty of others in exotic places, and have paid for it with ailments and aches, as you know. But the point is that hepatitis is a serious disease, and you must take it seriously, something I suspect you don't do, to judge by your flippant references to the experience. Remember that your great-grandmother Gray caught it on a trip to Mexico and died of it, and very quickly. So for God's sake stay put, there at Mount Holyoke, and don't add to my insomnia by going to places you know may be dangerous.

It's a help to know you don't drink. A heavy diet of cannabis can be almost as harmful to the liver, you know. (Likewise tobacco and coffee!) Your doctor must have told you all this, but that doesn't mean that you listened. Having withstood an attack doesn't make you immune; on the contrary, you're more vulnerable to another attack.

Forgive me if I lapse into pedantry, but you spoke of 'convincing' the manager of the bookshop to extend credit. It's not possible to convince 'to'. If you're going to use *convince*, you need either 'of' or 'that'. Otherwise use *persuade*. End of lecture, and until soon.

(*sent to Pamela Loeffler*)

There's no point in asking for news from here. News isn't generally made in this part of the world, or if something occurs here which becomes news in the rest of the world, we hear about it in foreign broadcasts. And the broadcasts of course are full of talk about terrorism. For most Europeans and Americans the word *terrorist* is unqualifiedly pejorative; while to the people here it suggests a patriot. Thus actions some consider criminal and contemptible are to others heroic. How can the two ever see eye to eye?

A theatrical agency in Sydney! I didn't know thay had them. I understand her being called Fronda Farquhar if that's where she's from. You make the picnics sound like something out of Waugh or early Angus Wilson. How did you weather three of them, all with F. Farquhar as well as Ruth P.? My suspicion is that the reason Dick refused to go with you is that he was loath to get too far away from the source of supply: your refrigerator. He's always been a glutton. I shan't ask your opinion on that: you're too far away to put irrelevant questions to. But it must be something of a relief to have all of them gone, in spite of feeling alone and missing them. I can't believe you actually miss those three particular people, though. Isn't what you miss the presence of someone, anyone, to talk to now and then? That's not an irrelevant question, by the way, and I do put it to you. Because it's occurred to me that Sue Choate, my father's sister's great-granddaughter, will be visiting a college friend in Honolulu, and might enjoy a visit with you. (I think I told you I was financing her education, so it's of great interest to me where she spends her vacations.) The last time she was out of the States she went to Haiti and caught hepatitis. One can't ask a seventeen-year-old to be circumspect in matters like that, of course. Haiti was there, she was invited, it sounded exciting, so she went.

Let me know about that. I think it might be pleasant for you both. She's charming, lively, and very attractive. Talkative, but intelligently so, and can be turned off with ease. (I'm describing her as she was at the age of fifteen; I haven't seen her since.)

If you have crowds of people scheduled to arrive, and Suky would be in the way, that's of course another story. But let me know when you can, so I can plan her summer.

What happened to those people from California who lived only six miles from you? Don't they like picnics?

See enclosed sheet with Sue's address and phone number at Mount Holyoke, in case.

(sent to Susan Choate)

It was good of you to write so soon, even if I wasn't exactly pleased to hear you'd sold the caftan. And without ever wearing it! I admit that you got an unbelievable price for it. Your friend Myra must be wallowing in dollars. But that wasn't why I sent it to you, so that you could sell it to have spending money. I was hoping it would be a very special item of your wardrobe. You say that one has to get used to doing without things when one becomes poor, and that you couldn't face asking me for money when I was paying for the hospital. All that I appreciate completely. Still, I'm sorry you didn't bring the subject up before getting rid of the garment. I'd have tried to dissuade you, even though I couldn't have sent you the twelve hundred you got for it – at least, not all at once, which is obviously the way you wanted it.

Have you thought of how you'll spend the summer? Much as I'd like to see you, I wouldn't advise your coming here. There's nothing much here to interest you, I'm afraid. Hotels are relatively inexpensive, yes, but not cheap enough for my purse. And the friends with guest-houses where you might have stayed gratis have died or moved away.

It has occurred to me that you might like to visit Hawaii.

I know the suggestion sounds absurd, coming directly after the song of poverty. But there I do know someone who might put you up, and probably would be delighted to do so. You've never met her, but you may have heard me speak of her when you were a child. More likely not. Your summer would cost me only the round-trip fare and what's more, I shouldn't be worrying that you might have sneaked off to Mexico or Jamaica, or, God forbid, Haiti. You, of course, know what you want and how you feel like spending your vacation. This is just one suggestion; others may appear in the course of time.

I should add that I do appreciate your concern about money, and understand that you sold the caftan to help me, so I'm not too chagrined that you never wore it, and that I haven't a photo of you modelling it. The postal system, incidentally, is worse than ever.

(sent to Susan Choate)

I can't help wondering why you're so eager to know how much I paid for that caftan. It's clear that you hope it was very little, as if that would somehow justify your having sold it. But your logic is ailing. It's not a question of how much *I* paid for it; it's a question rather of how much *you* paid for it, and the answer is nothing. Therefore you cleared your twelve hundred and ought not to bother your head with what it cost me. I can see how your mind is working, and I suppose it shows family solidarity: that is, what's mine is ours. Since you write about practically nothing else in your short letter, I have to assume that it's important to you to know how much more your selling price was than my purchase price. You want to know how much 'we' made on the deal. So in spite of your not seeming to be aware that it's unheard-of to inquire the price of a gift, I think you deserve an answer, since you made 'us' a profit of an even thousand, minus the mailing charges. Does that please you?

You don't seem to take my suggestion about Hawaii very seriously. I can see why, with all our talk about scarce money. Nevertheless I meant it in all seriousness, as a way of solving the vacation problem. I can see that you may not be eager to be the guest of a woman you don't know , or of anyone else, for that matter. But Pamela is what's called easy-going – tolerant and gregarious. She gives the impression of being twenty years younger than she really is. (She's in her late fifties, and may have had cosmetic surgery, but I somehow doubt it. That sort of thing she'd be secretive about.) Do I make her sound like someone to be avoided? I hope not, as I'd be delighted to see you established there for the summer. Besides solving the vacation problem, your sojourn there could prove advantageous in other ways.

Or perhaps I'm crazy, in which case nothing I've said makes sense.

Anyway, let me hear.

                                        (sent to Susan Choate)

Your friend McCall sounds like a real slob. Why would he drive you to Hartford knowing you were going to have to take the bus back, and not mention it to you beforehand? You didn't seem to find that unusual; I suppose this sort of irresponsible rudeness is part of today's etiquette. I don't find it appealing, but then, young people go out of their way to be as unattractive as possible, both in their persons and their behaviour. So your date from Amherst is probably no worse than the rest.

I can see you're beginning to give the Hawaiian idea a little thought. You're wrong, however, to use the word *directive,* and to suggest that I've been 'pressuring' you, as you put it. To issue a directive is one thing, and to request a favour is something else. Perhaps I didn't make myself clear in the last letter. Staying with Pamela out there you would be in a position, if you were clever enough, to receive financial assistance for the coming year. That wouldn't have occurred to you in your youthful innocence. But it occurred to me, and I see it as a distinct possibility. Pamela has more money than she can spend, and she's generous. She and I are old friends as you know, and if she took a fancy to you and offered to help you, she'd know she was also helping me. Obviously, once you were there it would be up to you to decide how to play it. A question of choosing the right moment in which to be perfectly truthful. Clearly it's in my interest that you go (and even more in your own, I suspect).

Meditate some more, and when you come up with an answer, let me know. But don't wait too long.

(*sent to Susan Choate*)

Pamela has risen to the occasion. She's asked me to tell you that she'd be delighted to have you stay with her for as long as it suits you – the entire summer if you like. As soon as she knows what you've decided she'll be in touch directly with you. But if you make up your mind to go, wire or phone her immediately, even before you let me know. Because if you accept her invitation through me, it will take the rest of the spring. Massachusetts–Morocco, Morocco–Hawaii.

If I had access to a telephone I'd call you. And if sending a telegram didn't involve standing in line for an hour first, I'd wire you, and save that much more time. But I'm not up to that.

In any case, the machinery has been set in motion. Let me hear.

(*sent to Susan Choate*)

Your letter was the best sort of news. Thank God for Lucy Piper! Knowing that you had a friend who lived in Hawaii, I went out on a limb and lied a bit to Pamela, telling her that you'd been asked by this girl's family for a visit. I needed a pretext on which to hang my suggestion that Pamela invite you to Maui. (Since you were going to be in Hawaii, etc.) Now it turns out not to be a lie, after all. The two weeks in Honolulu ought to be fun, particularly if her parents aren't going to be there. The Pipers may be paragons of charm for all I know, but things are generally better when families are not around.

I'll have the New York bank send you fifteen hundred. With what you have, that should be enough for fare both ways. Send me a wire when you get to San Francisco before the Hawaii flight. I shan't write more now. I only wanted to let you know how delighted I am that you decided to go.

(*sent to Susan Choate*)

The wire Pamela sent you is essentially the same as the one she sent me. She'll pick you up at the Pipers' June 20th and fly you on to Maui. It's an ideal solution. Providential. She wanted to be in Honolulu anyway that week, so she's not putting herself out for you. It just happened to fall right.

In spite of your trepidation, I'd say the possibility that Pamela will be bored by your presence is nil. You by her, who knows? But very unlikely.

What do you mean, 'procedure' to follow with Pamela? Of course there is none. You simply play everything by ear. How can I advise you from here, or dictate a course of behaviour? Or foresee the complex choreography of subterfuges and dissimulations which will make up your conversation? Women know how to handle each other, and need no man's advice.

Don't think about these things now. It will just interfere with your studying. Time enough for that later. Finish up your work and go with Lucy Piper. I hope she's fun to travel with.

Postscriptum: Destroy my letters once you've read them. There won't be all that many, in any case. The summer's too short.

(*sent to Pamela Loeffler*)

So everything meshed, *grace à Dieu*. And now Suky's with you. Could you gauge her immediate reaction to the new environment? I ask you because I don't expect her to tell me accurately in her letters, if she ever decides to write me. I'm a little surprised that she hasn't sent me even a few words. I suppose she thought a letter from you would be enough.

While we're still talking about Suky, I'm so glad you find her companionable. One never knows with the very young; their moods are mercurial. She's been alone far too much. Her parents both died when she was twelve, and I've seen her only once, and briefly, since then. She will have changed.

There never was such a thing as hashish in Morocco; it was the Americans who first manufactured it here. Kif is volatile, and they were looking for a more compact and durable form of it, so they used a vice. This made an ersatz sort of hashish. The Moroccans, not knowing hashish, good or bad, followed suit, and found the product saleable abroad. They've been pressing this inferior merchandise ever since, and are still making great fortunes exporting it. There's a direct relationship between the commerce in hashish and the prevalence of corruption. A huge sum can silence anyone. I take it the situation is very different where you are; do you know anything about it? That is, more than you can read in the press?

Suggest to Sue that she write me a note at least, if she can find the time between dates. Two boy-friends? Who are they? I imagined you as fairly isolated. Apparently you're not.

What makes you say I'm 'obsessed' by the girl? If you've even suggested such an idea to her, inevitably she'll see it in a Freudian light. This would give her a perfect pretext for not writing. In what other way could she take it? And in what way did *you* mean it, for that matter? 'Obsessed' is a word used too often.

(*sent to Pamela Loeffler*)

I can't help feeling some anxiety over not having had some word from Sue. I know you say she's fine, but I'm not convinced. If she were her usual self, she'd write. It's clear that something is troubling her that she shrinks from telling me, something more than this nonsense she's been feeding you about being 'terrified' of me. She knows that's laughable. How can she speak of me as 'authoritarian'? We haven't seen each other in several years, and no one can terrify by mail.

What's got into her? The difficulty is that you don't know her, so you can't notice any little changes that might have come over her recently. Have you tried to persuade her to sit down and scribble a few words?

It goes without saying that I don't expect you to choose her friends for her. I have no objection to her seeing a Japanese mechanic three nights a week, or every night, so you needn't feel uneasy on my account. Please understand that I don't consider you in any way responsible for her behaviour. She's old enough to account for it herself. As she undoubtedly has told you, she's a partisan of feminine 'liberation'.

(*sent to Susan Choate*)

I saw something this morning that amused me. Two little boys about five years old were playing at bullfighting. The bull was a perambulator containing a strapped-in baby under blankets, and the one pushing the pram was making frantic attempts to gore the torero, who dodged and sidestepped the attacks. At one point the bull made an all-out desperate attempt and charged with such force that it banged into a telephone pole. Torero delighted. Baby jolted but impervious.

Do write a few lines about the place, about the general set-up. Remember, I've never been there, and am curious. A few sentences in a personal report mean more than pages of a travel article. I'm not asking for an essay; you can tell it all in two paragraphs. One on the place and the other on Pamela. *Finis.*

(sent to Susan Choate)

And now you write me, when you're just about ready to leave, so that I can't even be sure this will reach you in time. At least you gave what it probably an honest reason for your silence: you were having too good a time. That is of course the best reason, and I'm glad it turned out that way. It would have been awful if you'd hated the place and been bored by Pamela. But what a peculiar creature you are, to keep me waiting all summer for a sheet of paper it would have taken five minutes to cover.

The last message I had from you was the wire you sent from San Francisco, so I have no idea of your present finances, or even whether you bought a round-trip passage. One can only worry so much, however; then one becomes philosophical. I suppose philosophy is merely sublimated worry. If this were a telephone conversation I could say: Let me speak to Pamela. So I shall speak to her, in a letter I'll write as soon as I get this one into its envelope. I'm very happy you've loved your vacation.

(sent to Pamela Loeffler)

I just finished a note to the culprit. As you probably know, she finally decided to write me before she returned to college. She describes everything and all in glowing terms – particularly you, about whom she made some highly astute observations, all favourable. I think she has seen the entire spectrum of your personality, complex though it is, and for that I give her good marks. I can see from your last letter that you loved having her there with you.

Does she seem at all preoccupied by the thought of money? If she's been sensible, she should have more than enough to get her back to Massachusetts. Nevertheless, if you get this in time, and think she should have a bit more, please let her have it. I'll repay you immediately.

I'll try to write an actual letter soon, which this is not. What I'd call a true letter ought to be an amalgam of personal conversation, diary (what happened) and journal (what one thinks about what happened). But anyway.

(sent to Pamela Loeffler)

Your letter was indeed bad news. Are you really satisfied with the doctor? I ask because I'm surprised that he didn't seem to be sure whether it was a return of the hepatitis she caught in Haiti, or simple dysentery (non-amoebic, I mean).

Poor Suki! Tell her to relax, and not to worry about being late in getting back to classes. She can make up the work easily.

I wonder if it occurred to your doctor that she might have sunstroke. You spoke of her long hours at the beach. Her symptoms sound a little like my own when I was struck by the sun in Cuba. It's at times like this that I wish I had a telephone. Wire me if there's any sudden change for the worse in her condition.

I saw something incredible in a French magazine last week. A friend of de Gaulle was being interviewed. One question: 'Then de Gaulle was not anti-Semitic?' The reply: 'Well, in 1940, I remember that André Maurois came and asked to speak to de Gaulle privately. The general turned to someone beside him and said: "What's that kike doing here?" But that was just his way of speaking. De Gaulle was never anti-Semitic.' Little things like that make life worth living.

The dog may be man's best friend, but only if he has a master who feeds him. Here the dogs with no human ties are a menace. They hunt in packs of fifteen or twenty and have formed the habit of attacking tethered donkeys when night comes. They crowd around the donkey's head, trying to reach its neck. It backs up, and slowly winds its chain tightly around the tree. When it can no longer move, it belongs to the dogs, which devour it. In Tangier there used to be a dog-catcher, who piled ownerless dogs into his little truck and took them to the pound. Now there's neither catcher nor pound. The dogs are considered a natural hazard, like wild boars and snakes.

I hope it doesn't make too much extra bother for you to have Suki laid up in bed. I'm sorry I was instrumental in bringing this on you. You're an angel, as always. Write me soon.

(sent to Pamela Loeffler)

You don't sound very sanguine about Sue's improvement. Of course she hasn't written me, but I can scarcely expect her to if she feels miserable. She knows you keep in touch.

So now Florence pays her visit, and unannounced. And naturally she defends herself with the story of the letter she sent from Santa Barbara, even though she saw that it hadn't arrived until three days after her own arrival. And of course she appears just when you've got Suky in bed sick. I know you say guests never bother you, but it always takes a lot of one's time to care for a sick person. I hope by now that sick person is on her feet. It's almost a month since she came down with whatever she has.

Still the doctor doesn't want to commit himself on what's wrong with her? After all the laboratory tests? I find that unheard-of, but apparently you don't, since you calmly quote him as though he were Pasteur. This sort of thing strikes me as one of the disadvantages of living in Kahului. You can see that I'm not at home with illness. I'd much rather be ill myself than have to cope with a sufferer.

And you, are you all right? I'm sorry that Sue's holiday had to end this way. I hope she's already on her way back to Mount Holyoke.

In any case, I'll be waiting to hear from you. And tell me more about Florence; she's always amused me. (At a distance.)

(sent to Pamela Loeffler)

You're as bad as Suky herself, if not worse, for as far as I know you're in good health, whereas I have to assume she's still in bed, having heard nothing to the contrary. How can you let an entire month go by without sending me some sort of word? I'm not berating you, but I'm curious and *blessé* at the same time. I get an indistinct impression that in spite of my being what you call 'obsessed' by Suky, you think I don't care deeply about her.

It's true that I don't really know her; I've never had the opportunity. But that's beside the point. I've taken on the responsibility for her education and I want it to go well. Surely you can understand that.

As I was waking up this morning (a moment when things of the distant past can suddenly reappear in detail) I recalled the opening lines of two songs my mother used to sing when I was very young. They were both songs of rejection, I now realize. One went: 'Take back your gold, for gold will never buy me', and the other, even more absurd: 'I don't want to play in your yard; I don't love you any more.' According to her, they were both very popular ditties. Have you ever heard of either?

I'm in a hurry to get this off, because I have a forlorn hope that in the event you haven't written, my pleas will make you decide to do so. Consider this note to be one long supplication. Let me hear about Sue!

(*sent to Pamela Loeffler*)

Your postcard from Fiji was a slap in the face. You think I'll be 'amused' to see where you are, but I'm not. I'm astounded and exasperated that you should be dragging Sue off on a South Pacific trip when she should be in college. And I don't subscribe to your theory that such a voyage is a part of her convalescence. In fact, I think you don't believe it yourself. Obviously you imagine that old age makes people ingenuous. Or was that remark merely the first pretext that came to your mind? Do you find it incredible that having invested nervous energy, time and money in her education, I should want to see her complete it?

It goes without saying that this year is lost. It strikes me as an irresponsible act to gather the girl under your wing and fly off with her to God knows where and for God knows how long.

I suppose you won't receive this for many weeks. Tell S. that I'm disappointed to see how basically indifferent she is to her own well-being. Tell her I'm glad she's well (if indeed she ever was as ill as you gave me to believe) and tell her that when she gives a sign of life I'll reply. But she probably feels guilty and doesn't want to be in touch with me.

I'll get over my shock and indignation, but it won't be right away.

(*sent to Pamela Loeffler*)

In the past ten weeks I've had three postcards from you: from Fiji, Apia and Papeete, plus Sue's silly attempt at humour: 'Having wonderful time. Glad you're not here.' Tell her that message doesn't count. (Although it does show me it was only thanks to the security she felt in your presence that she was able to express her hostility toward me.) She'll have to write me a letter if she wants to hear from me.

If you've followed the schedule you outlined on your card from Papeete, you're back at home now. I'll expect to hear from you.

I'm still at a loss to understand why you went on that senseless trip. Perhaps when you're settled again you'll feel like explaining. Or perhaps you won't. It really doesn't matter. I think I perceive the general pattern.

(*sent to Pamela Loeffler*)

We seem to have arrived at an impasse: mutual misunderstandings due to IPI (insufficient preliminary information). You take exception to whatever I say. You're unreasonable. I get the impression that you two are arrayed against me. I can also see that S. confided in you completely, and at my expense. I did tell her you were generous, which you always have been.

My mistake with her, I think, was in advising her to destroy my letters. It was foolish because there was nothing incriminating in them, as I'm sure you're aware, having read them. But it must have set her to thinking, so that she now imagines I used her as a 'pawn' in my own 'financial planning'. It must be clear to you that this line of reasoning is unjustified. If it's not clear, there's nothing I can do about it, and it doesn't matter.

I had a brief note from Florence – the first in at least fifteen years. She wanted me to know what a fine time she'd had with you, and how much she liked Sue. Loved the climate, the landscape, the picnics and the bathing, and incidentally had not a word to say about anyone being sick in bed. According to her you all went everywhere together, and it was perfect. This deviates considerably from the official version.

(sent to Pamela Loeffler)

A few postmortem thoughts. You can tell S. that I've written her Aunt Emily West (who became her guardian when her parents died) informing her that her niece has left college and has an address in Hawaii where she can reach her. I've also been in touch with my lawyer in New York, explaining that my financial obligations to Susan Choate terminated with the end of her academic career, and asking him to cancel whatever future arrangements he had expected to make.

As to my writing S. herself, there doesn't seem to be any reason for it. She's made it very clear that she prefers not to hear from me. And what could I say at this point? 'I hope you won't regret your decision'? As you tell me, she already suspects that I disapprove of that decision, so that anything I might say would change suspicion to conviction. It would be hard to get her to believe that I have no objection to what she's doing. She probably prefers to imagine me as being scandalized by her behaviour; it would be more fun for her that way. She expects me to mind that things didn't work out in the way I thought they would. But that's only because she doesn't know me. What she must consider to be my archaic epistolary style has helped her to think of me as an opinionated and uncompromising old bastard.

Nevertheless, please believe me when I tell you that she

can fall in love with a Japanese garage mechanic, sleep with you, and marry an orang-utan, and it will all be the same to me. There's not enough time in life for recriminations.

Hugh Harper

Hugh Harper could have been Dr Hugh Harper, had he completed his medical training. But somewhere along the way he lost interest. Perhaps it was the realization that he did not need the extra money which might be got from a practice in Harley Street or elsewhere. He saw that he could have a comfortable life without expending all that unnecessary effort.

Like most hedonists, Harper was eccentric and secretive. In his case the secretiveness is not surprising, since his eccentricity consisted in a taste for human blood. He was in no way ashamed of his unusual predilection since it had no sexual facet; it was purely gastronomical. On the other hand, he saw no reason to extend the circle of those who knew of his fondness for the flavour of blood beyond the group of neighbourhood youths who regularly sold him small quantities of it. The difficulty proved to be, as he might have guessed it would, that inevitably the mother of one of the boys learned what was going on. She was thoroughly outraged, of course, and there was the threat of a scandal. The Harper family decided that Hugh must immediately disappear.

Naively, he objected, claiming that what he had been doing was not illegal. His older brother replied that if this was so, it was only because there was no precedent for such behaviour in civilized society, and that he himself was putting Hugh on the ferry for Calais that very evening. He accompanied him to Dover and got him on to the ferry; then he heaved a sigh of relief and returned to London. Even though he realized that there were no sexual overtones in the affair, he knew that the indignant mothers, once they got together, would be quick to supply them.

At Pozzuoli, outside Naples, Hugh Harper installed himself in an apartment and set to work gathering a group of young proletarian blood donors who would not be likely to confide in their mothers (and whose mothers in any case would not have been particularly interested in such information). What did not occur to him was that the Italian police often seem to know about things even before they happen. According to them, here was a foreigner who, not satisfied with supplying drugs to teenagers, insisted upon administering the shots himself. The youths naturally were unanimous in denying this, maintaining with Italian pride that they submitted to the Englishman's senseless requests solely because they were well paid to do so.

Very well, no drugs, said the police, but the thing is illegal in any case, because the foreigner has no permit to practise medicine in Italy, and for one person to use a hypodermic needle, no matter for what purpose, on another person, requires a medical certificate.

To avoid a trial and possible incarceration Harper was obliged to part with several substantial sums of money, after which he was ordered to leave the country and not return.

It was to be expected that the next place for Hugh Harper to settle in would be Morocco. He rented a small house on the Marshan in Tangier, in whose *sala* he installed a gigantic refrigerator. Here on the brightly lighted shelves were the small glasses of blood, each bearing a sticker with the name of the donor and the date the liquid had been drawn. The young Moroccans found it perfectly natural that this Englishman should have need of supplementary blood for his health, since it was common knowledge that English blood was thin and cold. The idea that he might want it because he appreciated its flavour would have been inconceivable to them.

It seemed that at last he had found the right place; here he could indulge his very special tastes without thought of outside interference. During the two years he lived there on the Marshan he came little by little to think of his tastes as not much more special than as if the small glasses contained wine. It was all so easy, and no one objected. At this point his euphoria destroyed his common sense. The neat display of little glasses on the shelves of his refrigerator seemed to him irresistible, and he began to imagine that his European acquaintances would find them equally attractive. 'Have a glass,' he would urge a visitor. 'It's delicious chilled.'

The Europeans, duly shocked, were not in a position to do more than add this latest wonderful scandal to their repertory of gossip. The sinister novelty of Harper's behaviour delighted them. 'Of course the man is completely mad,' they assured one another at the end of each discussion. In a sense they were right. Had he been wholly sane, he would have continued to admire the display of the glasses and partake of their contents in strict privacy as he had done when he first arrived in Tangier. Instead, he would read aloud the names on them to his guests: 'Abdeslam, Mohammed, Abderrahman, Omar. Which tempts you? Ali?'

The Europeans thus importuned talked so much about the strange Mr Harper that their Moroccan servants could not help overhearing their accounts. In this way a fqih of Souq el Bqar came to know about the unusual Englishman. He gave the matter much thought. Even though the blood served a therapeutic purpose, he sensed something objectionable in the consuming by a Nazarene of so much Muslim blood. He felt sure that there must be Koranic strictures prohibiting such practices, but not being conversant with the holy scripture, he was unable to do more than conjecture. At length he consulted an imam from a mosque in Dradeb, who assured him that the partaking of human blood was an abomination in the eyes of Allah. The Christian must be prevented from drinking any more Muslim blood.

When religious leaders in Islam reach a decision, it is implemented with surprising speed. Hugh Harper received a *procès-verbal*: he must leave Tangier within eight days. No reason was given, but none was necessary. Where he went after being declared *persona non grata* in Morocco is not known.

Dinner at Sir Nigel's

In those days the social life of the city was sharply divided between the Moroccans and the Europeans, whose relationship to the former was the traditional one of master–servant. The average European household was normally run by a staff or five or six Moroccans. A larger establishment understandably needed a good many more, and the native work-force was often fortified with a European chef, housekeeper and chauffeur. An unaccountable exception, according to local gossip, was the house of Sir Nigel Renfrew, who would have been expected to need a good-sized staff, but who was reported as employing only one man and one maid. This anomaly was repeatedly discussed by the members of the British Colony, and one heard vague reports hinting that there was more than mere parsimony behind Sir Nigel's spartan limiting of his help.

The year of his arrival in Tangier is uncertain; apparently it was immediately after the close of the Second World War. He must have brought a considerable fortune with him (either legally or clandestinely, which is more likely) for he lost no time in putting up a series of large apartment houses on what were then the outskirts of town. It's doubtful that he recuperated his investment on any of these constructions, since there were dozens of empty apartments all over town, waiting for occupancy.

The first eye-witness account I had of Sir Nigel came from two English friends whom he had invited to lunch. They waited for an hour and a half for him to appear, which he did without offering any apology or explanation; then they waited another half-hour for the single manservant to arrange the dining table and bring the food. Their account of the ordeal was brief; they agreed that he was 'insufferable'. As far as I'm aware, neither of them ever returned to his house. All this did not deter me, two or three years later, from accepting, along with a group of British and Canadian journalists, an invitation to dinner at Sir Nigel's.

We had to leave our cars at some distance from the house and walk through an untended pasture where a few sheep grazed. It was still daylight, but I wondered aloud how we should find our way back to the road in the dark. One of the journalists, however, had a flashlight with him.

Sir Nigel's unprepossessing appearance surprised me. He was a short man, very thin, with a seamed face and small colourless eyes set very close together. He seated himself between two correspondents whom he evidently knew fairly well, and spoke with them, paying no attention whatever to the rest of us. I studied his face, and decided that it was incapable of smiling, or indeed of replacing its expression of permanent displeasure with any other. He radiated hostility, and it was clear that the guests felt this; they ceased talking among themselves, and sat silently listening to their host's scratchy voice.

A black manservant brought whisky, soda and ice. When he had gone out, Sir Nigel waved his arm and said: 'You see that man? I brought him from Zanzibar. He's my cook, butler and gardener. You'd need half a dozen of your Moors to do the same job. Pack of lazy buggers, lolling about, smoking their pipes and cadging food. Useless sods.' He glared at us as if he suspected us of being disguised Moroccans, and I saw that he was already drunk.

On the floor in a dim part of the room there were several drums of varying sizes and shapes, all of them covered in zebra hide. In the hope of providing him with a different topic of conversation, I asked Sir Nigel if they also had been imported from Zanzibar. Looking at me with an expression which I could only interpret as one of acute rancour and contempt, he answered rapidly: 'I have a house there', and returned to his excoriation of Moroccans.

Of the dinner, I recall only that we ate seated on hassocks in groups of three, at three low tables, and that as the meal progressed our host became visibly more excited. He had forgotten the Moroccans, and was now heaping maledictions and obscenities upon the French and Spanish. They had no idea of how to run a colony, or of how to manage the ignorant and slothful natives. I had an unreasoning conviction that our Amphitryon's mounting frenzy was the result of a decision he had made to involve us in an unpleasantness of some sort.

'You know, he's out of his mind,' I muttered to the Canadian beside me. He nodded, not looking away from the malevolent face.

When the Zanzibari brought on the fruit, Sir Nigel sprang to his feet. 'In a minute', he shouted, 'you're going to see something you'll not forget, by God. And remember, they come of their own accord.' With that he rushed from the room, and we remained, staring at one another.

Soon we heard a slight commotion. A curtain moved in the wall behind the drums, and a tall, muscular black woman strode in, not looking in our direction, and proceeded to light several lamps in that part of the room. Then she turned to lift the curtain while five girls in their mid-teens ambled in and sank to the floor, each beside a drum. They were clad in diaphanous white gowns, and their hair fell loosely about their shoulders. Three of them were what would be called raving beauties; the other two were merely pretty. The sight was impressive. Sir Nigel had been right in saying we would not forget it.

The girls began to thump indiscriminately on the drums, which, being so much more resonant than the hand-drums Moroccan girls are used to playing, filled the room with a chaos of rhythmless pounding. Like the black woman who had ushered them in, they behaved as though the Europeans in front of them were invisible. No one attempted to say anything.

Suddenly Sir Nigel stood before us, brandishing a long circus whip. He had changed into jodhpurs and black leather boots, and his face had turned such a dangerously dark red that I wondered if we might not be going to witness then and there the death from apoplexy of Sir Nigel Renfrew. Although his movements appeared to be uncoordinated, he had no difficulty in cracking his whip with a maximum of sound, and this he proceeded to do above the heads of the cowering girls, who gave little shrieks of simulated terror as they writhed at his feet among the drums.

And now Sir Nigel gave a great shout, to which the girls responded by attacking each other in a wild free-for-all, yanking hair, ripping open the bodices of the filmy gowns and uttering prolonged, hair-raising screams. Sir Nigel hopped up and down, emitting little grunts, cracking the whip and from time to time actually lashing one of the frantic girls with it. A moment before, they had been play-acting, but now they began to sob, and to use their fingernails in the fight. No signal was given that I could detect, but once again the curtain was lifted and the black woman advanced upon the crazy group, forcing them apart and pulling them to their feet. Then she shoved them under the curtain and we were left with Sir Nigel, who still flicked his whip as he strode in our direction.

His exertions of a minute ago had left him short of breath. 'They're locked into their rooms now, you see.' He cracked the whip over our heads and stared into our faces, one after the other, as he pulled a heavy key from his pocket and shook it at us. 'But if anybody feels like spending a little time with one of them, this is the master key.' His eyes flashed; they were the eyes of an enraged chimpanzee. I realized that for him the evening had been leading up to this moment. The others were clearly of the same mind, for no one said anything, and there was a long silence. Then Sir Nigel uttered a scornful 'Hah!' and tossed the whip in the direction of the drums.

'I'm afraid I must be getting back to the hotel,' someone said. There were general murmurs of assent, and we all rose and thanked our host, who saw us to the door. He bowed. 'Good night,' he said in mellifluous tones. 'Good night, you bloody swine, good night.'

As we went up through the dark pasture, one of the Englishmen who knew Sir Nigel gave us some of the details. It was true that the girls came of their own accord, from villages in the hills round about. Each one was locked up for a month, and upon leaving was given an expensive caftan, something she could never have hoped otherwise to possess. It was the sight of the garment which inspired other girls to come to Tangier and seek out Sir Nigel. They were not really mistreated, he said. Each had her own room in the servants' quarters, and was supplied with food by the black woman. Now I understood why Sir Nigel would not have Moroccan servants; it would have been impossible. If any Moroccan had got wind of what went on in the house, there would have been an immediate scandal.

As a matter of fact, trouble did break out some months later, and one can only assume that it was linked to the presence of the girls. Sir Nigel left the country and was absent for several years. He did return, however, to die of a heart attack sitting at a table on the terrace of the Café de Paris, in the centre of Tangier, at noon.

Abacus now offers an exciting range of quality fiction and non-fiction by both established and new authors. All of the books in this series are available from good bookshops, or can be ordered from the following address:

Sphere Books
Cash Sales Department
P.O. Box 11
Falmouth
Cornwall, TR10 9EN.

Please send cheque or postal order (no currency), and allow 60p for postage and packing for the first book plus 25p for the second book and 15p for each additional book ordered up to a maximum charge of £1.90 in U.K.

B.F.P.O. customers please allow 60p for the first book, 25p for the second book plus 15p per copy for the next 7 books, thereafter 9p per book.

Overseas customers, including Eire, please allow £1.25 for postage and packing for the first book, 75p for the second book and 28p for each subsequent title ordered.